THE SHEIK

Edith Maude Hull

(E. M. Hull)

THE SHEIK

A Novel

BIBLIOBAZAAR

THE SHEIK

CHAPTER I

"Are you coming in to watch the dancing, Lady Conway?"

"I most decidedly am not. I thoroughly disapprove of the expedition of which this dance is the inauguration. I consider that even by contemplating such a tour alone into the desert with no chaperon or attendant of her own sex, with only native camel drivers and servants, Diana Mayo is behaving with a recklessness and impropriety that is calculated to cast a slur not only on her own reputation, but also on the prestige of her country. I blush to think of it. We English cannot be too careful of our behavior abroad. No opportunity is slight enough for our continental neighbours to cast stones, and this opportunity is very far from being slight. It is the maddest piece of unprincipled folly I have ever heard of."

"Oh, come, Lady Conway! It's not quite so bad as all that. It is certainly unconventional and—er—probably not quite wise, but remember Miss Mayo's unusual upbringing—"

"I am not forgetting her unusual upbringing," interrupted Lady Conway. "It has been deplorable. But nothing can excuse this scandalous escapade. I knew her mother years ago, and I took it upon myself to expostulate both with Diana and her brother, but Sir Aubrey is hedged around with an egotistical complacency that would defy a pickaxe to penetrate. According to him a Mayo is beyond criticism, and his sister's reputation her own to deal with. The girl herself seemed, frankly, not to understand the seriousness of her position, and was very flippant and not a little rude. I wash my hands of the whole affair, and will certainly not countenance tonight's entertainment by appearing at it. I have already warned the manager that if the noise is kept up beyond a reasonable hour I shall leave the hotel tomorrow." And, drawing her wrap around her with a little shudder, Lady Conway stalked majestically across the wide verandah of the Biskra Hotel.

The two men left standing by the open French window that led into the hotel ballroom looked at each other and smiled.

"Some peroration," said one with a marked American accent. "That's the way scandal's made, I guess."

"Scandal be hanged! There's never been a breath of scandal attached to Diana Mayo's name. I've known the child since she was a baby. Rum little cuss she was, too. Confound that old woman! She would wreck the reputation of the Archangel Gabriel if he came down to earth, let alone that of a mere human girl."

"Not a very human girl," laughed the American. "She was sure meant for a boy and changed at the last moment. She looks like a boy in petticoats, a damned pretty boy—and a damned haughty one," he added, chuckling. "I overheard her this morning, in the garden, making mincemeat of a French officer."

The Englishman laughed.

"Been making love to her, I expect. A thing she does not understand and won't tolerate. She's the coldest little fish in the world, without an idea in her head beyond sport and travel. Clever, though, and plucky as they are made. I don't think she knows the meaning of the word fear."

"There's a queer streak in the family, isn't there? I heard somebody yapping about it the other night. Father was mad and blew his brains out, so I was told."

The Englishman shrugged his shoulders.

"You can call it mad, if you like," he said slowly. "I live near the Mayos' in England, and happen to know the story. Sir John Mayo was passionately devoted to his wife; after twenty years of married life they were still lovers. Then this girl was born, and the mother died. Two hours afterwards her husband shot himself, leaving the baby in the sole care of her brother, who was just nineteen, and as lazy and as selfish then as he is now. The problem of bringing up a girl child was too much trouble to be solved, so he settled the difficulty by treating her as if she was a boy. The result is what you see."

They moved nearer to the open window, looking into the brilliantly lit ballroom, already filled with gaily chattering people. On a slightly raised platform at one end of the room the host and hostess were receiving their guests. The brother and sister were singularly unlike. Sir Aubrey Mayo was very tall and thin, the pallor of his face accentuated by the blackness of his smoothly brushed hair and heavy black moustache. His attitude was a mixture of well-bred courtesy and languid boredom. He seemed too tired even to keep the single eye-glass that he wore in position, for it dropped continually. By contrast the girl at his side appeared vividly alive. She was only of medium height and very slender, standing erect with the easy, vigorous carriage of an athletic boy, her small head poised proudly. Her scornful mouth and firm chin showed plainly an obstinate determination, and her deep blue eyes were unusually clear and steady. The long, curling black lashes that shaded her eyes and the dark eyebrows were a foil to the thick crop of loose, red-gold curls that she wore short, clubbed about her ears.

"The result is worth seeing," said the American admiringly, referring to his companion's last remark.

A third and younger man joined them.

"Hallo, Arbuthnot. You're late. The divinity is ten deep in would-be partners already."

A dull red crept into the young man's face, and he jerked his head angrily.

"I got waylaid by Lady Conway—poisonous old woman! She had a great deal to say on the subject of Miss Mayo and her trip. She ought to be gagged. I thought she was going on talking all night, so I fairly bolted in the end. All the same, I agree with her on one point. Why can't that lazy ass Mayo go with his sister?"

Nobody seemed to be able to give an answer. The band had begun playing, and the floor was covered with laughing, talking couples.

Sir Aubrey Mayo had moved away, and his sister was left standing with several men, who waited, programme in hand, but she waved them away with a little smile and a resolute shake of her head.

"Things seem to be getting a hustle on," said the American.

"Are you going to try your luck?" asked the elder of the two Englishmen.

The American bit the end off a cigar with a little smile.

"I sure am not. The haughty young lady turned me down as a dancer very early in our acquaintance. I don't blame her," he added, with a rueful laugh, "but her extreme candour still rankles. She told me quite plainly that she had no use for an American who could neither ride nor dance. I did intimate to her, very gently, that there were a few little openings in the States for men beside cattle-punching and cabaret dancing, but she froze me with a look, and I faded away. No, Sir Egotistical Complacency will be having some bridge later on, which will suit me much better. He's not a bad chap underneath if you can swallow his peculiarities, and he's a sportsman. I like to play with him. He doesn't care a durn if he wins or loses."

"It doesn't matter when you have a banking account the size of his," said Arbuthnot. "Personally, I find dancing more amusing and less expensive. I shall go and take my chance with our hostess."

His eyes turned rather eagerly towards the end of the room where the girl was standing alone, straight and slim, the light from an electrolier gilding the thick bright curls framing her beautiful, haughty little face. She was staring down at the dancers with an absent expression in her eyes, as if her thoughts were far away from the crowded ballroom.

The American pushed Arbuthnot forward with a little laugh.

"Run along, foolish moth, and get your poor little wings singed. When the cruel fair has done trampling on you I'll come right along and mop up the remains. If, on the other hand, your temerity meets with the success it deserves, we can celebrate suitably later on." And, linking his arm in his friend's, he drew him away to the card-room.

Arbuthnot went through the window and worked slowly round the room, hugging the wall, evading dancers, and threading his way through groups of chattering men and women of all nationalities. He came at last to the raised dais on which Diana Mayo was still standing, and climbed up the few steps to her side.

"This is luck, Miss Mayo," he said, with an assurance that he was far from feeling. "Am I really fortunate enough to find you without a partner?"

She turned to him slowly, with a little crease growing between her arched eyebrows, as if his coming were inopportune and she resented the interruption to her thoughts, and then she smiled quite frankly.

"I said I would not dance until everybody was started," she said rather doubtfully, looking over the crowded floor.

"They are all dancing. You've done your duty nobly. Don't miss this ripping tune," he urged persuasively.

She hesitated, tapping her programme-pencil against her teeth.

"I refused a lot of men," she said, with a grimace. Then she laughed suddenly. "Come along, then. I am noted for my bad manners. This will only be one extra sin."

Arbuthnot danced well, but with the girl in his arms he seemed suddenly tongue-tied. They swung round the room several times, then halted simultaneously beside an open window and went out into the garden of the hotel, sitting down on a wicker seat under a gaudy Japanese hanging lantern. The band was still playing, and for the moment the garden was empty, lit faintly by coloured lanterns, festooned from the palm trees, and twinkling lights outlining the winding paths.

Arbuthnot leaned forward, his hands clasped between his knees.

"I think you are the most perfect dancer I have ever met," he said a little breathlessly.

Miss Mayo looked at him seriously, without a trace of self-consciousness.

"It is very easy to dance if you have a musical ear, and if you have been in the habit of making your body do what you want. So few people seem to be trained to make their limbs obey them. Mine have had to do as they were told since I was a small child," she answered calmly.

The unexpectedness of the reply acted as a silencer on Arbuthnot for a few minutes, and the girl beside him seemed in no hurry to break the silence. The dance was over and the empty garden was thronged for a little time. Then the dancers drifted back into the hotel as the band started again.

"It's rather jolly here in the garden," Arbuthnot said tentatively. His heart was pounding with unusual rapidity, and his eyes, that he kept fixed on his own clasped hands, had a hungry look growing in them.

"You mean that, you want to sit out this dance with me?" she said with a boyish directness that somewhat nonplussed him.

"Yes," he stammered rather foolishly.

She held her programme up to the light of the lantern. "I promised this one to Arthur Conway. We quarrel every time we meet. I cannot think why he asked me; he disapproves of me even more than his mother does—such an interfering old lady. He will be overjoyed to be let off. And I don't want to dance tonight. I am looking forward so tremendously to tomorrow. I shall stay and talk to you, but you must give me a cigarette to keep me in a good temper."

His hand shook a little as he held the match for her. "Are you really determined to go through with this tour?"

She stared at him in surprise. "Why not? My arrangements have been made some time. Why should I change my mind at the last moment?"

"Why does your brother let you go alone? Why doesn't he go with you? Oh, I haven't any right to ask, but I do ask," he broke out vehemently.

She shrugged her shoulders with a little laugh. "We fell out, Aubrey and I. He wanted to go to America. I wanted a trip into the desert. We quarrelled for two whole days and half one night, and then we compromised. I should have my desert tour, and Aubrey should go to New York; and to mark his brotherly appreciation of my gracious promise to follow him to the States without fail at the end of a month he has consented to grace my caravan for the first stage, and dismiss me on my way with his blessing. It annoyed him so enormously that he could not order me to go with him, this being the first time in our wanderings that our inclinations have not jumped in the same direction. I came of age a few months ago, and, in future, I can do as I please. Not that I have ever done anything else," she conceded, with another laugh, "because Aubrey's ways have been my ways until now."

"But for the sake of one month! What difference could it make to him?" he asked in astonishment.

"That's Aubrey," replied Miss Mayo drily.

"It isn't safe," persisted Arbuthnot.

She flicked the ash from her cigarette carelessly. "I don't agree with you. I don't know why everybody is making such a fuss about it. Plenty of other women have travelled in much wilder country than this desert."

He looked at her curiously. She seemed to be totally unaware that it was her youth and her beauty that made all the danger of the expedition. He fell back on the easier excuse.

"There seems to be unrest amongst some of the tribes. There have been a lot of rumours lately," he said seriously.

She made a little movement of impatience. "Oh, that's what they always tell you when they want to put obstacles in your way. The authorities have already dangled that bogey in front of me. I asked for facts and they only gave me generalities. I asked definitely if they had any power to stop me. They said they had not, but strongly advised me not to make the attempt. I said I should go, unless the French Government arrested me . . . Why not? I am not afraid. I don't admit that there is anything to be afraid of. I don't believe a word about the tribes being restless. Arabs are always moving about, aren't they? I have an excellent caravan leader, whom even the authorities vouch for, and I shall be armed. I am perfectly able to take care of myself. I can shoot straight and I am used to camping. Besides, I have given my word to Aubrey to be in Oran in a month, and I can't get very far away in that time."

There was an obstinate ring in her voice, and when she stopped speaking he sat silent, consumed with anxiety, obsessed with the loveliness of her, and tormented with the desire to tell her so. Then he turned to her suddenly, and his face was very white. "Miss Mayo—Diana—put off this trip only for a little, and give me the right to go with you. I love you. I want you for my wife more than anything on earth. I shan't always be a penniless subaltern. One of these days I shall be able to give you a position that is worthy of you; no, nothing could be that, but one at least that I am not ashamed to offer to you. We've been very good friends; you know all about me. I'll give my whole life to make you happy. The world has been a different place to me since you came into it. I can't get away from you. You are in my thoughts night and day. I love you; I want you. My God, Diana! Beauty like yours drives a man mad!"

"Is beauty all that a man wants in his wife?" she asked, with a kind of cold wonder in her voice. "Brains and a sound body seem much more sensible requirements to me."

"But when a woman has all three, as you have, Diana," he whispered ardently, his hands closing over the slim ones lying in her lap.

But with a strength that seemed impossible for their smallness she disengaged them from his grasp. "Please stop. I am sorry. We have been good friends, and it has never occurred to me that there could be anything beyond that. I never thought that you might love me. I never thought of you in that way at all, I don't understand it. When God made me He omitted to give me a heart. I have never loved any one in my life. My brother and I have tolerated each other, but there has never been any affection between us. Would it be likely? Put yourself in Aubrey's place. Imagine a young man of nineteen, with a cold, reserved nature, being burdened with the care of a baby sister, thrust into his hands unwanted and unexpected. Was it likely that he would have any affection for me? I never wanted it. I was born with the same cold nature as his. I was brought up as a boy, my training was hard. Emotion and affection have been barred out of my life. I simply don't know what they mean. I don't want to know. I am very content with my life as it is. Marriage for a woman means the end of independence, that is, marriage with a man who is a man, in spite of all that the most modern woman may say. I have never obeyed any one in my life; I do not wish to try the experiment. I am very sorry to have hurt you. You've been a splendid pal, but that side of life does not exist for me. If I had thought for one moment that my friendship was going to hurt you I need not have let you become so intimate, but I did not think, because it is a subject that I never think of. A man to me is just a companion with whom I ride or shoot or fish; a pal, a comrade, and that's just all there is to it. God made me a woman. Why, only He knows."

Her quiet, even voice stopped. There had been a tone of cold sincerity in it that Arbuthnot could not help but recognise. She meant everything that she said. She said no more than the truth. Her reputation for complete indifference to admiration and her unvarying attitude towards men were as well known as her dauntless courage and obstinate determination. With Sir Aubrey Mayo she behaved like a younger brother, and as such entertained his friends. She was popular with everybody, even with the mothers of marriageable daughters, for, in spite of her wealth and beauty, her notorious peculiarities made her negligible as a rival to plainer and less well-dowered girls.

Arbuthnot sat in silence. It was hardly likely, he thought bitterly, that he should succeed where other and better men had failed. He had been a fool to succumb to the temptation that had been too hard for him to resist. He knew her well enough to know beforehand what her answer would be. The very real fear for her safety that the thought of the coming expedition gave him, her nearness in the mystery of the Eastern night, the lights, the music, had all combined to rush to his lips words that in a saner moment would never have passed them. He loved her, he would love her always, but he knew that his love was as hopeless as it was undying. But it was men who were men whom she wanted for her friends, so he must take his medicine like a man.

"May I still be the pal, Diana?" he said quietly.

She looked at him a moment, but in the dim light of the hanging lanterns his eyes were steady under hers, and she held out her hand frankly. "Gladly," she said candidly. "I have hosts of acquaintances, but very few friends. We are always travelling, Aubrey and I, and we never seem to have time to make friends. We rarely stay as long in one place as we have stayed in Biskra. In England they call us very bad neighbours, we are so seldom there. We generally go home for three months in the winter for the hunting, but the rest of the year we wander on the face of the globe."

He held her slender fingers gripped in his for a moment, smothering an insane desire to press them to his lips, which he knew would be fatal to the newly accorded friendship, and then let them go. Miss Mayo continued sitting quietly beside him. She was in no way disturbed by what had happened. She had taken him literally at his word, and was treating him as the pal he had asked to be. It no more occurred to her that she might relieve him of her society than it occurred to her that her continued presence might be distressing to him. She was totally unembarrassed and completely un-self-conscious. And as they sat silent, her thoughts far away in the desert, and his full of vain longings and regrets, a man's low voice rose in the stillness of the night. *"Pale hands I loved beside the Shalimar. Where are you now? Who lies beneath your spell?"* he sang in a passionate, vibrating baritone. He was singing in English, and yet the almost indefinite slurring from note to note was strangely un-English. Diana Mayo leaned forward, her head raised, listening intently, with shining eyes. The voice seemed to come from the dark shadows at the end of the garden, or it might have been further away out in the road beyond the cactus hedge. The singer sang slowly, his voice lingering caressingly on the words; the last verse dying away softly and clearly, almost imperceptibly fading into silence.

For a moment there was utter stillness, then Diana lay back with a little sigh. "The Kashmiri Song. It makes me think of India. I heard a man sing it in Kashmere last year, but not like that. What a wonderful voice! I wonder who it is?"

Arbuthnot looked at her curiously, surprised at the sudden ring of interest in her tone, and the sudden animation of her face.

"You say you have no emotion in your nature, and yet that unknown man's singing has stirred you deeply. How do you reconcile the two?" he asked, almost angrily.

"Is an appreciation of the beautiful emotion?" she challenged, with uplifted eyes. "Surely not. Music, art, nature, everything beautiful appeals to me. But there is nothing emotional in that. It is only that I prefer beautiful things to ugly ones. For that reason even pretty clothes appeal to me," she added, laughing.

"You are the best-dressed woman in Biskra," he acceded. "But is not that a concession to the womanly feelings that you despise?"

"Not at all. To take an interest in one's clothes is not an exclusively feminine vice. I like pretty dresses. I admit to spending some time in thinking of colour schemes to go with my horrible hair, but I assure you that my dressmaker has an easier life than Aubrey's tailor."

She sat silent, hoping that the singer might not have gone, but there was no sound except a cicada chirping near her. She swung round in her chair, looking in the direction from which it came. "Listen to him. Jolly little chap! They are the first things I listen for when I get to Port Said. They mean the East to me."

"Maddening little beasts!" said Arbuthnot irritably.

"They are going to be very friendly little beasts to me during the next four weeks . . . You don't know what this trip means to me. I like wild places. The happiest times of my life have been spent camping in America and India, and I have always wanted the desert more than either of them. It is going to be a month of pure joy. I am going to be enormously happy."

She stood up with a little laugh of intense pleasure, and half turned, waiting for Arbuthnot. He got up reluctantly and stood silent beside her for a few moments. "Diana, I wish you'd let me kiss you, just once," he broke out miserably.

She looked up swiftly with a glint of anger in her eyes, and shook her head. "No. That's not in the compact. I have never been kissed in my life. It is one of the things that I do not understand." Her voice was almost fierce.

She moved leisurely towards the hotel, and he paced beside her wondering if he had forfeited her friendship by his outburst, but on the verandah she halted and spoke in the frank tone of camaraderie in which she had always addressed him. "Shall I see you in the morning?"

He understood. There was to be no more reference to what had passed between them. The offer of friendship held, but only on her own terms. He pulled himself together.

"Yes. We have arranged an escort of about a dozen of us to ride the first few miles with you, to give you a proper send-off."

She made a laughing gesture of protest. "It will certainly need four weeks of solitude to counteract the conceit I shall acquire," she said lightly, as she passed into the ballroom.

A few hours later Diana came into her bedroom, and, switching on the electric lights, tossed her gloves and programme into a chair. The room was empty, for her maid had had a *vertige* at the suggestion that she should accompany her mistress into the desert, and had been sent back to Paris to await Diana's return. She had left during the day, to take most of the heavy luggage with her.

Diana stood in the middle of the room and looked at the preparations for the early start next morning with a little smile of satisfaction. Everything was *en train*; the final arrangements had all been concluded some days before. The camel caravan with the camp equipment was due to leave Biskra a few hours before the time fixed for the Mayos to start with Mustafa Ali, the reputable guide whom the French authorities had reluctantly recommended. The two big suit-cases that Diana was taking with her stood open, ready packed, waiting only for the last few necessaries, and by them the steamer trunk that Sir Aubrey would take charge of and leave in Paris as he passed through. On a chaise-longue was laid out her riding kit ready for the morning. Her smile broadened as she looked at the smart-cut breeches and high brown boots. They were the clothes in which most of her life had been spent, and in which she was far more at home than in the pretty dresses over which she had laughed with Arbuthnot.

She was glad the dance was over; it was not a form of exercise that appealed to her particularly. She was thinking only of the coming tour. She stretched her arms out with a little happy laugh.

"It's the life of lives, and it's going to begin all over again tomorrow morning." She crossed over to the dressing-table, and, propping her elbows on it, looked at herself in the glass, with a little friendly smile at the reflection. In default of any other confidant she had always talked to herself, with no thought for the beauty of the face staring back at her from the glass. The only comment she ever made to herself on her own appearance was sometimes to wish that her hair was not such a tiresome shade. She looked at herself now with a tinge of curiosity. "I wonder why I'm so especially happy tonight. It must be because we have been so long in Biskra. It's been very jolly, but I was beginning to get very bored." She laughed again and picked up her watch to wind. It was one of her peculiarities that she would wear no jewellery of any kind. Even the gold repeater in her hand was on a plain leather strap. She undressed slowly and each moment felt more wide-awake. Slipping a thin wrap over her pyjamas and lighting a cigarette she went out on to the broad balcony on to which her bedroom gave. The room was on the first floor, and opposite her window rose one of the ornately carved and bracketed pillars that supported the balcony, stretching up to the second story above her head. She looked down into the gardens below. It was an easy climb, she thought, with a boyish grin—far easier than many she had achieved successfully when the need of a solitary ramble became imperative. But the East was inconvenient for solitary ramble; native servants had a disconcerting habit of lying down to sleep wherever drowsiness overcame them, and it was not very long since she had slid down from her balcony and landed plumb on a slumbering bundle of humanity who had roused half the hotel with his howls. She leant far over the rail, trying to see into the verandah below, and she thought she caught a glimpse of white drapery. She looked again, and this time there was nothing, but she shook her head with a little grimace, and swung herself up on to the broad ledge of the railing. Settling herself comfortably with her back against the column she looked out over the hotel gardens into the night, humming softly the Kashmiri song she had heard earlier in the evening.

The risen moon was full, and its cold, brilliant light filled the garden with strong black shadows. She watched some that seemed even to move, as if the garden were alive with creeping, hurrying figures, and amused herself tracking them until she traced them to the palm tree or cactus bush that caused them. One in particular gave her a long hunt till she finally ran it to its lair, and it proved to be the shadow of a grotesque lead statue half hidden by a flowering shrub. Forgetting the hour and the open windows all around her, she burst into a rippling peal of laughter, which was interrupted by the appearance of a figure, imperfectly seen through the lattice-work which divided her balcony from the next one, and the sound of an irritable voice.

"For Heaven's sake, Diana, let other people sleep if you can't."

"Which, being interpreted, is let Sir Aubrey Mayo sleep," she retorted, with a chuckle. "My dear boy, sleep if you want to, but I don't know how you can on a night like this. Did you ever see such a gorgeous moon?"

"Oh, damn the moon!"

"Oh, very well. Don't get cross about it. Go back to bed and put your head under the clothes, and then you won't see it. But I'm going to sit here."

"Diana, don't be an idiot! You'll go to sleep and fall into the garden and break your neck."

"Tant pis pour moi. Tant mieux pour toi," she said flippantly. "I have left you all that I have in the world, dear brother. Could devotion go further?"

She paid no heed to his exclamation of annoyance, and looked back into the garden. It was a wonderful night, silent except for the cicadas' monotonous chirping, mysterious with the inexplicable mystery that hangs always in the Oriental night. The smells of the East rose up all around her; here, as at home, they seemed more perceptible by night than by day. Often at home she had stood on the little stone balcony outside her room, drinking in the smells of the night—the pungent, earthy smell after rain, the aromatic smell of pine trees near the house. It was the intoxicating smells of the night that had first driven her, as a very small child, to clamber down from her balcony, clinging to the thick ivy roots, to wander with the delightful sense of wrong-doing through the moonlit park and even into the adjoining gloomy woods. She had always been utterly fearless.

Her childhood had been a strange one. There had been no near relatives to interest themselves in the motherless girl left to the tender mercies of a brother nearly twenty years her senior, who was frankly and undisguisedly horrified at the charge that had been thrust upon him. Wrapped up in himself, and free to indulge in the wander hunger that gripped him, the baby sister was an intolerable burden, and he had shifted responsibility in the easiest way possible. For the first few years of her life she was left undisturbed to nurses and servants who spoiled her indiscriminately. Then, when she was still quite a tiny child, Sir Aubrey Mayo came home from a long tour, and, settling down for a couple of years, fixed on his sister's future training, modelled rigidly on his own upbringing. Dressed as a boy, treated as a boy, she learned to ride and to shoot and to fish—not as amusements, but seriously, to enable her to take her place later on as a companion to the man whose only interests they were. His air of weariness was a mannerism. In reality he was as hard as nails, and it was his intention that Diana should grow up as hard. With that end in view her upbringing had been Spartan, no allowances were made for sex or temperament and nothing was spared to gain the desired result. And from the first Diana had responded gallantly, throwing herself heart and soul into the arduous, strenuous life mapped out for her. The only drawback to a perfect enjoyment of life were the necessary lessons that had to be gone through, though even these might have been worse. Every morning she rode across the park to the rectory for a couple of hours' tuition with the rector, whose heart was more in his stable than in his parish, and whose reputation was greater across country than it was in the pulpit. His methods were rough and ready, but she had brains, and acquired an astonishing amount of diverse knowledge. But her education was stopped with abrupt suddenness when she was fifteen by the arrival at the rectory of an overgrown young cub who had been sent by a despairing parent, as a last resource, to the muscular rector, and who quickly discovered what those amongst whom she had grown up had hardly realised, that Diana Mayo, with the clothes and manners of a boy, was really an uncommonly beautiful young woman. With the assurance belonging to his type, he had taken the earliest opportunity of telling her so, following it with an attempt to secure the kiss that up to now his own good looks had always secured for him. But in this case he had to deal with a girl who was a girl by accident of birth only, who was quicker with her hands and far finer trained than he was, and whose natural strength was increased by furious rage. She had blacked his eyes before he properly understood what was happening, and was dancing around him like an infuriated young gamecock when the rector had burst in upon them, attracted by the noise.

What she left he had finished, and then, breathless and angry, had ridden back across the park with her and had briefly announced to Sir Aubrey, who happened to be at home upon one of his rare visits, that his pupil was both too old and too pretty to continue her studies at the rectory, and had taken himself off as hurriedly as he had come, leaving Sir Aubrey to settle for himself the new problem of Diana. And, as before, it was settled in the easiest possible way. Physically she was perfectly able to take up the role for which he had always intended her; mentally he presumed that she knew as much as it was necessary for her to know, and, in any case, travelling itself was an education, and a far finer one than could be learned from books. So Diana grew up in a day, and in a fortnight the old life was behind her and she had started out on the ceaseless travels with her brother that had continued for the last six years—years of perpetual change, of excitements and dangers.

She thought of it all, sitting on the broad rail of the balcony, her head slanted against the column on which she leaned. "It's been a splendid life," she murmured, "and tomorrow—today begins the most perfect part of it." She yawned and realised suddenly that she was desperately sleepy. She turned back into her room, leaving the windows wide, and, flinging off her wrap, tumbled into bed and slept almost before her head was on the pillow.

It must have been about an hour later when she awoke, suddenly wide awake. She lay quite still, looking cautiously under her thick lashes. The room was flooded with moonlight, there was nothing to be seen, but she had the positive feeling that there was another presence in the room beside her own; she had had a half-conscious vision in the moment of waking of a shadowy something that had seemed to fade away by the window. As the actual reality of this thought pierced through the sleep that dulled her brain and became a concrete suggestion, she sprang out of the bed and ran on to the balcony. It was empty. She leaned over the railing, listening intently, but she could see nothing and hear nothing. Puzzled, she went back into her room and turned on the lights. Nothing seemed to be missing: her watch lay where she had left it on the dressing table; and the suit-cases had apparently not been tampered with. By the bedside the ivory-mounted revolver that she always carried was lying as she had placed it. She looked around the room again, frowning. "It must have been a dream," she said doubtfully, "but it seemed very real. It looked tall and white and solid, and I *felt* it there." She waited a moment or two, then shrugged her shoulders, turned out the lights, and got into bed. Her nerves were admirable, and in five minutes she was asleep again.

CHAPTER II

The promised send-off had been enthusiastic. The arrangements for the trip had been perfect; there had been no hitch anywhere. The guide, Mustafa Ali, appeared capable and efficient, effacing himself when not wanted and replying with courteous dignity when spoken to. The day had been full of interest, and the long, hot ride had for Diana been the height of physical enjoyment. They had reached the oasis where the first night was to be passed an hour before, and found the camp already established, tents pitched, and everything so ordered that Sir Aubrey could find nothing to criticise; even Stephens, his servant, who had travelled with him since Diana was a baby, and who was as critical as his master on the subject of camps, had no fault to find.

Diana glanced about her little travelling tent with complete content. It was much smaller than the ones to which she had always been accustomed, ridiculously so compared with the large one she had had in India the previous year, with its separate bath—and dressing-rooms. Servants, too, had swarmed in India. Here service promised to be inadequate, but it had been her whim on this tour to dispense with the elaborate arrangements that Sir Aubrey cultivated and to try comparative roughing it. The narrow camp cot, the tin bath, the little folding table and her two suit-cases seemed to take up all the available space. But she laughed at the inconvenience, though she had drenched her bed with splashing, and the soap had found its way into the toe of one of her long boots. She had changed from her riding clothes into a dress of clinging jade-green silk, swinging short above her slender ankles, the neck cut low, revealing the gleaming white of her soft, girlish bosom. She came out of the tent and stood a moment exchanging an amused smile with Stephens, who was hovering near dubiously, one eye on her and the other on his master. She was late, and Sir Aubrey liked his meals punctually. The baronet was lounging in one deck-chair with his feet on another.

Diana wagged an admonishing forefinger. "Fly, Stephens, and fetch the soup! If it is cold there will be a riot." She walked to the edge of the canvas cloth that had been thrown down in front of the tents and stood revelling in the scene around her, her eyes dancing with excitement as they glanced slowly around the camp spread out over the oasis—the clustering palm trees, the desert itself stretching away before her in undulating sweeps, but seemingly level in the evening light, far off to the distant hills lying like a dark smudge against the horizon. She drew a long breath. It was the desert at last, the desert that she felt she had been longing for all her life. She had never known until this moment how intense the longing had been. She felt strangely at home, as if the great, silent emptiness had been waiting for her as she had been waiting for it, and now that she had come it was welcoming her softly with the faint rustle of the whispering sand, the mysterious charm of its billowy, shifting surface that seemed beckoning to her to penetrate further and further into its unknown obscurities.

Her brother's voice behind her brought her down to earth suddenly. "You've been a confounded long time."

She turned to the table with a faint smile. "Don't be a bear, Aubrey. It's all very well for you. You have Stephens to lather your chin and to wash your hands, but thanks to that idiot Marie, I have to look after myself."

Sir Aubrey took his heels down leisurely from the second chair, pitched away his cigar, and, screwing his eyeglass into his eye with more than usual truculence, looked at her with disapproval. "Are you going to rig yourself out like that every evening for the benefit of Mustafa Ali and the camel-drivers?"

"I do not propose to invite the worthy Mustafa to meals, and I am not in the habit of 'rigging myself out,' as you so charmingly put it, for any one's benefit. If you think I dress in camp to please you, my dear Aubrey, you flatter yourself. I do it entirely to please myself. That explorer woman we met in London that first year I began travelling with you explained to me the real moral and physical value of changing into comfortable, pretty clothes after a hard day in breeches and boots. You change yourself. What's the difference?"

"All the difference," he snapped. "There is no need for you to make yourself more attractive than you are already."

"Since when has it occurred to you that I am attractive? You must have a touch of the sun, Aubrey," she replied, with uplifted eyebrows, drumming impatiently with her fingers on the table.

"Don't quibble. You know perfectly well that you are good-looking—too good-looking to carry through this preposterous affair."

"Will you please tell me what you are driving at?" she asked quietly. But the dark blue eyes fixed on her brother's face were growing darker as she looked at him.

"I've been doing some hard thinking today, Diana. This tour you propose is impossible."

"Isn't it rather late in the day to find that out?" she interrupted sarcastically; but he ignored the interruption.

"You must see for yourself, now that you are face to face with the thing, that it is impossible. It's quite unthinkable that you can wander for the next month all alone in the desert with those damned niggers. Though my legal guardianship over you terminated last September I still have some moral obligations towards you. Though it has been convenient to me to bring you up as a boy and to regard you in the light of a younger brother instead of a sister, we cannot get away from the fact that you are a woman, and a very young woman. There are certain things a young woman cannot do. If you had been the boy I always wished you were it would have been a different matter, but you are not a boy, and the whole thing is impossible—utterly impossible." There was a fretful impatience in his voice.

Diana lit a cigarette slowly, and swung round on her chair with a hard laugh. "If I had not lived with you all my life, Aubrey, I should really be impressed with your brotherly solicitude; I should think you really meant it. But knowing you as I do, I know that it is not anxiety on my behalf that is prompting you, but the disinclination that you have to travel alone without me. You have come to depend on me to save you certain annoyances and inconveniences that always occur in travelling. You were more honest in Biskra when you only objected to my trip without giving reasons. Why have you waited until tonight to give me those reasons?"

"Because I thought that here, at least, you would have sense enough to see them. In Biskra it was impossible to argue with you. You made your own arrangements against my wishes. I left it, feeling convinced that the impossibility of it would be brought home to you here, and that you would see for yourself that it was out of the question. Diana, give up this insane trip."

"I will not."

"I've a thundering good mind to make you."

"You can't. I'm my own mistress. You have no right over me at all. You have no claim on me. You haven't even that of ordinary brotherly affection, for you have never given me any, so you cannot expect it from me. We needn't make any pretence about it, I am not going to argue any more. I will not go back to Biskra."

"If you are afraid of being laughed at—" he sneered; but she took him up swiftly.

"I am not afraid of being laughed at. Only cowards are afraid of that, and I am not a coward."

"Diana, listen to reason!"

"Aubrey! I have said my last word. Nothing will alter my determination to go on this trip. Your arguments do not convince me, who know you. It is your own considerations and not mine that are at the bottom of your remonstrances. You do not deny it, because you can't, because it is true."

They were facing each other across the little table. An angry flush rose in Sir Aubrey's face, and his eyeglass fell with a little sharp tinkle against a waistcoat button.

"You're a damned obstinate little devil!" he said furiously.

She looked at him steadily, her scornful mouth firm as his own. "I am what you have made me," she said slowly. "Why quarrel with the result? You have brought me up to ignore the restrictions attached to my sex; you now round on me and throw them in my face. All my life you have set me an example of selfishness and obstinacy. Can you wonder that I have profited by it? You have made me as hard as yourself, and you now profess surprise at the determination your training has forced upon me. You are illogical. It is your fault, not mine. There was bound to be a clash some day. It has come sooner than I expected, that's all. Up till now my inclinations have gone with yours, but this seems to be the parting of the ways. As I reminded you before, I am my own mistress, and

I will submit to no interference with my actions. Please understand that clearly, Aubrey. I don't want to wrangle any more. I will join you in New York as I promised. I am not in the habit of breaking my promises, but my life is my own to deal with, and I will deal with it exactly as I wish and not as any one else wishes. I will do what I choose when and how I choose, and I will *never* obey any will but my own."

Sir Aubrey's eyes narrowed suddenly. "Then I hope to Heaven that one day you will fall into the hands of a man who will make you obey," he cried wrathfully.

Her scornful mouth curled still more scornfully. "Then Heaven help him!" she retorted scathingly, and turned away to her tent.

But, alone, her anger gave way to amusement. It had been something, after all, to rouse the lazy Aubrey to wrath. She knew exactly the grievance he had been nursing against her during the last few weeks in Biskra. Though he travelled perpetually and often in remote and desolate places, he travelled with the acme of comfort and the minimum of inconveniences. He put himself out for nothing, and the inevitable difficulties that accrued fell on Diana's younger and less blase shoulders. She had always known the uses he put her to and the convenience she was to him. He might have some latent feelings with regard to the inadvisability of her behavior, he might even have some prickings of conscience on the subject of his upbringing of her, but it was thoughts of his own comfort that were troubling him most. That she knew, and the knowledge was not conducive to any kinder feeling towards him. He always had been and always would be supremely selfish. The whole of their life together had been conducted to suit his conveniences and not hers. She knew, too, why her company was particularly desired on his visit to America. It was a hunting trip, but not the kind that they were usually accustomed to: it was a wife and not big game that was taking Sir Aubrey across the ocean on this occasion. It had been in his mind for some time as an inevitable and somewhat unpleasant necessity. Women bored him, and the idea of marriage was distasteful, but a son to succeed him was imperative—a Mayo must be followed by a Mayo. An heir was essential for the big property that the family had held for hundreds of years. No woman had ever attracted him, but of all women he had met American women were less actively irritating to him, and so it was to America that he turned in search of a wife. He proposed to take a house in New York for a few months and later on in Newport, and it was for that that Diana's company was considered indispensable. She would save him endless trouble, as all arrangements could be left in her hands and Stephens'. Having made up his mind to go through with a proceeding that he regarded in the light of a sacrifice on the family altar, his wish was to get it over and done with as soon as possible, and Diana's interference in his plans had exasperated him. It was the first time that their wills had crossed, and she shrugged her shoulders impatiently, with a grimace at the recollection. A little more and it would have degenerated into a vulgar quarrel. She banished Aubrey and his selfishness resolutely from her mind. It was very hot, and she lay very still in the narrow cot, wishing she had not been so rigid in the matter of its width, and wondering if a sudden movement in the night would precipitate her into the bath that stood alongside. She thought regretfully of a punkah, and then smiled derisively at herself.

"Sybarite!" she murmured sleepily. "You need a few discomforts."

She was almost aggressively cheerful next morning at breakfast and for the time that they lingered at the oasis after the baggage camels had started. Sir Aubrey was morose and silent, and she exchanged most of her badinage with Stephens, who was superintending the packing of the tiffin basket that would accompany her in charge of the man who had been selected as her personal servant, and who was waiting, with Mustafa Ali and about ten men, to ride with her.

The time for starting came. Stephens was fussing about the horse that Diana was to ride.

"Everything all right, Stephens? Up to your standard? Don't look so glum. I wish you were coming to look after me, but it couldn't be done. Sir Aubrey would be lost without you."

The idea of a tour without Stephens in the background seemed suddenly momentous, and the smile she gave him was more serious than she meant it to be. She went back to her brother, who was pulling his moustache savagely. "I don't think there's any use waiting any longer. You won't want to hurry yourself too much, and you will want to be in Biskra in time for dinner," she said as casually as she could.

He swung towards her. "Diana, it's still not too late to change your mind. For Heaven's sake give up this folly. It's tempting Providence." For the first time there was a genuine ring in his voice, and for a moment Diana wavered, but only for a moment. Then she looked at him with a slow smile.

"Do I fall on your neck and say, 'Take me back, dear Guardian; I will be good,' or do I prostrate myself at your feet and knock my head on your boots, and whine, in the language of the country, 'Hearing is obeying'? Don't be ridiculous, Aubrey. You can't expect me to change my mind at the eleventh hour. It's perfectly safe. Mustafa Ali will take care that everything goes smoothly. He has his reputation in Biskra to think of. You know the character the authorities gave him. He is not likely to throw that away. In any case I can take care of myself, thanks to your training. I don't mind owning to being conceited about my shooting. Even you admit that I am a credit to your teaching."

With a gay little laugh she whipped out the ivory-mounted revolver, and aiming at a low flat rock, some distance away, fired. She was an unusually good revolver shot, but this time she seemed to have missed. There was no mark on the stone. Diana stared at it stupidly, a frown of perplexity creasing her forehead. Then she looked at her brother, and back to the revolver in her hand.

Sir Aubrey swore. "Diana! What a senseless piece of bravado!" he cried angrily.

She took no notice of him. She was still staring at the smooth rock fate. "I don't understand it. How could I miss? It's as big as a house," she murmured thoughtfully, and raised the revolver again.

But Sir Aubrey caught her wrist. "For God's sake don't make a fool of yourself a second time. You have lowered your prestige quite enough already," he said in a low voice, with a glance at the group of watching Arabs.

Diana jerked the little weapon back into its place reluctantly. "I don't understand it," she said again. "It must be the light." She mounted and wheeled her horse alongside of Sir Aubrey's, and held out her hand. "Goodbye, Aubrey. Expect me a month after you arrive. I will cable to you from Cherbourg. Good luck! I shall roll up in time to be best man," she added, laughing, and with a nod to Mustafa Ali she turned her horse's head southwards.

For a long time she rode in silence. The quarrel with Aubrey had left a nasty taste in her mouth. She knew that what she was doing was considered unconventional, but she had been brought up to be unconventional. She had never even thought, when she planned her tour, of possible criticism; it would have made no difference to her if she had thought, and she had been amazed and amused at the sensation that her proposed trip had caused. The publicity to which it had given rise had annoyed her intensely; she had been scornful that people could not occupy themselves with their own affairs and leave her to deal with hers. But that Aubrey should join in the general criticism and present such a complete *volte-face* to the opinions he had always held was beyond her comprehension. She was angry with him, and contempt was mingled with her anger. It was inconsistent with the whole of his lifelong attitude toward her, and the discovery of his altered ideas left her rather breathless and more than ever determined to adhere to her own deeply-rooted convictions. Aubrey was responsible for them, he had instilled them, and if he chose now to abandon them that was his look-out. For her own part she saw no reason to change principles she had been brought up in. If Aubrey really thought there was danger in this expedition he could have sacrificed himself for once and come with her. As Jim Arbuthnot had said, it was only a month, a negligible length of time, but Aubrey's selfishness would not allow him to make that concession any more than her own obstinacy would allow her to give way. It was too much to expect. And this was the desert! It was the expedition that she had dreamed of and planned for years. She could not give it up. The idea of danger brought a little laugh to her lips. How could anything in the desert hurt her? It had been calling to her always. There was nothing strange about the scene that lay all around her. Her surroundings seemed oddly familiar. The burning sun overhead in the cloudless sky, the shimmering haze rising from the hot, dry ground, the feathery outline of some clustering palm trees in a tiny distant oasis were like remembrances that she watched again with a feeling of gladness that was fuller and deeper than anything that she had been conscious of before. She was radiantly happy—happy in the sense of her youth and strength, her perfect physical fitness, happy in the capacity of her power of enjoyment, happy with the touch of the keen, nervous horse between her knees, exhilarated with her new authority. She had looked forward so eagerly, and realisation was proving infinitely greater than anticipation. And for a whole month this perfect happiness was to be hers. She thought of her promise to Aubrey with impatience. To give up the joyous freedom of the desert for the commonplace round of American social life seemed preposterous. The thought of the weeks in New York were frankly tedious; Newport would be a little less bad, for there were alleviations. The only hope was that Aubrey would find the wife he was looking for quickly and release her from an obligation that was going to be very wearisome. Aubrey was counting on her, and it would be unsporting to let him down; she would have to keep her promise, but she would be glad when it was over. Aubrey married would settle definitely the possibility of any further disagreements between them. She wondered vaguely what the future Lady Mayo would be like, but she did not expend much pity on her. American girls as a rule were well able to care for themselves. She stroked her horse with a little smile. Aubrey and his possible wife seemed singularly uninteresting beside the vivid interest of the moment. A caravan that had been visible for a long time coming towards them drew nearer, and Diana reined in to watch the long line of slow, lurching camels passing. The great beasts, with their disdainful tread and long, swaying necks, never failed to interest her. It was a large caravan; the bales on the camels' backs looked heavy, and beside the merchants on riding camels and a motley crowd of followers—some on lean little donkeys and others on foot—there was an armed guard of mounted men. It took some time to pass. One of two of the camels carried huddled figures, swathed and shapeless with a multitude of coverings, that Diana knew must be women. The contrast between them and herself was almost ridiculous. It made her feel stifled even to look at them. She wondered what their lives were like, if they ever rebelled against the drudgery and restrictions that were imposed upon them, if they ever longed for the freedom that she was revelling in, or if custom and usage were so strong that they had no thoughts beyond the narrow life they led. The thought of those lives filled her with aversion. The idea of marriage—even in its highest form, based on mutual consideration and mutual forbearance—was repugnant to her. She thought of it with a shiver of absolute repulsion. To Aubrey it was distasteful, but to her cold, reserved temperament it was a thing of horror and disgust. That women could submit to the degrading intimacy and fettered existence of married life filled her with scornful wonder. To be bound irrevocably to the will and pleasure of a man who would have the right to demand obedience in all that constituted marriage and the strength to enforce those claims revolted her. For a Western woman it was bad enough, but for the women of the East, mere slaves of the passions of the men who owned them, unconsidered, disregarded, reduced to the level of animals, the bare idea made her quiver and bring her hand down heavily on her horse's neck. The nervous creature started sharply and she let him go, calling to Mustafa Ali as she cantered past him. He had ridden to meet the caravan and was dismounted, deep in conversation with the chief of the armed guard. With the thoughts that it had provoked the caravan had lost all interest for Diana. She wanted to get away from it, to forget it, and she rode on unmindful of her escort, who, like her guide, had stopped to speak with the traders. Diana's horse was fleet, and it was some time before they caught her up. There was a look of annoyance on Mustafa Ali's face as she turned on hearing them behind her and signed to him to ride beside her.

"Mademoiselle is not interested in the caravan?" he asked curiously.

"No," she replied shortly, and asked for some details connected with her own expedition. The man talked easily and well, in fluent French, and after giving the required information, volunteered anecdotes relating to various well-known people whom he had guided in the desert. Diana watched him interestedly. He seemed a man of about middle age, though it was difficult to guess more than approximately, for the thick, peaked beard that hid both mouth and chin made him look older than he really was. His beard had been his only drawback from Diana's point of view, for she judged men by their mouths. Eyes were untrustworthy evidences of character in an Oriental, for they usually wavered under a European's. Mustafa Ali's were wavering now as she looked at him, and it occurred to her that they had not seemed nearly so shifty in Biskra when she had engaged him. But she attached no importance to the thought, and dismissed it as much less interesting than the great difference displayed in their respective modes of riding. The Arab's exaggeratedly short stirrup would have given her agonies of cramp. She pointed the difference with a laugh of amusement and drew the man on to speak of his horses. The one Diana was riding was an unusually fine beast, and had been one of the greatest points in the guide's favour when he had brought it for her inspection. He was enthusiastic in its praise, but volubly vague as to its antecedents, which left Diana with the conviction that the animal had either been stolen or acquired in some irregular manner and that it would be tactless to pursue further inquiries. After all it was no business of hers. It was enough that her trip was to be conducted on the back of a horse that it was a pleasure to ride and whose vagaries promised to give interest to what otherwise might have been monotonous. Some of the horses that she had seen in Biskra had been the veriest jades.

She asked Mustafa Ali about the country through which they were passing, but he did not seem to have much information that was really of interest, or what seemed important to him appeared trivial to her, and he constantly brought the conversation back to Biskra, of which she was tired, or to Oran, of which she knew nothing. The arrival at a little oasis where the guide suggested that the midday halt might be made was opportune. Diana swung to the ground, and, tossing down her gloves, gave herself a shake. It was hot work riding in the burning sun and the rest would be delightful. She had a thoroughly healthy appetite, and superintended the laying out of her lunch with interest. It was the last time that it would be as daintily packed. Stephens was an artist with a picnic basket. She was going to miss Stephens. She finished her lunch quickly, and then, with her back propped against a palm tree, a cigarette in her mouth, her arms clasped round her knees, she settled down happily, overlooking the desert. The noontime hush seemed over everything. Not a breath of wind stirred the tops of the palms; a lizard on a rock near her was the only living thing she could see. She glanced over her shoulder. The men, with their big cloaks drawn over their heads, were lying asleep, or at any rate appeared to be so; only Mustafa Ali was on foot, standing at the edge of the oasis, staring fixedly in the direction in which they would ride later.

Diana threw the end of her cigarette at the lizard and laughed at its precipitant flight. She had no desire to follow the example of her escort and sleep. She was much too happy to lose a minute of her enjoyment by wasting it in rest that she did not require. She was perfectly content and satisfied with herself and her outlook. She had not a care or a thought in the world. There was not a thing that she would have changed or altered. Her life had always been happy; she had extracted the last ounce of pleasure out of every moment of it. That her happiness was due to the wealth that had enabled her to indulge in the sports and constant travel that made up the sum total of her desires never occurred to her. That what composed her pleasure in life was possible only because she was rich enough to buy the means of gratifying it did not enter her head. She thought of her wealth no more than of her beauty. The business connected with her coming of age, when the big fortune left to her by her father passed unreservedly into her own hands, was a wearisome necessity that had been got through as expeditiously as possible, with as little attention to detail as the old family lawyer had allowed, and an absence of interest that was evidenced in the careless scrawl she attached to each document that was given her to sign. The mere money in itself was nothing; it was only a means to an end. She had never even realised how much was expended on the continuous and luxurious expeditions that she had made with Sir Aubrey; her own individual tastes were simple, and apart from the expensive equipment that was indispensable for their hunting trips, and which was Aubrey's choosing, not hers, she was not extravagant. The long list of figures that had been so boring during the tedious hours that she had spent with the lawyer, grudging every second of the glorious September morning that she had had to waste in the library when she was longing to be out of doors, had conveyed nothing to her beyond the fact that in future when she wanted anything she would be put to the trouble of writing out an absurd piece of paper herself, instead of leaving the matter in Aubrey's hands, as she had done hitherto.

She had hardly understood and had been much embarrassed by the formal and pedantic congratulations with which the lawyer had concluded his business statement. She was not aware that she was an object of congratulation. It all seemed very stupid and uninteresting. Of real life she knew nothing and of the ordinary ties and attachments of family life less than nothing. Aubrey's cold, loveless training had debarred her from all affection; she had grown up oblivious of it. Love did not exist for her; from even the thought of passion she shrank instinctively with the same fastidiousness as she did from actual physical uncleanliness.

That she had awakened an emotion that she did not understand herself in certain men had been an annoyance that had become more intolerable with repetition. She had hated them and herself impartially, and she had scorned them fiercely. She had never been so gentle and so human with any one as she had been with Jim Arbuthnot, and that only because she was so radiantly happy that night that not even the distasteful reminder that she was a woman whom a man coveted was able to disturb her happiness. But here there was no need to dwell on annoyances or distasteful reminders.

Diana dug her heels into the soft ground with a little wriggle of content; here she would be free from anything that could mar her perfect enjoyment of life as it appeared to her. Here there was nothing to spoil her pleasure. Her head had drooped during her thoughts, and for the last few minutes her eyes had been fixed on the dusty tips of her riding-boots. But she raised them now and looked up with a great content in them. It was the happiest day of her life. She had forgotten the quarrel with Aubrey. She had put from her the chain of ideas suggested by the passing caravan. There was nothing discordant to disturb the perfect harmony of her mind.

A shade beside her made her turn her head. Mustafa Ali salaamed obsequiously. "It is time to start, Mademoiselle."

Diana looked up in surprise and then back over her shoulder at the escort. The men were already mounted. The smile faded from her eyes. Mustafa Ali was guide, but she was head of this expedition; if her guide had not realised this he would have to do so now. She glanced at the watch on her wrist.

"There is plenty of time," she said coolly.

Mustafa Ali salaamed again. "It is a long ride to reach the oasis where we must camp tonight," he insisted hurriedly.

Diana crossed one brown boot over the other, and scooping up some sand in the palm of her hand trickled it through her fingers slowly. "Then we can ride faster," she replied quietly, looking at the shining particles glistening in the sun.

Mustafa Ali made a movement of impatience and persisted doggedly. "Mademoiselle would do well to start."

Diana looked up swiftly with angry eyes. Under the man's suave manner and simple words a peremptory tone had crept into his voice. She sat quite still, her fingers raking the warm sand, and under her haughty stare the guide's eyes wavered and turned away. "We will start when I choose, Mustafa Ali," she said brusquely. "You may give orders to your men, but you will take your orders from me. I will tell you when I am ready. You may go."

Still he hesitated, swaying irresolutely backwards and forwards on his heels.

Diana snapped her fingers over her shoulder, a trick she had learned from a French officer in Biskra. "I said go!" she repeated sharply. She took no notice of his going and did not look back to see what orders he gave the men. She glanced at her watch again. Perhaps it was growing late, perhaps the camp was a longer ride than she had thought; but Mustafa Ali must learn his lesson if they rode till midnight to reach the oasis. She pushed her obstinate chin out further and then smiled again suddenly. She hoped that the night would fall before they reached their destination. There had been one or two moonlight riding picnics out from Biskra, and the glamour of the desert nights had gone to Diana's head. This riding into the unknown away from the noisy, chattering crowd who had spoiled the perfect stillness of the night would be infinitely more perfect. She gave a little sigh of regret as she thought of it. It was not really practical. Though she would wait nearly another hour to allow the fact of her authority to sink into Mustafa Ali's brain she would have to hasten afterwards to arrive at the camp before darkness set in. The men were unused to her ways and she to theirs. She would not have Stephens' help tonight; she would have to depend on herself to order everything as she wished it, and it was easier done in daylight. One hour would not make much difference. The horses had more in them than had been taken out of them this morning; they could be pushed along a bit faster with no harm happening to them. She eyed her watch from time to time with a grin of amusement, but suppressed the temptation to look and see how Mustafa Ali was taking it, for her action might be seen and misconstrued.

When the time she had set herself was up she rose and walked slowly towards the group of Arabs. The guide's face was sullen, but she took no notice, and, when they started, motioned him to her side again with a reference to Biskra that provoked a flow of words. It was the last place she wanted to hear of, but it was one of which he spoke the readiest, and she knew it was not wise to allow him to remain silent to sulk. His ill-temper would evaporate with the sound of his own voice. She rode forward steadily, silent herself, busy with her own thoughts, heedless of the voice beside her, and unconscious of the fact when it became silent.

She had been quite right about the capabilities of the horses. They responded without any apparent effort to the further demand made of them. The one in particular that Diana was riding moved in a swift, easy gallop that was the perfection of motion.

They had been riding for some hours when they came to the first oasis that had been sighted since leaving the one where the midday halt was made. Diana pulled up her horse to look at it, for it was unusually beautiful in the luxuriousness and arrangement of its group of palms and leafy bushes. Some pigeons were cooing softly, hidden from sight amongst the trees, with a plaintive melancholy that somehow seemed in keeping with the deserted spot. Beside the well, forming a triangle, stood what had been three particularly fine palm trees, but the tops had been broken off about twenty feet up from the ground, and the mutilated trunks reared themselves bare and desolate-looking. Diana took off her heavy helmet and tossed it to the man behind her, and sat looking at the oasis, while the faint breeze that had sprung up stirred her thick, short hair, and cooled her hot head. The sad notes of the pigeons and the broken palms, that with their unusualness vaguely suggested a tragedy, lent an air of mystery to the place that pleased her.

She turned eagerly to Mustafa Ali. "Why did you not arrange for the camp to be here? It would have been a long enough ride."

The man fidgeted in his saddle, fingering his beard uneasily, his eyes wandering past Diana's and looking at the broken trees. "No man rests here, Mademoiselle. It is the place of devils. The curse of Allah is upon it," he muttered, touching his horse with his heel, and making it sidle restlessly—an obvious hint that Diana ignored.

"I like it," she persisted obstinately.

He made a quick gesture with his fingers. "It is accursed. Death lurks beside those broken palm trees," he said, looking at her curiously.

She jerked her head with a sudden smile. "For you, perhaps, but not for me. Allah's curse rests only upon those who fear it. But since you are afraid, Mustafa Ali, let us go on." She gave a little light laugh, and Mustafa Ali kicked his horse savagely as he followed.

The distance before her spread out cleanly with the sharp distinctness that precedes the setting sun. She rode on until she began to wonder if it would indeed be night-fall before she reached her destination. They had ridden longer and faster than had ever been intended. It seemed odd that they had not overtaken the baggage camels. She looked at her watch with a frown. "Where is your caravan, Mustafa Ali?" she called. "I see no sign of an oasis, and the darkness will come."

"If Mademoiselle had started earlier—" he said sullenly.

"If I had started earlier it would still have been too far. Tomorrow we will arrange it otherwise," she said firmly.

"Tomorrow—" he growled indistinctly.

Diana looked at him keenly. "What did you say?" she asked haughtily.

His hand went to his forehead mechanically. "Tomorrow is with Allah!" he murmured with unctuous piety.

A retort trembled on Diana's lips, but her attention was distracted from her annoying guide to a collection of black specks far off across the desert. They were too far away for her to see clearly, but she pointed to them, peering at them intently. "See!" she cried. "Is that the caravan?"

"As Allah wills!" he replied more piously than before, and Diana wished, with a sudden feeling of irritation, that he would stop relegating his responsibilities to the Deity and take a little more active personal interest in his missing camel train.

The black specks were moving fast across the level plain. Very soon Diana saw that it was not the slow, leisurely camels that they were overtaking, but a band of mounted men who were moving swiftly towards them. They had seen nobody since the traders' caravan had passed them in the morning. For Diana the Arabs that were approaching were even more interesting than the caravan had been. She had seen plenty of caravans arriving and departing from Biskra, but, though she had seen small parties of tribesmen constantly in the vicinity of the town, she had never seen so large a body of mounted men before, nor had she seen them as they were here, one with the wild picturesqueness of their surroundings. It was impossible to count how many there were, for they were riding in close formation, the wind filling their, great white cloaks, making each man look gigantic. Diana's interest flamed up excitedly. It was like passing another ship upon a hitherto empty sea. They seemed to add a desired touch to the grim loneliness of the scene that had begun to be a little awe-inspiring. Perhaps she was hungry, perhaps she was tired, or perhaps she was only annoyed by the bad arrangements of her guide, but before the advent of the mounted Arabs Diana had been conscious of a feeling of oppression, as if the silent desolation of the desert was weighing heavily upon her, but the body of swiftly moving men and horses had changed the aspect utterly. An atmosphere of life and purpose seemed to have taken the place of the quiet stagnation that had been before their coming.

The distance between the two parties decreased rapidly. Diana, intent on the quickly advancing horsemen, spurred ahead of her guide with sparkling eyes. They were near enough now to see that the horses were beautiful creatures and that each man rode magnificently. They were armed too, their rifles being held in front of them, not slung on their backs as she had seen in Biskra. They passed quite close to her, only a few yards away—a solid square, the orderly ranks suggesting training and discipline that she had not looked for. Not a head turned in her direction as they went by and the pace was not slackened. Fretted by the proximity of the galloping horses, her own horse reared impatiently, but Diana pulled him in, turning in her saddle to watch the Arabs pass, her breath coming quick with excitement.

"What are they?" she called out to Mustafa Ali, who had dropped some way behind her. But he, too, was looking back at the horsemen, and did not seem to hear her question. Her escort had lagged still further behind her guide and were some distance away. Diana watched the rapidly moving, compact square eagerly with appreciatory eyes—it was a beautiful sight. Then she gave a little gasp. The galloping horses had drawn level with the last stragglers of her own party, and just beyond they stopped suddenly. Diana would not have believed it possible that they could have stopped so suddenly and in such close formation while travelling at such a pace. The tremendous strain on the bridles flung the horses far back on their haunches. But there was no time to dwell on the wonderful horsemanship or training of the men. Events moved too rapidly. The solid square split up and lengthened out into a long line of two men riding abreast. Wheeling behind the last of Mustafa's men they came back even faster than they had passed, and circled widely round Diana and her attendants. Bewildered by this manoeuvre she watched them with a puzzled frown, striving to soothe her horse, who was nearly frantic with excitement. Twice they galloped round her little band, their long cloaks fluttering, their rifles tossing in their hands. Diana was growing impatient. It was very fine to watch, but time and the light were both going. She would have been glad if the demonstration had occurred earlier in the day, when there would have been more time to enjoy it. She turned again to Mustafa Ali to suggest that they had better try to move on, but he had gone further from her, back towards his own. She wrestled with her nervous mount, trying to turn him to join her guide, when a sudden burst of rifle shots made her start and her horse bound violently. Then she laughed. That would be the end of the demonstration, a parting salute, the *decharge de mousqueterie* beloved of the Arab. She turned her head from her refractory horse to look at them ride off, and the laugh died away on her lips. It was not a farewell salute. The rifles that the Arabs were firing were not pointing up into the heavens, but aiming straight at her and her escort. And as she stared with suddenly startled eyes, unable to do anything with her plunging horse, Mustafa Ali's men were blotted out from her sight, cut off by a band of Arabs who rode between her and them. Mustafa Ali himself was lying forward on the neck of his horse, who was standing quiet amidst the general confusion. Then there came another volley, and the guide slid slowly out of his saddle on to the ground, and at the same time Diana's horse went off with a wild leap that nearly unseated her.

Until they started shooting the thought that the Arabs could be hostile had not crossed her mind. She imagined that they were merely showing off with the childish love of display which she knew was characteristic. The French authorities had been right after all. Diana's first feeling was one of contempt for an administration that made possible such an attempt so near civilisation. Her second a fleeting amusement at the thought of how Aubrey would jeer. But her amusement passed as the real seriousness of the attack came home to her. For the first time it occurred to her that her guide's descent from his saddle was due to a wound and not to the fear that she had at first disgustedly attributed to him. But nobody had seemed to put up any kind of a fight, she thought wrathfully. She tugged angrily at her horse's mouth, but the bit was between his teeth and he tore on frantically. Her own position made her furious. Her guide was wounded, his men surrounded, and she was ignominiously being run away with by a bolting horse. If she could only turn the wretched animal. It would only be a question of ransom, of that she was positive. She must get back somehow to the others and arrange terms. It was an annoyance, of course, but after all it added a certain piquancy to her trip, it would be an experience. It was only a "hold-up." She did not suppose the Arabs had even really meant to hurt any one, but they were excited and some one's shot, aimed wide, had found an unexpected billet. It could only be that. It was too near Biskra for any real danger, she argued with herself, still straining on the reins. She would not admit that there was any danger, though her heart was beating in a way that it had never done before. Then as she hauled ineffectually at the bridle with all her strength there came from behind her the sound of a long, shrill whistle. Her horse pricked up his ears and she was conscious that his pace sensibly lessened. Instinctively she looked behind. A solitary Arab was riding after her and as she looked she realised that his horse was gaining on hers. The thought drove every idea of stopping her runaway from her and made her dig her spurs into him instead. There was a sinister air of deliberation in the way in which the Arab was following her; he was riding her down.

Diana's mouth closed firmly and a new keenness came into her steady eyes. It was one thing to go back voluntarily to make terms with the men who had attacked her party; it was quite another thing to be deliberately chased across the desert by an Arab freebooter. Her obstinate chin was almost square. Then the shadow of a laugh flickered in her eyes and curved her mouth. New experiences were crowding in upon her today. She had often wondered what the feelings of a hunted creature were. She seemed in a fair way of finding out. She had always stoutly maintained that the fox enjoyed the run as much as the hounds; that remained to be proved, but, in any case, she would give this hound a run for his money. She could ride, and there seemed plenty yet in the frightened animal under her. She bent down, lying low against his neck with a little, reckless laugh, coaxing him with all her knowledge and spurring him alternately. But soon her mood changed. She frowned anxiously as she looked at the last rays of the setting sun. It would be dark very soon. She could not go chasing through the night with this tiresome Arab at her heels. The humour seemed to have died out of the situation and Diana began to get angry. In the level country that surrounded her there were no natural features that could afford cover or aid in any way; there seemed nothing for it but to own herself defeated and pull up—if she could. An idea of trying to dodge him and of returning of her own free will was dismissed at once as hopeless. She had seen enough in her short glimpse of the Arabs' tactics when they had passed her to know that she was dealing with a finished horseman on a perfectly trained horse, and that her idea could never succeed. But, perversely, she felt that to that particular Arab following her she would never give in. She would ride till she dropped, or the horse did, before that.

The whistle came again, and again, in spite of her relentless spurring, her horse checked his pace. A sudden inspiration came to her. Perhaps it was the horse she was riding that was the cause of all the trouble. It was certainly the Arab's whistle that had made it moderate its speed; it was responding clearly to a signal that it knew. Her guide's reluctance to give any particulars of his acquisition of the horse came back to her. There could not be much doubt about it. The animal had unquestionably been stolen, and either belonged to or was known to the party of Arabs who had met them.

The *naivete* that paraded a stolen horse through the desert at the risk of meeting its former owner made her smile in spite of her annoyance, but it was not a pleasant smile, as her thoughts turned from the horse to its present owner. The sum of Mustafa Ali's delinquencies was mounting up fast. But it was his affair, not hers. In the meantime she had paid for the horse to ride through the desert, not to be waylaid by Arab bandits. Her temper was going fast.

She urged the horse on with all her power, but perceptibly he was slowing up. She flashed another backward look. The Arab was close behind her—closer than she had been aware. She had a momentary glimpse of a big white figure, dark piercing eyes, and white gleaming teeth, and passionate rage filled her. With no thought of what the consequences or retaliation might be, with no thought at all beyond a wild desire to rid herself of her pursuer, driven by a sudden madness which seemed to rise up in her and which she could not control, she clutched her revolver and fired twice, full in the face of the man who was following her. He did not even flinch and a low laugh of amusement came from him. And at the sound of his laugh Diana's mouth parched suddenly, and a cold shiver rippled across her spine. A strange feeling that she had never experienced before went through her. She had missed again as she had missed this morning. How, she did not know; it was inexplicable, but it was a fact, and a fact that left her with a feeling of powerlessness. She dropped the useless revolver, trying vainly to force her horse's pace, but inch by inch the fiery chestnut that the Arab was riding crept up nearer alongside. She would not turn to look again, but glancing sideways she could see its small, wicked-looking head, with flat laid ears and vicious, bloodshot eyes, level with her elbow. For a moment or two it remained there, then with a sudden spurt the chestnut forged ahead, and as it shot past it swerved close in beside her, and the man, rising in his stirrups and leaning towards her, flung a pair of powerful arms around her, and, with a jerk, swung her clear of the saddle and on to his own horse in front of him. His movement had been so quick she was unprepared and unable to resist. For a moment she was stunned, then her senses came back to her and she struggled wildly, but, stifled in the thick folds of the Arab's robes, against which her face was crushed, and held in a grip that seemed to be slowly suffocating her, her struggles were futile. The hard, muscular arm round her hurt her acutely, her ribs seemed to be almost breaking under its weight and strength, it was nearly impossible to breathe with the close contact of his body. She was unusually strong for a girl, but against this steely strength that held her she was helpless. And for a time the sense of her helplessness and the pain that any resistance to the arm wrapped round her gave her made her lie quiet. She felt the Arab check his horse, felt the chestnut wheel, spinning high on his hind legs, and then bound forward again.

Her feelings were indescribable. She did not know what to think. Her mind felt jarred. She was unable to frame any thoughts coherently. What had happened was so unexpected, so preposterous, that no conclusion seemed adequate. Only rage filled her—blind, passionate rage against the man who had dared to touch her, who had dared to lay his hands on her, and those hands the hands of a native. A shiver of revulsion ran through her. She was choking with fury, with anger and with disgust. The ignominy of her plight hurt her pride badly. She had been outridden, swept from her saddle as if she were a puppet, and compelled to bear the proximity of the man's own hateful body and the restraint of his arms. No one had ever dared to touch her before. No one had ever dared to handle her as she was being handled now. How was it going to end? Where were they going? With her face hidden she had lost all sense of direction. She had no idea to what point the horse had turned when he had wheeled so suddenly. He was galloping swiftly with continual disconcerting bounds that indicated either temper or nerves, but the man riding him seemed in no way disturbed by his horse's behavior. She could feel him swaying easily in the saddle, and even the wildest leaps did not cause any slackening of the arm around her.

But by degrees as she continued to lie still the pressure on her body was relieved slightly, and she was able to turn her head a little towards the air for which she was almost fainting, but not enough to enable her to see what was passing around her. She drank in the cool air eagerly. Though she could not see she knew that the night had come, the night that she had hoped would fall before she reached her destination, but which now seemed horrible. The fresh strength that the air gave her fanned the courage that still remained with her. Collecting all her force she made a sudden desperate spring, trying to leap clear of the arm that now lay almost loosely about her, her spurred heels tearing the chestnut's flank until he reared perpendicularly, snorting and trembling. But with a quick sweep of his long arm the Arab gathered her back into his hold, still struggling fiercely. His arms were both round her; he was controlling the maddened horse only with the pressure of his knees.

"Doucement, doucement." She heard the slow, soft voice indistinctly, for he was pressing her head again closely to him, and she did not know if the words were applied to herself or to the horse. She fought to lift her head, to escape the grip that held her, straining, striving until he spoke again.

"Lie still, you little fool!" he snarled with sudden vehemence, and with brutal hands he forced her to obey him, until she wondered if he would leave a single bone unbroken in her body, till further resistance was impossible. Gasping for breath she yielded to the strength that overpowered her, and ceased to struggle. The man seemed to know intuitively that she was beaten, and turned his undivided attention to his horse with the same low laugh of amusement that had sent the strange feeling through her when her shots had missed him. It had puzzled her then, but it grew now with a horrible intensity, until she knew that it was fear that had come to her for the first time in her life—a strange fear that she fought against desperately, but which was gaining on her with a force that was sapping her strength from her and making her head reel. She did not faint, but her whole body seemed to grow nerveless with the sudden realisation of the horror of her position.

After that Diana lost all sense of time, as she had already lost all sense of direction. She did not know if it was minutes or hours that passed as they still galloped swiftly through the night. She did not know if they were alone or if the band of Arabs to which this man belonged were riding with them, noiseless over the soft ground. What had happened to her guide and his men? Had they been butchered and left where they fell, or were they, too, being hurried unwillingly into some obscure region of the desert? But for the moment the fate of Mustafa Ali and his companions did not trouble her very much; they had not played a very valiant part in the short encounter, and her own situation swamped her mind to the exclusion of everything else.

The sense of fear was growing on her. She scorned and derided it. She tried to convince herself it did not exist, but it did exist, torturing her with its strangeness and with the thoughts that it engendered. She had anticipated nothing like this. She had never thought of a contingency that would end so, that would induce a situation before which her courage was shuddering into pieces with the horror that was opening up before her—a thing that had always seemed a remote impossibility that could never touch her, from even the knowledge of which her life with Aubrey had almost shielded her, but which now loomed near her, forcing its reality upon her till she trembled and great drops of moisture gathered on her forehead.

The Arab moved her position once, roughly, but she was glad of the change for it freed her head from the stifling folds of his robes. He did not speak again—only once when the chestnut shied violently he muttered something under his breath. But her satisfaction was short-lived. A few minutes afterwards his arm tightened round her once more and he twined a fold of his long cloak round her head, blinding her. And then she understood. The galloping horse was pulled in with almost the same suddenness that had amazed her when she had first seen the Arabs. She felt him draw her close into his arms and slip down on to the ground; there were voices around her—confused, unintelligible; then they died away as she felt him carry her a few paces. He set her down and unwound the covering from her face. The light that shone around her seemed by contrast dazzling with the darkness that had gone before. Confused, she clasped her hands over her eyes for a moment and then looked up slowly. She was in a big, lofty tent, brightly lit by two hanging lamps. But she took no heed of her surroundings; her eyes were fixed on the man who had brought her there. He had flung aside the heavy cloak that enveloped him from head to foot and was standing before her, tall and broad-shouldered, dressed in white flowing robes, a waistcloth embroidered in black and silver wound several times about him, and from the top of which showed a revolver that was thrust into the folds.

Diana's eyes passed over him slowly till they rested on his brown, clean-shaven face, surmounted by crisp, close-cut brown hair. It was the handsomest and cruellest face that she had ever seen. Her gaze was drawn instinctively to his. He was looking at her with fierce burning eyes that swept her until she felt that the boyish clothes that covered her slender limbs were stripped from her, leaving the beautiful white body bare under his passionate stare.

She shrank back, quivering, dragging the lapels of her riding jacket together over her breast with clutching hands, obeying an impulse that she hardly understood.

"Who are you?" she gasped hoarsely.

"I am the Sheik Ahmed Ben Hassan."

The name conveyed nothing. She had never heard it before. She had spoken without thinking in French, and in French he replied to her.

"Why have you brought me here?" she asked, fighting down the fear that was growing more terrible every moment.

He repeated her words with a slow smile. "Why have I brought you here? Bon Dieu! Are you not woman enough to know?"

She shrank back further, a wave of colour rushing into her face that receded immediately, leaving her whiter than she had been before. Her eyes fell under the kindling flame in his. "I don't know what you mean," she whispered faintly, with shaking lips.

"I think you do." He laughed softly, and his laugh frightened her more than anything he had said. He came towards her, and although she was swaying on her feet, desperately she tried to evade him, but with a quick movement he caught her in his arms.

Terror, agonising, soul-shaking terror such as she had never imagined, took hold of her. The flaming light of desire burning in his eyes turned her sick and faint. Her body throbbed with the consciousness of a knowledge that appalled her. She understood his purpose with a horror that made each separate nerve in her system shrink against the understanding that had come to her under the consuming fire of his ardent gaze, and in the fierce embrace that was drawing her shaking limbs closer and closer against the man's own pulsating body. She writhed in his arms as he crushed her to him in a sudden access of possessive passion. His head bent slowly down to her, his eyes burned deeper, and, held immovable, she endured the first kiss she had ever received. And the touch of his scorching lips, the clasp of his arms, the close union with his warm, strong body robbed her of all strength, of all power of resistance.

With a great sob her eyes closed wearily, the hot mouth pressed on hers was like a narcotic, drugging her almost into insensibility. Numbly she felt him gather her high up into his arms, his lips still clinging closely, and carry her across the tent through curtains into an adjoining room. He laid her down on soft cushions. "Do not make me wait too long," he whispered, and left her.

And the whispered words sent a shock through her that seemed to wrench her deadened nerves apart, galvanising her into sudden strength. She sprang up with wild, despairing eyes, and hands clenched frantically across her heaving breast; then, with a bitter cry, she dropped on to the floor, her arms flung out across the wide, luxurious bed. It was not true! It was not true! It could not be—this awful thing that had happened to her—not to her, Diana Mayo! It was a dream, a ghastly dream that would pass and free her from this agony. Shuddering, she raised her head. The strange room swam before her eyes. Oh, God! It was not a dream. It was real, it was an actual fact from which there was no escape. She was trapped, powerless, defenceless, and behind the heavy curtains near her was the man waiting to claim what he had taken. Any moment he might come; the thought sent her shivering closer to the ground with limbs that trembled uncontrollably. Her courage, that had faced dangers and even death without flinching, broke down before the horror that awaited her. It was inevitable; there was no help to be expected, no mercy to be hoped for. She had felt the crushing strength against which she was helpless. She would struggle, but it would be useless; she would fight, but it would make no difference. Within the tent she was alone, ready to his hand like a snared animal; without, the place was swarming with the man's followers. There was nowhere she could turn, there was no one she could turn to. The certainty of the accomplishment of what she dreaded crushed her with its surety. All power of action was gone. She could only wait and suffer in the complete moral collapse that overwhelmed her, and that was rendered greater by her peculiar temperament. Her body was aching with the grip of his powerful arms, her mouth was bruised with his savage kisses. She clenched her hands in anguish. "Oh, God!" she sobbed, with scalding tears that scorched her cheeks. "Curse him! Curse him!"

And with the words on her lips he came, silent, noiseless, to her side. With his hands on her shoulders he forced her to her feet. His eyes were fierce, his stern mouth parted in a cruel smile, his deep, slow voice half angry, half impatiently amused. "Must I be valet, as well as lover?"

CHAPTER III

The warm sunshine was flooding the tent when Diana awoke from the deep sleep of exhaustion that had been almost insensibility, awoke to immediate and complete remembrance. One quick, fearful glance around the big room assured her that she was alone. She sat up slowly, her eyes shadowy with pain, looking listlessly at the luxurious appointments of the tent. She looked dry-eyed, she had no tears left. They had all been expended when she had grovelled at his feet imploring the mercy he had not accorded her. She had fought until the unequal struggle had left her exhausted and helpless in his arms, until her whole body was one agonised ache from the brutal hands that forced her to compliance, until her courageous spirit was crushed by the realisation of her own powerlessness, and by the strange fear that the man himself had awakened in her, which had driven her at last moaning to her knees. And the recollection of her abject prayers and weeping supplications filled her with a burning shame. She loathed herself with bitter contempt. Her courage had broken down; even her pride had failed her.

She wound her arms about her knees and hid her face against them. "Coward! Coward!" she whispered fiercely. Why had she not scorned him? Or why had she not suffered all that he had done to her in silence? It would have pleased him less than the frenzied entreaties that had only provoked the soft laugh that made her shiver each time she heard it. She shivered now. "I thought I was brave," she murmured brokenly. "I am only a coward, a craven."

She lifted her head at last and looked around her. The room was a curious mixture of Oriental luxury and European comfort. The lavish sumptuousness of the furnishings suggested subtly an unrestrained indulgence, the whole atmosphere was voluptuous, and Diana shrank from the impression it conveyed without exactly understanding the reason. There was nothing that jarred artistically, the rich hangings all harmonised, there were no glaring incongruities such as she had seen in native palaces in India. And everything on which her eyes rested drove home relentlessly the hideous fact of her position. His things were everywhere. On a low, brass-topped table by the bed was the half-smoked cigarette he had had between his lips when he came to her. The pillow beside her still bore the impress of his head. She looked at it with a growing horror in her eyes until an uncontrollable shuddering seized her and she cowered down, smothering the cry that burst from her in the soft pillows and dragging the silken coverings up around her as if their thin shelter were a protection. She lived again through every moment of the past night until thought was unendurable, until she felt that she would go mad, until at last, worn out, she fell asleep.

It was midday when she awoke again. This time she was not alone. A young Arab girl was sitting on the rug beside her looking at her with soft brown eyes of absorbed interest As Diana sat up she rose to her feet, salaaming, with a timid smile.

"I am Zilah, to wait on Madame," she said shyly in stumbling French, holding out a wrap that Diana recognised with wonder as her own. She looked behind her. Her suit-cases were lying near her, open, partially unpacked. The missing baggage camels had been captured first, then. She was at least to be allowed the use of her own belongings. A gleam of anger shot into her tired eyes and she swung round with a sharp question; but the Arab girl shook her head uncomprehendingly, drawing back with frightened eyes; and to all further questions she remained silent, with down-drooping mouth like a scared child. She was little more. She evidently only half understood what was said to her and could give no answer to what she did understand, and turned away with obvious relief when Diana stopped speaking. She went across the tent and pulled aside a curtain leading into a bathroom that was as big and far better equipped than the one that Diana had had in the Indian tent, and which, up to now, had seemed the last word in comfort and luxury. Though the girl's knowledge of French was limited her hands were deft enough, but her ignorance of the intricacies of a European woman's toilette was very apparent, and constantly provoked in her a girlish giggle that changed hurriedly to a startled gravity when Diana looked at her. Laughter was very far from Diana, but she could not help smiling now and again at her funny mistakes.

The girl, with her big, wondering eyes, her shy, hesitating French and childish curiosity, in some indefinable way gave back to Diana the self-control that had slipped from her. Her pride reasserted itself, rigidly suppressing any sign of feeling or emotion that could be noticed by the gentle, inquisitive eyes fixed on her.

The hot bath that took the soreness out of her limbs brought back the colour to her face and lips. She even tubbed her head, rubbing the glistening curls dry with fierce vigour, striving to rid herself of the contamination that seemed to have saturated her. Yet the robes against which they had been pressed were spotless, and the hands that had held her were fastidiously clean, even to the well-kept nails.

She came back into the bedroom to find Zilah on her knees poring over her scanty but diverse wardrobe with bewilderment, fingering the evening dresses with shy hands, and finally submitting tentatively to Diana the tweed skirt that had been packed with her other things for the journey when Oran should be reached. But Diana put it aside, and pointed to the riding clothes she had worn the previous day. In them she felt more able to face what might be before her, the associations connected with them seemed to give her moral strength, in them she would feel herself again—Diana the boy, not the shivering piece of womanhood that had been born with tears and agony last night. She bit her lip as she stamped her foot down into the long boot.

She sent the girl away at last, and noticed that she avoided passing into the adjoining room, but vanished instead through the curtains leading into the bathroom. Did that mean that in the outer room the Arab Sheik was waiting? The thought banished the self-control she had regained and sent her weakly on to the side of the bed with her face hidden in her hands. Was he there? Her questions to the little waiting-girl had only been concerned with the whereabouts of the camp to which she had been brought and also of the fate of the caravan; of the man himself she had not been able to bring herself to speak. The strange fear that he had inspired in her filled her with rage and humiliation. The thought of seeing him again brought a shame that was unspeakable. But she conquered the agitation that threatened to grow beyond restraint, pride helping her again. It was better to face the inevitable of her own free will than be fetched whether she would or not. For she knew now the strength of the man who had abducted her, knew that physically she was helpless against him. She raised her head and listened. It was very silent in the next room. Perhaps she was to be allowed a further respite. She jerked her head impatiently at her own hesitation. "Coward!" she whispered again contemptuously, and flung across the room. But at the curtains she halted for a moment, then with set face drew them aside and went through.

The respite had been granted, the room appeared to be empty. But as she crossed the thick rugs her heart leapt suddenly into her throat, for she became aware of a man standing in the open doorway. His back was turned to her, but in a moment she saw that the short, slim figure in white linen European clothes bore no resemblance to the tall Arab she had expected to see. She thought her footsteps were noiseless, but he turned with a little quick bow. A typical Frenchman with narrow, alert, clean-shaven face, sleek black hair and dark restless eyes. His legs were slightly bowed and he stooped a little; his appearance was that of a jockey with the manners of a well-trained servant. Diana coloured hotly under his glance, but his eyes were lowered instantly.

"Madame is doubtless ready for lunch." He spoke rapidly, but his voice was low and pleasant. His movements were as quick and as quiet as his voice, and in a dream Diana found herself in a few moments before a lunch that was perfectly cooked and daintily served. The man hovered about her solicitously, attending to her wants with dexterous hands and watchful eyes that anticipated every need. She was bewildered, faint from want of food, everything seemed unreal. For the moment she could just sit still and be waited on by the soft-footed, soft-spoken manservant who seemed such a curious adjunct to the household of an Arab chief.

"Monseigneur begs that you will excuse him until this evening. He will return in time for dinner," he murmured as he handed her a cous-cous.

Diana looked up blankly. "Monseigneur?"

"My master. The Sheik."

She flushed scarlet and her face hardened. Hypocritical, Oriental beast who "begged to be excused"! She refused the last dish curtly, and as the servant carried it away she propped her elbows on the table and rested her aching head on her hands. A headache was among the new experiences that had overwhelmed her since the day before. Suffering in any form was new to her, and her hatred of the man who had made her suffer grew with every breath she drew.

The Frenchman came back with coffee and cigarettes. He held a match for her, coaxing the reluctant flame with patience that denoted long experience with inferior sulphur.

"Monseigneur dines at eight. At what hour will Madame have tea?" he asked, as he cleared away and folded up the table.

Diana choked back the sarcastic retort that sprang to her lips. The man's quiet, deferential manner, that refused to see anything extraordinary in her presence in his master's camp, was almost harder to bear than flagrant impertinence would have been. That she could have dealt with; this left her tingling with a feeling of impotence, as if a net were gradually closing round her in whose entangling meshes her vaunted liberty was not only threatened, but which seemed destined even to stifle her very existence. She pulled her racing thoughts up with a jerk. She must not think if she was going to keep any hold over herself at all. She gave him an answer indifferently and turned her back on him. When she looked again he was gone, and she heaved a sigh of relief. She had chafed under his watchful eyes until the feeling of restraint had grown unbearable.

She breathed more freely now that he was gone, flinging up her head and jerking her shoulders back with an angry determination to conquer the fear that made her ashamed. Natural curiosity had been struggling with her other emotions, and she gave way to it now to try and turn the channel of her thoughts from the fixed direction in which they tended, and wandered round the big room. The night before she had taken in nothing of her surroundings, her eyes had been held only by the man who had dominated everything. Here, also, were the same luxurious appointments as in the sleeping-room. She had knowledge enough to appreciate that the rugs and hangings were exquisite, the former were Persian and the latter of a thick black material, heavily embroidered in silver. The main feature of the room was a big black divan heaped with huge cushions covered with dull black silk. Beside the divan, spread over the Persian rugs, were two unusually large black bearskins, the mounted heads converging. At one end of the tent was a small doorway, a little portable writing-table. There were one or two

Moorish stools heaped with a motley collection of ivories and gold and silver cigarette cases and knick-knacks, and against the partition that separated the two rooms stood a quaintly carved old wooden chest. Though the furniture was scanty and made the tent seem even more spacious than it really was, the whole room had an air of barbaric splendour. The somber hangings gleaming with thick silver threads seemed to Diana like a studied theatrical effect, a setting against which the Arab's own white robes should contrast more vividly; she remembered the black and silver waistcloth she had seen swathed round him, with curling scornful lip. There was a strain of vanity in all natives, she generalised contemptuously. Doubtless it pleased this native's conceit to carry out the colour scheme of his tent even in his clothes, and pose among the sable cushions of the luxurious divan to the admiration of his retainers. She made a little exclamation of disgust, and turned from the soft seductiveness of the big couch with disdain.

She crossed the tent to the little bookcase and knelt beside it curiously. What did a Francophile-Arab read? Novels, probably, that would harmonise with the atmosphere that she dimly sensed in her surroundings. But it was not novels that filled the bookcase. They were books of sport and travel with several volumes on veterinary surgery. They were all in French, and had all been frequently handled, many of them had pencilled notes in the margins written in Arabic. One shelf was filled entirely with the works of one man, a certain Vicomte Raoul de Saint Hubert. With the exception of one novel, which Diana only glanced at hastily; they were all books of travel. From the few scribbled words in the front of each Diana could see that they had all been sent to the Arab by the author himself—one even was dedicated to "My friend, Ahmed Ben Hassan, Sheik of the Desert." She put the books back with a puzzled frown. She wished, with a feeling that she could not fathom, that they had been rather what she had imagined. The evidence of education and unlooked-for tastes in the man they belonged to troubled her. It was an unexpected glimpse into the personality of the Arab that had captured her was vaguely disquieting, for it suggested possibilities that would not have existed in a raw native, or one only superficially coated with a veneer of civilisation. He seemed to become infinitely more sinister, infinitely more horrible. She looked at her watch with sudden apprehension. The day was wearing away quickly. Soon he would come. Her breath came quick and short and the tears welled up in her eyes.

"I mustn't! I mustn't!" she whispered in a kind of desperation. "If I cry again I shall go mad." She forced them back, and crossing to the big black divan that she had scorned before dropped down among the soft cushions. She was so tired, and her head throbbed persistently.

She was asleep when the servant brought tea, but she started up as he put the tray on a stool beside her.

"It is Madame's own tea. If she will be good enough to say if it is made to her taste," he said anxiously, as if his whole happiness was contained in the tiny teapot at which he was frowning deprecatingly.

His assiduity jarred on Diana's new-found jangling nerves. She recognised that he was sincere in his efforts to please her, but just now they only seemed an added humiliation. She longed to shout "Go away!" like an angry schoolboy, but she managed to give him the information he wanted, and putting cigarettes and matches by her he went out with a little smile of satisfaction. The longing for fresh air and the desire to see what place she had been brought to grew irresistible as the evening came nearer. She went to the open doorway. A big awning stretched before it, supported on lances. She stepped out from under its shade and looked about her wonderingly. It was a big oasis—bigger than any she had seen. In front of the tent there was an open space with a thick belt of palm trees beyond. The rest of the camp lay behind the Chief's tent. The place was alive with men and horses. There were some camels in the distance, but it was the horses that struck Diana principally. They were everywhere, some tethered; some wandering loose, some exercising in the hands of grooms. Mounted Arabs on the outskirts of the oasis crossed her view occasionally. There were groups of men engaged on various duties all around her. Those who went by near her salaamed as they passed, but took no further notice of her. A strange look came into Diana's eyes. This was the desert indeed, the desert as she had never expected to see it, the desert as few could expect to see it. But the cost! She shuddered, then turned at a sudden noise near her. A biting, screaming chestnut fury was coming past close to the tent, taking complete charge of the two men who clung, yelling, to his head. He was stripped, but Diana recognised him at once. The one brief view she had had of his small, vicious head as he shot past her elbow the evening before was written on her brain for all time. He came to a halt opposite Diana, refusing to move, his ears laid close to his head, quivering all over, snatching continually at his grooms, who seemed unable to cope with him. Once he swung up on his hind legs and his cruel teeth flashed almost into the face of one of the men, who was taken off his guard, and who dropped on to the ground, rolling out of the way with a howl that provoked a shout of laughter from a knot of Arabs who had gathered to watch the usual evening eccentricities of the chestnut. The French servant, coming from behind the tent, stopped to speak to the man as he picked himself up and made a grab at the horse's head, and then turned to Diana with his pleasant smile.

"He is rightly named Shaitan, Madame, for he is assuredly possessed of a devil," he said, indicating the chestnut, who, at that moment, with a violent plunge, broke away from the men who were holding him and headed for the edge of the oasis with the Arabs streaming after him. "The mounted men will catch him," he added with a little laugh, in response to Diana's exclamation.

"Is he amusing himself, or is it really vice?" she asked.

"Pure vice, Madame. He has killed three men."

Diana looked at him incredulously, for his tone was casual and his manner did not indicate any undue feeling.

"He ought to be shot," she said indignantly.

The man shrugged. "Monseigneur is fond of him," he said quietly.

And so because Monseigneur was fond of him the vicious animal was surrounded with every care that his master's pleasure might not be interfered with. Evidently the lives of his wretched people were of less value to him than that of a favourite horse. It sounded compatible with the mercilessness she had herself experienced. What she would not have believed yesterday today seemed terribly credible. The courage that the relief of his absence brought back was sinking fast, as fast as the red ball glowing in the heavens was sinking down towards the horizon. She turned from her own fearful thoughts to look at some more horses that were being led away to the lines on the other side of the camp.

"The horses are magnificent, but they are bigger than any Arabs I have seen before."

"They are a special breed, Madame," replied the Frenchman. "The tribe has been famous for them for generations. Monseigneur's horses are known through all the Barbary States, and as far as France," he added, with a little accent of pride creeping into his voice.

Diana looked at him speculatively. There was an inflection in his voice each time he mentioned his master that indicated a devotion that she was unable to accredit to the brute for whose treatment she was still suffering. But her thoughts were broken into abruptly.

"There is Monseigneur," said the servant suddenly. He spoke as if she, too, must be glad of his coming. Did the valet imagine for one moment that she was here of her own free will? Or was it all a part of the hypocrisy in which she seemed to be enveloped? She flashed one glance at the horseman riding through the belt of trees that fringed the oasis and an icy perspiration chilled her from head to foot. She shrank back under the awning and into the coolness of the tent, raging against the mastering fear that she could not overcome. But just inside the open doorway she stood firm; even her fear could make her go no further. She would meet him here, not cowering into the inner room like a trembling creature skulking in the furthest corner of its cage. That much pride at least was left.

From the shelter of the tent she watched the troop arrive at the open space before her. The horse the Sheik was riding was jet black, and Diana looked from the beautiful creature's satiny coat to the man's white robes with angry contempt.

"Black and white! Black and white! Mountebank!" she muttered through her clenched teeth. Then as he swung to the ground every thought fell from her but the terror he inspired. She waited, breathless, the swift racing of her heart an actual physical pain.

He lingered, fondling the great black horse, and even after it had been led away he stood looking after it, talking to a tall young Arab who had ridden in with him. At last he turned and came leisurely towards the tent. He paused at the door to speak to the Frenchman, a picturesque, barbaric figure, with flowing robes and great white cloak, the profile of his lean face clean cut against the evening sky, the haughty poise of his head emphasised by the attitude in which he was standing, arrogant, dominating. He moved his hands when he spoke with quick, expressive gestures, but his voice was slow and soft, pitched in a deep musical key, but with all its softness unmistakably authoritative. He pointed with outstretched, steady hand to something beyond her line of vision, and as he turned to enter the tent he laughed softly, and she shivered involuntarily. Then he swept in, and she drew back from him with lowered eyes. She would not look at him; she would not meet his look. His presence was an offence, she was scorched with shame. Every fibre of her being cried out in protest at his proximity. She wished with passionate fierceness that she could die. She shook feverishly and caught her quivering lip between her teeth to keep it still, and the red-gold curls lay wet against her forehead. Her breast heaved stormily with the rapid beating of her heart, but she held herself proudly erect. He crossed the tent with a long noiseless stride.

"I hope that Gaston took care of you properly and gave you everything that you wanted?" he said easily, stooping to a little table to light a cigarette. The coolness of his words and manner were like a dash of cold water. She had been prepared for anything but this calm nonchalance in a situation that was intolerable. His tone conveyed the perfunctory regret of a host for an unavoidable absence. Her fear gave way to rage, her body stiffened, her hands clenched.

"Is it not time that this ended? Haven't you done enough?" she burst out passionately. "Why have you committed this outrage?"

A thin thread of smoke drifted towards her, as if the hand holding the cigarette had moved in her direction in one of the gestures that she had noticed outside, but there was no answer. His silence infuriated her and she grew utterly reckless.

"Do you think that you can keep me here, you fool? That I can vanish into the desert and no notice be taken of my disappearance— that no inquiries will be made?"

"There will be no inquiries," he answered calmly.

She ground the heel of her boot into the soft carpet. "There *will* be inquiries," she choked furiously. "I am not such a nonentity that nothing will be done when I am missed. The English authorities will make the French Government find out who is responsible, and you will have to pay for what you have done."

He laughed—the little amused laugh that sent the same cold feeling of dread through her that she had felt the day before.

"The French Government has no jurisdiction over me. I am not subject to it. I am an independent chief, my own master. I recognise no government. My tribe obey me and only me."

Her shaking fingers found the handkerchief for which they were groping, and she wiped the moisture that had gathered on the palms of her hands.

"When I am missed—" she began desperately, trying to keep a bold front, but her assurance was leaving her.

"You will not be missed for so long that it will be too late," he replied drily.

"Too late! What do you mean?" she gasped.

"Your own plans will stop any possibility of inquiry for some time to come." He paused, and behind her, Diana heard him strike another match. The banal little incident nearly snapped her nerves that were stretched to breaking-point. She put her hands to her head to try and stop the throbbing in her temples.

"You engaged a caravan in charge of Mustafa Ali," he went on evenly, "to travel in the desert for a month. You set out from Biskra, but your intention was at the end of the time to travel northward to Oran and there dismiss the caravan. From there you were to cross to Marseilles, then to Cherbourg, where you would embark for America to follow your brother, who has already started."

She listened breathlessly with an ever-increasing fear growing in her eyes. The slow, casual voice detailing her itinerary with the quiet certainty of perfect knowledge filled her with a terror that made her want to scream. She swayed a little as she stood, her eyes fixed on the endless strip of desert and gold-flecked sky visible through the opening of the tent, but she saw nothing of the undulating sand, nor the red glory of the setting sun.

"How do you know—all—this?" she whispered with dry lips that trembled.

"I wished to know. It was quite simple." The answer was given carelessly, and again the thin thread of smoke drifted across her face.

Her anger flamed up again. "Is it money that you want? Are you holding me for ransom?" But her scornful voice faltered and died away on the last word, and it did not need his silence to convince her that it was no question of ransom. She had only spoken to try and stifle the inner conviction that grew despite her efforts to crush it. Her hands were locked together tightly, her eyes still staring out unseeing at the wonderful sunset. She felt dazed, hopeless, like a fugitive who has turned into a cul-de-sac, hemmed in on every side; there seemed no way out, no loophole of escape. She wrung her hands convulsively and a great shudder shook her. Then in her despair a faint ray of hope came.

"Mustafa Ali, or one of the caravan men may have given the alarm already in Biskra—if you have not—murdered them all," she whispered jerkily.

"I have not murdered them all," he rejoined shortly, "but Mustafa Ali will not give any alarm in Biskra."

"Why?" She tried to keep silent, but the question was forced from her, and she waited tense for his answer. Tales of ruthless Arab cruelty surged through her mind. What had been the fate of the unfortunate caravan leader? Her eyes closed and her throat grew dry.

"There was no need for any murder," he continued sarcastically. "When you come to know me better you will realise that I do not leave too much to chance. 'All things are with Allah, blessed be his name.' Good! But it is well to remember that Allah does not always concern himself with the affairs of men, and arrange accordingly. If I had left this affair to chance there might very easily have been, as you suggest, murder done—though we do not call it murder in the desert. It was very simple. *Voyons!* You paid Mustafa Ali well to guide you in the desert. I paid him better to lead you to me. I paid him well enough to make him content to remove himself from Biskra, where awkward questions might be asked, to another sphere of usefulness where he is not known, and where he can build up for himself a new reputation as a caravan leader."

There was another silence and her hands went groping to her throat. It had been no chance affair then—no accidental meeting that the Arab chief had turned to his own account, but an organised outrage that had been carefully planned from the beginning. From the very outset she had been a dupe. She ground her teeth with rage. Her suave, subservient guide had been leading her the whole time, not in the direction that had been mapped out in Biskra, but towards the man who had bought him to betray his trust. Mustafa Ali's shifting eyes, his desire to hurry her from the oasis where they had rested at mid-day, his tone were all explained. He had acted well. The last touch—the imaginary wound that had toppled him slowly out of his saddle had been a masterpiece, she reflected bitterly. Nothing had been omitted to make the attempt a success. The horse that had been given her to ride was the Sheik's beyond all doubt, trained to his whistle. Even her revolver had been tampered with. She had not missed, as she had thought. She remembered the noise, the fleeting vision she had had in the hotel at Biskra. It had been some one in her room, Mustafa Ali himself, or one of his men, who had stolen in and substituted the blank cartridges. The possibility of Aubrey changing his mind and accompanying her must also have been thought of, for the Sheik had provided against the resistance that would certainly have then been made by the number of followers he had brought with him—a large enough force to frustrate easily any attempted opposition to the attack.

The net that she had felt closing round her earlier in the afternoon seemed wrapped round her now inextricably, drawing tighter and tighter, smothering her. She gasped for breath. The sinking sun seemed suddenly to leap up wildly into the heavens; then she pulled herself together with a tremendous effort. "Why have you done this?" she murmured faintly.

Then for a moment her heart stood still, her eyes dilating. He had come close behind her, and she waited in an agony, until he caught her to him, crushing her against him, forcing her head back on his arm.

"Because I wanted you. Because one day in Biskra, four weeks ago, I saw you for a few moments, long enough to know that I wanted you. And what I want I take. You played into my hands. You arranged a tour in the desert. The rest was easy."

Her eyes were shut, the long dark lashes quivering on her pale cheeks so that she could not see his face, but she felt him draw her closer to him and then his fierce kisses on her mouth. She struggled frantically, but she was helpless, and he laughed softly as he kissed her lips, her hair, her eyes passionately. He stood quite still, but she felt the heavy beating of his heart under her cheek, and understood dimly the passion that she had aroused in him. She had experienced his tremendous strength. She realised from what he had told her that he recognised no law beyond his own wishes, and was prepared to go to any lengths to fulfil them. She knew that her life was in his hands, that he could break her with his lean brown fingers like a toy is broken, and all at once she felt pitifully weak and frightened. She was utterly in his power and at his mercy—the mercy of an Arab who was merciless.

She gave in suddenly, lying quiet in his arms. She had touched the lowest depths of degradation; he could do nothing more to her than he had done. For the moment she could fight no further, she was worn out and utterly weary. A numb feeling of despair came over her and with it a sense of unreality, as if it were a hideous nightmare from which she would wake, for the truth seemed too impossible, the setting too theatrical. The man himself was a mystery. She could not reconcile him and the barbaric display in which he lived with the evidences of refinement and education that the well-worn books in the tent evinced. The fastidious ordering of his appointments puzzled her; it was strange to find in such a place. A dozen incongruities that she had noticed during the day crowded into her recollection until her head reeled. She turned from them wearily; she was too tired to think, too spent in mind and body. And with the despair a kind of indifference stole over her. She had suffered so much that nothing more mattered.

The strong arms around her tightened slowly. "Look at me," he said in the soft slow voice that seemed habitual to him, and which contrasted oddly with the neat, clipping French that he spoke. She shivered and her dark lashes flickered for a moment. "Look at me." His voice was just as slow, just as soft, but into it had crept an inflection that was unmistakable.

Twenty-four hours ago Diana Mayo had not known the meaning of the word fear, and had never in all her life obeyed any one against her inclination, but in twenty-four hours she had lived through years of emotions. For the first time she had pitted her will against a will that was stronger than her own, for the first time she had met an arrogance that was greater and a determination that was firmer than hers. For the first time she had met a man who had failed to bow to her wishes, whom a look had been powerless to transform into a willing slave. In a few hours that had elapsed she had learned fear, a terrible fear that left her sick with apprehension, and she was learning obedience. Obedient now, she forced herself to lift her eyes to his, and the shamed blood surged slowly into her cheeks. His dark, passionate eyes burnt into her like a hot flame. His encircling arms were like bands of fire, scorching her. His touch was torture. Helpless, like a trapped wild thing, she lay against him, panting, trembling, her wide eyes fixed on him, held against their will. Fascinated she could not turn them away, and the image of the brown, handsome face with its flashing eyes, straight, cruel mouth and strong chin seemed searing into her brain. The faint indefinite scent of an uncommon Turkish tobacco clung about him, enveloping her. She had been conscious of the same scent the previous day when he had held her in his arms during the wild ride across the desert.

He smiled down at her suddenly. *"Bon Dieu*! Do you know how beautiful you are?" he murmured. But the sound of his voice seemed to break a spell that had kept her dumb. She struggled again to free herself.

"Let me go!" she cried piteously, and it was her complete immunity from him that she prayed for, but he chose wilfully to misunderstand her. The passion faded from his eyes, giving place to a gleam of mockery.

"There is plenty of time. Gaston is the most discreet servant. We shall hear him when he comes," he said with a low laugh.

But she persisted with the courage of desperation. "When will you let me go?"

With an exclamation of impatience he put her from him roughly, and going to the divan flung himself down on the cushions, lit another cigarette and picked up a magazine that was lying on an inlaid stool beside him.

She bit her lips to keep back the hysterical sobs that rose in her throat, nerving herself with clenched hands, and followed him. "You *must* tell me. I *must* know. When will you let me go?"

He turned a page with deliberation, and flicked the ash from his cigarette before looking up. A heavy scowl gathered on his face, and his eyes swept her from head to foot with a slow scrutiny that made her shrink. "When I am tired of you," he said coldly.

She shuddered violently and turned away with a little moan, stumbling blindly towards the inner room, but as she reached the curtains his voice arrested her. He had thrown aside the magazine and was lying back on the divan, his long limbs stretched out indolently, his hands clasped behind his head.

"You make a very charming boy," he said lightly, with a faint smile, "but it was not a boy that I saw in Biskra. You understand?"

Beyond the curtains she stood a moment, shaking all over, her face hidden in her hands, able to relax a little the hold she was keeping on herself. Yes! She understood, plainly enough. The understanding had already been forced upon her. It was an order from one who was prepared to compel his commands, to make herself more attractive with all that it implied in the eyes of the man who held her in his power and who looked at her as no other man had ever dared to look, with appraising criticism that made her acutely conscious of her sex, that made her feel like a slave exposed for sale in a public market.

She must take off the boyish clothes that somehow seemed to lend her courage and substitute, to gratify the whim of the savage in the next room, the womanly dress that revealed more intimately the slender lines of her figure and intensified the uncommon beauty of her face.

She went to the dressing table with lagging feet and stared resentfully at the white face and haggard eyes that looked back at her from the mirror. It was like the face of a stranger. Aubrey's words came back to her with an irony that was horrible. Tonight she did not dress to please herself. Her face was set, her eyes almost black with rage, but behind the rage there was lurking apprehension. She started at every sound that came from the adjoining room. Her fingers, wet with perspiration, seemed almost unable to fulfil their task. She hated him, she hated herself, she hated her beauty that had brought this horror upon her. She would have rebelled if she had dared, but instinctively she hurried—fear had already driven her so far. But when she was ready she did not move from the table beside which she stood. Fear had forced her to haste, but her still struggling pride would not permit her to obey her fear any further. She raised her eyes to the glass again, glowering angrily at the pale reflection, and the old obstinacy mingled with the new pain that filled them. Must she endure his mocking glance with chalk-like cheeks and eyes like a beaten hound? Had she not even courage enough left to hide the fear that filled her with self-contempt? The wave of anger that went through her rushed the colour into her face and she leaned nearer the glass with a little murmur of satisfaction that stopped abruptly as her fingers gripped the edge of the table, and she continued staring into the mirror not at her own face, but at the white robes that appeared behind her head, blotting out the limited view she had had of the room.

The Sheik was standing behind her. He had come with the peculiar noiseless tread that she had noticed before. He swung her round to look at her and she writhed under his eyes of admiration, straining from him as far as his grip allowed. Holding her with one hand he took her chin in the other and tilted her face up to his with a little smile. "Don't look so frightened. I don't want anything more deadly than some soap and water. Surely even an Arab may be allowed to wash his hands?"

His mocking voice and his taunt of fear stung her, but she would not answer and, with a laugh and a shrug, he lot her go, picking up a razor from the table and lounging into the bathroom.

With crimson cheeks Diana fled into the outer room, His manner could not have been more casual if she had been his wife a dozen years. She waited for him in a tumult of emotions, but with the advent of Gaston and dinner he returned to the attitude of dispassionate, courteous host that he had assumed when he first came in. He was a few minutes late, and apologised gravely as he sat down opposite her. He maintained the attitude throughout dinner, and conscious of the watching manservant Diana made herself reply to his easy conversation.

He talked mainly of the desert and the sport that it offered, as if he had studied her tastes and chosen the topic to please her. He spoke well; what he said was interesting, and showed complete knowledge of the subject, and at any other time Diana would have listened fascinated and absorbed, but now the soft, slow, cultured voice only seemed to add to the incongruity of the situation. The role of willing guest that he was forcing upon her was almost more than she could play, and the necessity of sitting still and responding was taxing her endurance to the utmost. And all the time she was aware acutely of his constant surveillance. Reluctantly her own furtive glance was drawn frequently to his face, and always his dark fierce eyes were watching her with a steadiness that racked her nerves, till she was reminded irresistibly of an exhibition that she had seen in a circus in Vienna, where a lion tamer had concluded an unusually daring performance by dining in the lions' cage, surrounded by savage snarling brutes very different from the sleepy half-drugged creatures ordinarily shown. Interested in the animals, she had gone behind with Aubrey after the performance, and while fondling some tiny lion cubs that had been brought for her to see had chatted with the tamer, a girl little older than herself. She had been somewhat unapproachable until she had realised from Diana's friendly manner that her questions were prompted by real interest and not mere curiosity, and had unbent with surprising swiftness, accepting Diana's proffered cigarettes and taking her to see her special lions, who were boxed for the night. Diana had wandered up and down before the narrow cages, looking at the big brutes still restless from the show, rubbing her cheek on the soft little round head of the cub she was holding in her arms, smiling at its sleepy rasping purr.

"Are you ever afraid?" she had asked suddenly—"not of the ordinary performance, but of that last act, when you dine all alone with them?"

The girl shrugged her shoulders, blowing a little cloud of smoke into the cub's face, and her eyes had met Diana's slowly over his little yellow body. "One does not taste very much," she had said drily.

And it was so with Diana. She had eaten mechanically everything that had been put before her, but she had tasted nothing. She had one thought in her mind that excluded everything else—to hide from the probing eyes that watched her ceaselessly the overmastering fear that augmented every moment. One thing she had noticed during the meal. For her only the servant poured out the light French wine that he had brought. Her eyes wandered to the Sheik's empty glass, and meeting her glance he smiled, with a little inclination.

"Excuse me. I do not drink wine. It is my only virtue," he added, with a sudden gleam leaping into his eyes that drove the blood into her cheeks and her own eyes on to her plate.

She had forgotten that he was an Arab.

The dinner seemed interminable, and yet she wished that it would never end. While the servant was in the room she was safe; the thought of his going sent a cold shudder through her. With the coffee came a huge Persian hound, almost upsetting the Frenchman in the entrance in his frantic endeavour to precede him through the doorway. He flung his long grey body across the Sheik's knees with a whine of pleasure and then turned his head to growl at Diana. But the growl died away quickly, and he lumbered down and came to her side curiously, eyeing her for a moment and then thrusting his big head against her.

The Sheik laughed. "You are honoured. Kopec makes few friends."

She did not answer. The natural reply was almost certain to provoke a retort that she did not desire, so she remained silent, smoothing the hound's rough coat. With her heart turning slowly to lead she lingered over her coffee until there was no further possible pretext for remaining at the table, then rose with a short, sharp sigh.

For some minutes the Sheik had sat silent, his own coffee long since finished. He made no comment when she got up, and went himself to the big divan, followed by the hound, who had gone back to him as soon as he moved.

Diana turned to the little bookcase, snatching at the opportunity it offered for further silence, and took a book at random. She did not know what she was looking at, she did not care. She only prayed fervently that she might be left alone, that the sudden silent fit that had come over him might continue.

Near her Gaston was clearing away the table and as he finished he paused to speak to his master. Diana heard the words "le petit Sheik," but the rest was in Arabic and unintelligible to her. The Sheik frowned with a gesture of annoyance, then nodded, and the servant left the tent.

A few moments after a voice that she had not heard before made her look up.

The young Arab who had ridden in with the Sheik was standing beside the divan. The fierce eyes that were watching her every movement met hers, and his cigarette was waved towards the young man. "My lieutenant, Yusef, a son of the desert with the soul of a *flaneur*. His body is here with me, but his heart is on the *trottoirs* of Algiers."

The tall lad laughed and salaamed profoundly, then straightened himself, posing magnificently until a curt word from the Sheik recalled him to his errand and his swagger changed swiftly to a deference of which the significance was not lost on Diana. The Arab might unbend to his people if it so pleased him, but he kept them well in hand. She looked at the lieutenant as he stood before his chief. He was tall and slender as a girl, with an air of languid indolence that was obviously a pose, for it was slipping from him now fast as he talked. His face was strikingly handsome, only saved from effeminacy by a firm chin. He was patently aware of his good looks. But he was also patently in awe of his chief, and the news that he brought was apparently not welcome.

Through her thick lashes Diana watched them intently. The younger man voluble, gesticulating, at times almost cringing. The Sheik silent, except for an occasional word, the heavy scowl back on his face, growing blacker every moment. At last with a shrug of impatience he got up and they went out together, the hound following them. Diana subsided on to the thick rug beside the bookcase. For a moment again she was alone, free of the watching eyes that seemed to be burning into her all the time, free of the hated proximity. She dropped her head on her knees with a little whimper of weariness. For a moment she need not check the tide of misery that rushed over her. She was tired in mind and body, exhausted with the emotion that had shaken her until she knew that no matter what happened in the future the Diana of yesterday was dead, and her new self was strange and unfamiliar. She did not trust it; she feared its capacity for maintaining the struggle she had resolved upon. The old courageous self had never failed her, this new shrinking fearful personality filled her with distrust. Her confidence in herself was gone. Her contempt of herself was unutterable. The strength that remained was not sufficient to conquer the fear that had taken so strong a hold upon her. She could only hope to hide it, to deny him at least that much satisfaction. She had grovelled at his feet once and it had amused him. He had laughed! She would die rather than afford him a similar amusement. She could never wipe out the recollection of her cowardice; he would remember always, and so would she; but she could atone for it if her strength held. And she prayed that it might hold, until a sob broke from her and her hands cramped around her knees. She pushed her hair off her forehead with a heavy sigh, and she looked back over her shoulder at the empty room. It had changed since this morning in the indefinable way a strange room does change after a few hours' association. If she could leave it now and never see it again in all her life no single detail of it would ever be forgotten. Its characteristics had been stamped upon her as familiarly as if the hours passed in it had been years. And yesterday was years ago, when the poor silly fool that had been Diana Mayo had ridden blindly into the trap from which her boasted independence had not been able to save her. She had paid heavily for the determination to ignore the restrictions of her sex laid upon her and the payment was not yet over. Her tired body shrank from the struggle that must recommence so soon. If he would only spare her until this numbing weariness that made her so powerless should lessen. She heard his voice at the door and her icy fingers grasped at the book that had slipped to the ground. The thick rugs deadened the sound of his movements, but she knew instinctively that he had come in and gone back to the divan where he had been sitting before. She knew that he was looking at her. She could feel his eyes fixed on her and she quivered with the consciousness of his stare. She waited, shivering, for him to speak or move. His methods of torture were diverse, she thought with dreary bitterness. Behind the tent in the men's lines a tom-tom was beating, and the irregular rhythm seemed hammering inside her own head. She could have shrieked with the agony of it.

"Come here—Diane."

She started, for a moment hardly recognising the Gallic rendering of her name, and then flushed angrily without answering or moving. It was a very little thing to stir her after all that had been done, but the use of her name flamed the anger that had been almost swamped in fear. The proprietory tone in his voice roused all her inherent obstinacy. She was not his to go at his call. What he wanted he must take—she would never give voluntarily. She sat with her hands gripped tightly in her lap, breathing rapidly, her eyes dark with apprehension.

"Come here," he repeated sharply.

Still she took no notice, but the face that he could not see was growing very white.

"I am not accustomed to having my orders disobeyed," he said at last, very slowly.

"And I am not accustomed to obeying orders," she retorted fiercely, though her lips were trembling.

"You will learn." The sinister accent of his voice almost shattered her remaining courage.

She crouched, gasping, on the ground, the same horrible terror that had come to her last night stealing over her irresistibly, paralysing her. Waiting, listening, agonising, the tom-tom growing louder and louder—or was it only the throbbing in her own head? With a choking cry she leaped to her feet suddenly and fled from him, back till the side of the tent stopped her and she stood, with wide-flung arms, gripping the black and silver hangings until he reached her.

Stooping he disengaged her clinging fingers from the heavy drapery and drew her hands slowly together up to his breast with a little smile. "Come," he whispered, his passionate eyes devouring her.

She fought against the fascination with which they dominated her, resisting him dumbly with tight-locked lips till he held her palpitating in his arms.

"Little fool," he said with a deepening smile. "Better me than my men."

The gibe broke her silence.

"Oh, you brute! You brute!" she wailed, until his kisses silenced her.

CHAPTER IV

"A month! Thirty-one days! Oh, God! Only thirty-one days. It seems a lifetime. Only a month since I left Biskra. A month! A month!"

Diana flung herself on to her face, burying her head deeply into the cushions of the divan, shutting out from her sight the barbaric luxury of her surroundings, shuddering convulsively. She did not cry. The complete breakdown of the first night had never been repeated. Tears of shame and anger had risen in her eyes often, but she would not let them fall. She would not give her captor the satisfaction of knowing that he could make her weep. Her pride was dying hard. Her mind travelled back slowly over the days and nights of anguished revolt, the perpetual clash of will against will, the enforced obedience that had made up this month of horror. A month of experience of such bitterness that she wondered dully how she still had the courage to rebel. For the first time in her life she had had to obey. For the first time in her life she was of no account. For the first time she had been made conscious of the inferiority of her sex. The training of years had broken down under the experience. The hypothetical status in which she had stood with regard to Aubrey and his friends was not tolerated here, where every moment she was made to feel acutely that she was a woman, forced to submit to everything to which her womanhood exposed her, forced to endure everything that he might put upon her—a chattel, a slave to do his bidding, to bear his pleasure and his displeasure, shaken to the very foundation of her being with the upheaval of her convictions and the ruthless violence done to her cold, sexless temperament. The humiliation of it seared her proud heart. He was pitiless in his arrogance, pitiless in his Oriental disregard of the woman subjugated. He was an Arab, to whom the feelings of a woman were non-existent. He had taken her to please himself and he kept her to please himself, to amuse him in his moments of relaxation.

To Diana before she had come to Africa the life of an Arab Sheik in his native desert had been a very visionary affair. The term sheik itself was elastic. She had been shown Sheiks in Biskra who drove hard bargains to hire out mangy camels and sore-covered donkeys for trips into the interior. Her own faithless caravan-leader had called himself "Sheik." But she had heard also of other and different Sheiks who lived far away across the shimmering sand, powerful chiefs with large followings, who seemed more like the Arabs of her imaginings, and of whose lives she had the haziest idea. When not engaged in killing their neighbours she visualized them drowsing away whole days under the influence of narcotics, lethargic with sensual indulgence. The pictures she had seen had been mostly of fat old men sitting cross-legged in the entrance of their tents, waited on by hordes of retainers, and looking languidly, with an air of utter boredom, at some miserable slave being beaten to death.

She had not been prepared for the ceaseless activity of the man whose prisoner she was. His life was hard, strenuous and occupied. His days were full, partly with the magnificent horses that he bred, and partly with tribal affairs that took him from the camp for hours at a time. Upon one or two occasions he had been away for the whole night and had come back at daybreak with all the evidences of hard riding. Some days she rode with him, but when he had not the time or the inclination, the French valet went with her. A beautiful grey thoroughbred called Silver Star was kept for her use, and sometimes on his back she was able to forget for a little time. So the moments of relaxation were less frequent than they might have been, and it was only in the evenings when Gaston had come and gone for the last time and she was alone with the Sheik that an icy hand seemed to close down over her heart. And, according to his mood, he noticed or ignored her. He demanded implicit obedience to his lightest whim with the unconscious tyranny of one who had always been accustomed to command. He ruled his unruly followers despotically, and it was obvious that while they loved him they feared him equally. She had even seen Yusef, his lieutenant, cringe from the heavy scowl that she had, herself, learned to dread.

"You treat them like dogs," she said to him once. "Are you not afraid that one day they will rise against you and murder you?"

And he had only shrugged his shoulders and laughed, the same low laugh of amusement that never failed to make her shiver.

The only person whose devotion seemed untinged by any conflicting sentiment was the French valet, Gaston.

It was the Sheik's complete indifference to everything beyond his own will, his Oriental egoism, that stung her most. He treated her supplications and invectives with a like unconcern. The paroxysms of wild rage that filled her periodically made no impression on him. He accorded them a shrug of ennui or watched her with cold curiosity, his lips parted in a little cruel smile, as if the dissection of her lacerated feelings amused him, until his patience was exhausted, and then, with one of the lithe, quick movements that she could never evade, his hands would grip and hold her and he would look at her. Only that, but in the grasp of his lean, brown fingers and under the stare of his dark, fierce eyes her own would drop, and the frantic words die from her lips. She was physically afraid of him, and she hated him and loathed herself for the fear he inspired. And her fear was legitimate. His strength was abnormal, and behind it was the lawlessness and absolutism that allowed free rein to his savage impulses. He held life and death in his hand.

A few days after he had taken her she had seen him chastise a servant. She did not know what the man's fault had been, but the punishment seemed out of all proportion to anything that could be imagined, and she had watched fascinated with horror, until he had tossed away the murderous whip, and without a second glance at the limp, blood-stained heap that huddled on the ground with suggestive stillness had strolled back unconcerned to the tent. The sight had sickened her and haunted her perpetually. His callousness horrified her even more than his cruelty. She hated him with all the strength of her proud, passionate nature. His personal beauty even was an additional cause of offence. She hated him the more for his handsome face and graceful, muscular body. His only redeeming virtue in her eyes was his total lack of vanity, which she grudgingly admitted. He was as unconscious of himself as was the wild animal with which she compared him.

"He is like a tiger," she murmured deep into the cushions, with a shiver, "a graceful, cruel, merciless beast." She remembered a tiger she had shot the previous winter in India. After hours of weary, cramped waiting in the machan the beautiful creature had slipped noiselessly through the undergrowth and emerged into the clearing. He had advanced midway towards the tree where she was perched and had stopped to listen, and the long, free stride, the haughty poise of the thrown-back head, the cruel curl of the lips and the glint in the ferocious eyes flashing in the moonlight, were identical with the expression and carriage of the man who was her master. Then it had been admiration without fear, and she had hesitated at wantonly destroying so perfect a thing, until the quick pressure of her shikari's fingers on her arm brought her back to facts and reminded her that the "perfect thing" was reported to have eaten a woman the previous week. And now it was fear with a reluctant admiration that she despised herself for according.

A hand on her shoulder made her start up with a cry. Usually her nerves were in better control, but the thick rugs deadened every sound, and she had not expected him so soon. He had been out since dawn and had come in much past his usual time, and had been having a belated siesta in the adjoining room.

Angry with herself she bit her lip and pushed the tumbled hair off her forehead. He dropped on to the divan beside her and lit the inevitable cigarette; he smoked continuously every moment he was not in the saddle. She glanced at him covertly. He was lying with his head thrown back against the cushions, idly blowing smoke-rings and watching them drift towards the open door-way. And as she looked he yawned and turned to her.

"Zilah is careless. Insist that she puts away your boots, and does not leave your clothes lying on the floor. There was a scorpion in the bathroom today," he said lazily, stretching out his long legs.

She flushed hotly, as she always did when he made any casual reference to the intimacy of their life. It was his casualness that frightened her, the carelessly implied continuance of a state that scorched her with shame. His attitude invariably suggested a duration of their relations that left her numb with a kind of helpless despair. He was so sure of himself, so sure of his possession of her.

She felt the warm blood pouring over her face now, up to the roots of her bright hair and dyeing her slender neck, and she put her hands up to her head, her fingers thrust through her loose curls, to shield her face from his eyes.

She gave a sigh of relief when Gaston came in bringing a little tray with two filigree-cased cups of coffee.

"I have brought coffee; Madame's tea is finished," he murmured in tones of deepest distress, and with a gesture that conveyed a national calamity.

There had been just enough tea taken on the tour to last a month. It was another pin-prick, another reminder. She set her teeth, moving her head angrily, and found herself looking into a pair of mocking eyes, and, as always, her own dropped.

Gaston said a few words in Arabic to his master, and the Sheik swallowed the boiling coffee and went out hastily. The valet moved about the tent with his usual deft noiselessness, gathering up cigarette ends and spent matches, and tidying the room with an assiduous orderliness that was peculiarly his own. Diana watched him almost peevishly. Was it the influence of the desert that made all these men cat-like in their movements, or was the servant consciously or unconsciously copying his master? With a sudden fit of childish irritability she longed to smash something, and, with an impetuous hand, sent the little inlaid table with the tray and coffee-cups flying. She was ashamed of the impulse even before the crash came, and looked at Gaston clearing up the debris with anxious eyes. What was the matter with her? The even temper on which she prided herself and the nerves that had been her boast had vanished, gone by the board in the last month. If her nerve failed her utterly what would become of her? What would she do?

Gaston had gone, and she looked around the tent with a hunted expression. There seemed no escape possible from the misery that was almost more than she could bear.

There was a way out that had been in her mind often, and she had searched frequently in the hope that she might find the means. But the Sheik had also thought and had taken precautions. One day it seemed as if her desperate wish might be fulfilled, and she had had only a moment's hesitation as she stretched out her hand to take the revolver that had been left lying on a table, but as her fingers closed on the butt a muscular hand closed over hers. He had come in with his usual silent step and was close to her without her knowing. He had taken the weapon from her quietly, holding her eyes with his own, and had jerked it open, showing the empty magazine. "Do you think that I am quite a fool?" he had asked without a trace of expression in his voice.

And since then she had been under a ceaseless, unobtrusive surveillance that had left her no chance of carrying out her terrible resolve. She buried her face in her hands. "Oh, my God! Is it never going to end? Am I never going to get away from him?"

She sprang to her feet and walked restlessly round the tent, her hands clasped behind her back, her head thrown up, and her lips pressed close together. She panted as if she had been running, and her eyes had a far-away, unseeing look. Gradually she got command of herself again and the nervous excitement died down, leaving her weary and very desolate. The solitude seemed suddenly horrible. Anything would be better than the silent emptiness of the great tent. A noise outside attracted her, and she wandered to the doorway and out under the awning. Near her the Sheik with Gaston and Yusef stood watching a mad, ramping colt that was being held with difficulty by two or three men, who clung to him tenaciously in spite of his efforts to break away, and beyond was a semi-circle of Arabs, some mounted and some on foot, leaving a wide, open space between them and the tent. They were intensely excited, talking and gesticulating, the mounted men riding round the outer ring that they formed. Diana leaned against one of the lances that supported the awning and watched the scene with growing interest. This camp was many miles to the south of the one to which she had first been brought, and which had been broken up a few days after her capture. The setting was wonderful, the far-off hills dusky in the afternoon light, the clustering palms behind the tents, the crowd of barbaric figures in picturesque, white robes, the horsemen moving continuously up and down, and in the midst of everything the beautiful, wild creature, frenzied by the noise, kicking and biting at the men holding him. After a moment the Sheik held up his hand, and a man detached himself from the chattering crowd and came to him salaaming. The Sheik said a few words, and with another salaam and a gleam of white teeth, the man turned and approached the struggling group in the centre of the ring.

Diana straightened up with interest. The frantic colt was going to be broken. It was already saddled. Several additional men ran forward, and between them the horse was forcibly held for a moment—only for a moment, but it was long enough for the man who leaped like a flash on to his back. The others fell away, racing from the reach of the terrible lashing heels. Amazed for the moment at the sudden unaccustomed weight, the colt paused, and then reared straight up, till it seemed to Diana that he must fall backward and crush the man who was clinging to him. But he came down at last, and for a few moments it was almost impossible to follow his spasmodic movements as he strove to rid himself of his rider. The end came quickly. With a twisting heave of his whole body he shot the Arab over his head, who landed with a dull thud and lay still, while the men who had been holding the colt dashed in and secured him before he was aware of his liberty. Diana looked towards the fallen man; a little crowd were gathered around him, and her heart beat faster as she thought that he was dead. Dead so quickly, and only a moment before he had been so full of life and strength. Death meant nothing to these savages, she thought bitterly, as she watched the limp body being carried away by three or four men, who argued violently over their burden. She glanced at the Sheik. He seemed perfectly unconcerned and did not even look in the direction of the man who had fallen. On the contrary, he laughed, and, turning to Yusef, put his hand en his shoulder and nodded towards the colt. Diana gave a gasp. He spared no one. He was going to make the young man take his chance as the rough-rider had taken his. She knew that the lieutenant rode well, as did all Ahmed Ben Hassan's followers, and that his languid manner was only a pose, but he looked so young and boyish, and the risk seemed enormous. She had seen colts broken before many times, but never a colt so madly savage as this one. But to Yusef the chance was evidently welcome. With an answering laugh, he swaggered out into the arena, where the men greeted him with shouts. There was the same procedure as before, and Yusef bounded up lightly into the saddle. This time, instead of rearing, the frightened beast dashed forward in a wild effort to escape, but the mounted men, closing up, headed him into the middle of the ring again, and he went back to his first tactics with a rapidity that was too much for the handsome lad on his back, and in a few moments he was thrown heavily. With a shrill scream the colt turned on him open-mouthed, and Yusef flung up one arm to save his face. But the men reached him in time, dragging the colt from him by main force. He rose to his feet unsteadily and limped to the tents behind. Diana could not see him easily for the throng around him.

Again she looked at the Sheik and ground her teeth. He was stooping to light a cigarette from a match that Gaston was holding, and then they walked together nearer to the colt. The animal was now thoroughly maddened, and it was increasingly difficult to hold him. They went up close to the struggling, yelling grooms, and the next minute Diana saw Gaston sitting firmly in the empty saddle. The little man rode magnificently, and put up a longer fight than the others had done, but at last his turn came, and he went flying over the colt's head. He came down lightly on his hands and knees, and scrambled to his feet in an instant amidst a storm of shouts and laughter. Laughing himself he came back to the Sheik with a shrug of the shoulders and outspread, eloquent hands. They spoke together for a moment, too low for Diana to hear, and then Ahmed Ben Hassan went again into the middle of the ring. Diana's breath came more quickly. She guessed his intention before he reached the colt, and she moved forward from under the awning and joined Gaston, who was wrapping his handkerchief round a torn hand.

"Monseigneur will try?" she asked a little breathlessly.

Gaston looked at her quickly. "Try, Madame?" he repeated in a queer voice. "Yes, he will try."

Again the empty saddle was filled, and a curious hush came over the watching crowd. Diana looked on with bright, hard eyes, her heart beating heavily. She longed passionately that the colt might kill him, and, at the same time, illogically, she wanted to see him master the infuriated animal. The sporting instinct in her acknowledged and responded to the fight that was going on before her eyes. She hated him and she hoped that he might die, but she was forced to admire the wonderful horsemanship that she was watching. The Sheik sat like a rock, and every effort made to unseat him was unsuccessful. The colt plunged wildly, making furious blind dashes backward and forward, stopping dead in the hope of dislodging his rider, twirling round suddenly until it seemed impossible that he could keep his feet. Then he started rearing, straight up, his forelegs beating the air, higher and higher, and then down, to commence again without a moment's breathing-space.

Diana heard Gaston's breath whistle through his teeth. "Look, Madame!" he cried sharply, and Diana saw the Sheik give a quick glance behind him, and, as the colt shot up again, almost perpendicular, with a jerk he pulled him deliberately over backwards, leaping clear with a tremendous effort as the horse crashed to the ground. He was in the saddle again almost before the dazed creature had struggled to its feet. And then began a scene that Diana never forgot. It was the final struggle that was to end in defeat for either man or horse, and the Sheik had decided that it was not to be for the man. It was a punishment of which the untamed animal was never to lose remembrance. The savagery and determination of the man against the mad determination of the horse. It was a hideous exhibition of brute strength and merciless cruelty. Diana was almost sick with horror from the beginning; she longed to turn away, but her eyes clung fascinated to the battle that was going on. The hush that had fallen on the crowd had given way to roars of excitement, and the men pressed forward eagerly, to give back precipitately when the still-fighting animal's heels flashed too near.

Diana was shaking all over and her hands were clenching and unclenching as she stared at the man, who seemed a part of the horse he was sitting so closely. Would it never end? She did not care now which killed the other so that it would only stop. The man's endurance seemed mere bravado. She clutched Gaston's arms with a hand that was wringing wet. "It is horrible," she gasped with an accent of loathing.

"It is necessary," he replied quietly.

"Nothing can justify that," she cried passionately.

"Your pardon, Madame. He must learn. He killed a man this morning, threw him, and what you call in English 'savaged' him."

Diana hid her face in her hands. "I can't bear it," she said pitifully.

A few minutes later Gaston clicked his tongue against his teeth. "See, Madame. It is over," he said gently.

She looked up fearfully. The Sheik was standing on the ground beside the colt, who was swaying slowly from side to side with heaving sides and head held low to the earth, dripping blood and foam. And as she looked he tottered and collapsed exhausted. There was a rush from all sides, and Gaston went towards his master, who towered above the crowd around him.

Diana turned away with an exclamation of disgust. It was enough to have seen a display of such brutality; it was too much to stand by while his fellow-savages acclaimed him for his cruelty.

She went slowly back into the tent, shaken with what she had seen, and stood in undecided hesitation beside the divan. The helpless feeling that she so often experienced swept over her with renewed force. There was nowhere that she could get away from him, no privacy, no respite. Day and night she must endure his presence with no hope of escape. She closed her eyes in a sudden agony, and then stiffened at the sound of his voice outside.

He came in laughing, a cigarette dangling from one blood-stained hand, while with the other he wiped the perspiration from his forehead, leaving a dull red smear. She shrank from him, looking at him with blazing eyes. "You are a brute, a beast, a devil! I hate you!" she choked furiously.

For a moment an ugly look crossed his face, and then he laughed again. "Hate me by all means, *ma belle*, but let your hatred be thorough. I detest mediocrity," he said lightly, as he passed on into the other room.

She sank down on to the couch. She had never felt so desperate, so powerless. She stared straight before her, shivering, as she went over the scene she had just witnessed, her fingers picking nervously at the jade-green silk of her dress. She longed for some power that would deaden her feelings and blunt her capacity for suffering. She looked at Gaston with hard eyes when he came in. He had approved of what the Sheik had done, would have done it himself if he had been able. They were all alike.

"The man who was hurt first," she asked abruptly, with a touch of her old hauteur in her voice, "is he dead?"

"Oh no, Madame. He has concussion but he will be all right. They have hard heads, these Arabs."

"And Yusef?"

Gaston grinned. *"Le petit* Sheik has a broken collar-bone. It is nothing. A few days' holiday to be petted in his harem, *et voilà!"*

"His harem?" echoed Diana in surprise. "Is he married?"

"Mais oui, Madame. He has two wives."

At Diana's exclamation he shrugged deprecatingly. *"Que voulez-vous?* It is the custom of the country," he said tolerantly, with the air of conceding a melancholy fact with the best grace possible.

The customs of the country was dangerous ground, and Diana changed the subject hastily. "Where did you learn to ride, Gaston?"

"In a racing-stable at Auteuil, Madame, when I was a boy. Then I was five years in the French cavalry. After that I came to Monseigneur."

"And you have been with him—how long?"

"Fifteen years, Madame."

"Fifteen years," she repeated wonderingly. "Fifteen years here, in the desert?"

"Here and elsewhere, Madame," he answered rather more shortly than usual, and with a murmur of excuse left the tent.

Diana leaned back against the cushions with a little sigh. Gaston need not have been afraid that she was trying to learn his master's secrets from him. She had not fallen as low as that. The mystery of the man whose path had crossed hers so terribly seemed to augment instead of lessen as the time went on. What was the power in him that compelled the devotion of his wild followers and the little French ex-cavalryman? She knit her forehead in perplexity and was still puzzling over it when he came back. Immaculate and well-groomed he was very different from the dishevelled, bloodstained savage of half-an-hour before. She shot a nervous glance at him, remembering her outburst, but he was not angry. He looked grave, but his gravity seemed centred in himself as he passed his lean fingers tenderly over his smooth chin. She had seen Aubrey do similarly hundreds of times. Occidental or Oriental, men seemed very alike. She waited for him to speak and waited vainly. One of the taciturn fits to which she had grown accustomed had come over him—hours sometimes in which he simply ignored her altogether. The evening meal was silent. He spoke once to Gaston, but he spoke in Arabic, and the servant replied only with a nod of compliance. And after Gaston was gone he did not speak for a long time, but sat on the divan, apparently absorbed in his thoughts.

Restless, Diana moved about the tent, listlessly examining objects that she knew by heart, and flirting over the pages of the French magazines she had read a dozen times. Usually she was thankful for his silent moods. Tonight with a woman's perversity she wanted him to speak. She was unstrung, and the utter silence oppressed her. She glanced over her shoulder at him once or twice, but his back looked unapproachable. Yet when he called her, with a swift revulsion of feeling, she wished he had kept silent. She went to him slowly. She was too unnerved tonight to struggle against him. What would be the use? she thought wearily; it would only end in defeat as it always did. He pulled her down on the divan beside him, and before she realised what he was doing slipped a long jade necklace over her head. For a moment she looked stupidly at the wonderful thing, almost unique in the purity of its colour and the marvellous carving on the uniform square pieces of which it was composed, and then with a low cry she tore it off and flung it on the ground.

"How dare you?" she gasped.

"You don't like it?" he asked in his low, unruffled voice, his eyebrows raised in real or assumed surprise. "Yet it matches your dress," and lightly his long fingers touched the folds of green silk swathed across the youthful curve of her breast. He glanced at an open box filled with shimmering stones on a low stool beside him.

"Pearls are too cold and diamonds too banal for you," he said slowly. "You should wear nothing but jade. It is the colour of the evening sky against the sunset of your hair."

He had never spoken like that to her before, or used that tone of voice. His methods had been more fierce than tender. She glanced up swiftly at his face, but it baffled her. There was no love in his eyes or even desire, nothing but an unusual gentleness. "Perhaps you would prefer the diamonds and the pearls," he went on, pointing disdainfully at the box.

"No, no. I hate them! I hate them all! I will not wear your jewels. You have no right to think that I am that kind of woman," she cried hysterically.

"You do not like them? *Bon Dieu!* None of the other women ever refused them. On the contrary, they could never get enough," he said with a laugh.

Diana looked up with a startled glance, a look of horror dawning in her eyes. "Other women?" she repeated blankly.

"You didn't suppose you were the first, did you?" he asked with brutal candour. "Don't look at me like that. They were not like you, they came to me willingly enough—too willingly. Allah! How they bored me! I tired of them before they tired of me."

She flung her arm across her eyes with a dry sob, straining away from him. She had never thought of that. In the purity of her mind it had never occurred to her. She was only one of many, one of a succession of mistresses, taken and discarded at his whim. She writhed with the shame that filled her. "Oh, you hurt me!" she whispered very low, and then anger killed all other feeling. He had loosened his arm about her and she wrenched herself free and sprang to her feet. "I hate you, do you understand? I hate you! I hate you!"

He lit a cigarette leisurely before answering and moved into a more comfortable position on the divan. "So you have already told me this afternoon," he said at length coolly, "and with reiteration your remark becomes less convincing, *ma cherie*."

Her anger ebbed away. She was too tired to be angry. She was humiliated and hurt, and the man before her had it in his power to hurt her more, but she was at his mercy and tonight she could not fight. She pushed the hair off her forehead with a heavy sigh and looked at the Sheik's long length stretched out on the couch, the steely strength of his limbs patent even in the indolent attitude in which he was lying, at his brown handsome face, inscrutable as it always was to her, and the feeling of helplessness came back with renewed force and with it the sense of her own pitiful weakness against his force, compelling her to speak. "Have you never felt pity for a thing that was weaker than yourself? Have you never spared anything or any one in all your life? Have you nothing in your nature but cruelty? Are all Arabs hard like you?" she said shakily. "Has love never even made you merciful?"

He glanced up at her with a harsh laugh, and shook his head. "Love? *Connais pas!* Yes, I do," he added with swift mockery, "I love my horses."

"When you don't kill them," she retorted.

"I am corrected. When I don't kill them."

There was something in his voice that made her reckless, that made her want to hurt him. "If you give no love to the—the women whom you bring here, do you give love to the women of your harem? You have a harem, I suppose, somewhere?" she braved him with curling lip and scornful voice, but as she spoke she knew that she had only hurt herself and her voice faltered.

His hand reached out suddenly and he dragged her down into his arms again with a laugh. "And if I have, are you jealous? What if the nights I spent away from you were passed in my harem—what then?"

"Then may Allah put it into the heart of one of your wives to poison you so that you never come back," she said fiercely.

"Allah! So beautiful and so bloodthirsty," he said in bantering reproof. Then he turned her face up to his, smiling into her angry eyes with amusement. "I have no harem and, thanks be to Allah, no wives, *cherie*. Does that please you?"

"Why should I care? It is nothing to me," she replied sharply, with a vivid blush.

He held her closer, looking deeply into her eyes, holding them as he could when he liked, in spite of her efforts to turn them away—a mesmerism she could not resist.

"Shall I make you care? Shall I make you love me? I can make women love me when I choose."

She went very white and her eyes flickered. She knew that he was only amusing himself, that he was utterly indifferent to her feelings, that he did not care if she hated or loved him, but it was a new form of torture that was more detestable than anything that had gone before it. It infuriated her that he could even suggest that she could come to care for him, that she could ever look on him as anything but a brutal savage who had committed a hideous outrage, that she could ever have any feeling for him except hatred and loathing. That he should class her with the other women he spoke of revolted her, she felt degraded, soiled as she had never done before, and she had thought that she had felt the utmost humiliation of her position.

The colour rushed back into her face. "I would rather you killed me," she cried passionately.

"So would I," he said drily, "for if you loved me you would bore me and I should have to let you go. While as it is"—he laughed softly—"as it is I do not regret the chance that took me into Biskra that day."

He let her go and got up with a yawn, watching her approvingly as she crossed the tent. The easy swing of her boyish figure and the defiant carriage of her head reminded him of one of his own thoroughbred horses. She was as beautiful and as wild as they were.

And as he broke them so would he break her. She was nearly tamed now, but not quite, and by Allah! it should be quite! As he turned his foot struck against the jade necklace lying on the rug where she had thrown it. He picked it up and called her back. She came reluctantly, slowly, with mutinous eyes.

He held out the necklace silently, and silently she stared not at it but at him. Her heart began to beat faster, and the colour slowly left her face. "Take it. I wish it," he said quietly.

"No." It was little more than a gasp.

"You will wear it to please me," he went on in the same soft voice, and the old hateful mockery crept into his eyes, "to please my artistic soul. I have an artistic soul even though I am only an Arab."

"I will not!"

The mockery was wiped out of his eyes in a flash, giving place to the usual ferocity, and his forehead knit in the dreaded heavy scowl. "Diane, obey me!"

She clenched her teeth on her lower lip until a rim of blood stained their whiteness. If he would only shout or bluster like the average angry man she felt that she could brave him longer, but the cold quiet rage that characterised him always was infinitely more sinister, and paralysed her with its silent force. She had never heard him raise his voice in anger or quicken his usual slow, soft tone, but there was an inflection that came into his voice and a look that came into his eyes that was more terrible than any outburst. She had seen his men shrink when, standing near him, she had barely been able to hear what he had said. She had seen a look from him silence a clamorous quarrel that had broken out among his followers too close to his own tent for his pleasure. And that inflection was in his voice and that look was in his eyes now. It was no longer use to resist. The fear of him was an agony. She would have to obey, as in the end he always forced her to obey. She wrenched her eyes away from his compelling stare, her bosom heaving under the soft silk, her chin quivering, and reached out blindly and took it from him. But the sudden chill of it against her bare breast seemed to revive the courage that was not yet dead in her. She flung up her head, the transient colour flaming into her cheeks, and her lips sprang open, but he drew her to him swiftly, and laid his hand over her mouth. "I know, I know," he said coldly. "I am a brute and a beast and a

devil. You need not tell me again. It commences to grow tedious."
His hand slipped to her shoulder, his fingers gripping the delicate, rounded arm. "How much longer are you going to fight? Would it not be wiser after what you have seen today to recognise that I am master?"

"You mean that you will treat me as you treated the colt this afternoon?" she whispered, her eyes drawn back irresistibly to his in spite of all her efforts.

"I mean that you must realise that my will is law."

"And if I do not?" He guessed rather than heard the words.

"Then I will teach you, and I think that you will learn—soon."

She quivered in his hands. It was a threat, but how much of it he meant to be taken literally she did not know. Again every ghastly detail of the afternoon passed with lightning speed through her mind. When he punished he punished mercilessly. To what lengths would he go? The Arab standards were not those of the men amongst whom she had lived. The position of a woman in the desert was a very precarious one. There were times when she forgot altogether that he was an Arab until some chance, as now, drove the hard fact home indisputably. He was an Arab, and as a woman she need expect no mercy at his hands. His hands! She looked down for a second sideways at the fingers gripping her shoulder and she saw them again stained with blood, saw them clenched round the dripping thong. She knew already by bitter experience the iron grip of his lean fingers and the compelling strength of his arms. Her quick imagination leaped ahead. What she had already suffered would be nothing compared with what would be. The remembrance of the stained, huddled figure of the servant he had chastised rose before her. And as she battled with herself, still torn in her passionate desire to make her strong will and courageous spirit triumph over her coward woman's body that shrank instinctively from physical torture, his arm tightened around her and she felt the hard muscles pressing against her shoulders and soft, bare neck, a suggestion of the force lying dormant beside her. She looked up at him slowly.

His expression was unchanged, his forehead was still drawn together in the heavy frown and there was no softening in his eyes. The cruel lines about his mouth were accentuated and the tiger-look in his face was more marked than ever. He was not threatening idly; he meant what he said.

"You had better kill me," she said drearily.

"That would be to admit my own defeat," he replied coolly. "I do not kill a horse until I have proved beyond all possible doubt that I cannot tame it. With you I have no such proof. I can tame you and I will. But it is for you to choose and to choose tonight if you will obey me willingly or if I must make you. I have been very patient—for me," he added, with an odd smile flitting across his face, "but my patience is exhausted. Choose quickly." Insensibly he drew her closer to him till his arm felt like an inflexible steel band about her, and she thought with a shudder of the coils of a great serpent closing round its victim. She made a final effort to conquer herself, but between her and the broad chest so close to her she seemed to see a horse's head held low in agony, blood and foam dripping from his lacerated mouth, and a horse's flanks heaving piteously, torn with the cruel punishment he had undergone. A sudden nausea came over her, everything seemed to swim before her eyes, and she swayed against the man who was holding her. Her bodily fear overruled her mind. She could not bear any more.

"I will obey you," she whispered heavily.

He took her chin in his fingers and jerked her head up sharply, staring at her intently until she felt he was looking into her very soul. The heavy scowl smoothed away but the fierceness lingered in his eyes. "Good!" he said at length briefly. "You are wise," he added significantly. He tilted her head further back, bending his own down until his lips were nearly touching hers. She shivered involuntarily, an anguished appeal leaping into her eyes. He smiled ironically. "Do you hate them so much, my kisses?"

She swallowed convulsively.

"You are at least candid if you are not complimentary;" and with that he released her and turned away.

She reached the curtain that divided the two rooms, her heart beating wildly, giddy with the strain that she had gone through. She paused a moment and looked back at him, amazed at her own temerity. He had unbuttoned the flap of the tent and was standing in the entrance looking out into the night. The scent of the peculiar tobacco he used drifted to her with the draught from the open door. Her eyes grew puzzled. Would she ever understand him?

Tonight he had given her a choice instead of simply enforcing his will, he had made her choose to save herself, he had proved his determination and his mastery over her. And with his last words the unexpected gentleness had come into his voice again and the cruel lines about his mouth had relaxed in a smile of amusement. It was the swift transition from ferocity to gentleness that she could never fathom. His complex nature was beyond her understanding. She would not try to understand him; she could never know the depths of his baffling personality. She only knew that for some reason of his own he had spared her, and she feared him more than ever.

CHAPTER V

Under the awning of the tent Diana was waiting for Gaston and the horses, pulling on her thick riding-gloves nervously. She was wrought up to the utmost pitch of excitement. Ahmed Ben Hassan had been away since the previous day and it was uncertain if he would return that night or the next. He had been vague as to how long he would be absent. There had been a constant coming and going amongst his followers—messengers arriving on exhausted horses at all hours of the day and night, and the Sheik himself had seemed unusually preoccupied. He had not condescended to give any reason for the special activity of his people and she had not asked him.

In the four weeks that had elapsed since she had promised him her obedience she had been very silent. The fear and hatred of him grew daily. She had learned to stifle the wild fits of rage and the angry words that leaped to her lips. She had learned to obey—a reluctant obedience given with compressed lips and defiant eyes, but given, and with a silence that surprised even herself. Day after day she had followed the usual routine, dumb unless he spoke to her; and with his own attention occupied with matters beyond the four walls of his tent he had not noticed or did not trouble to heed her silence. Lately he had left her very much alone; she had ridden with him almost daily until the last week, when he had announced curtly that in the meantime the length of her rides must be curtailed and that Gaston would accompany her. He had not offered any explanation, and she had not sought one. She had chosen to see in it merely another act of tyranny imposed on her by the man whose arbitrary exercise of power over her and whose tacit possession of her galled her continually. And under the sullen submission a wild fury of revolt was raging. She searched feverishly for means of flight, and now the Sheik's absence seemed to have given her the chance she had been waiting for. In the solitude of the previous night she had tossed impatiently from side to side of the big couch, vainly trying to find some means of taking advantage of her comparative freedom to effect her escape. Surely she could find some way of avoiding Gaston's vigilance. Excitement had kept her awake half the night, and in the morning she had had hard work to keep her agitation hidden and to appear as usual. She had even been afraid to order the horses any earlier in her nervous terror lest the valet should suspect there was any reason behind the simple request. After her *petit dejeuner* she had paced the tent, unable to sit still, dreading lest any moment might bring the return of the Sheik and frustrate her hopes. She looked back into the room with a shudder as her eyes travelled over the luxurious appointments and different objects that had become so curiously familiar in the last two months. The unexpected equipments and the man's own baffling personality would remain in her recollection always as an enigma that she would never be able to solve. So much had been so inexplicable in himself and in his mode of life. She drew a long breath and went out hastily into the sunshine.

The horses were waiting, and Gaston was standing ready to hold her stirrup. She fondled the beautiful grey horse's soft nose and patted his satiny neck with a hand that trembled a little. She loved the horse and today he should be the means of saving her. He responded to her caresses, gentling her with slobbering mouth and whinnying softly. With one last look at the big double tent and the rest of the camp behind it she mounted and rode away without another backward glance. She had to exercise a rigid control over herself. She longed to put Silver Star into a hand gallop at once and shake off Gaston, but she was still too near the camp. She must be patient and put a certain number of miles between herself and the possibility of pursuit before she attempted anything. Too early an endeavour would only bring the whole horde in wild chase at her heels. The thought of the promise she had given to the man from whom she was flying came back to her. She had promised obedience, but she had not promised that she would not try to escape, and, if she had, no promise wrung from her by fear was valid in her opinion.

She rode steadily forward at a slow, swinging canter, instinctively saving her horse, plan after plan passing through her brain to be rejected as impracticable. Silver Star fretted continually at the moderate pace, tossing his head and catching at his bit. She took no heed of the time beyond the fact that it was passing quickly, and that if anything was to be done it must be done as soon as possible. But Gaston, riding a few paces behind her, was very much alive to the hour and had looked several times at his watch. He ranged alongside of her now with a murmured apology. "Pardon, Madame. It grows late," and submitted his wrist watch for her inspection.

Diana glanced mechanically at her own wrist and then remembered that she had broken her watch the day before. She pulled up, and tilting her helmet back mopped her hot forehead, and, as she did so, a sharp breeze sprang up, the curious wind that comes and goes so rapidly in the desert. An idea flashed into her mind. It was a poor chance, but it might succeed. She shot a glance at Gaston. He was looking in the opposite direction, and, raising her hand, she fluttered her handkerchief a moment in the breeze and then let it go. The wind carried it some distance away. She gave a little cry and caught at the bridle of the valet's horse.

"Oh, Gaston, my handkerchief!" and pointed to where the morsel of cambric lay white against a rock. With a comical exclamation of dismay he slipped to the ground and started to run across the sand.

She waited until he had got well on his way, sitting tense with shining eyes and thumping heart, then, snatching off her helmet, she brought it down with a resounding smack on the hindquarters of the servant's horse, stampeding it in the direction of the camp, and, wheeling Silver Star, headed for the north, deaf to Gaston's cries.

Wild with excitement and free to go his own pace at last her mount galloped swiftly and the wind whistled past Diana's ears. To the possible fate of the little Frenchman left on foot so far from the encampment she gave no heed. For the moment she did not even think of him, she had no thought for anybody but herself. Her ruse by its very simplicity had succeeded. She was free and she did not care about anything else. She had no plans or ideas what she should do or where she should go beyond the fact that she would keep riding northward. She had vague hopes that she might fall in with friendly Arabs who, for a promised reward, would guide her to civilisation. Most of them could speak a little French, and for the rest her small stock of Arabic must do. She knew that she was mad to attempt to ride across the desert alone, but she did not mind. She was free. She was too excited to think coherently. She laughed and shouted like a mad thing and her madness communicated itself to the grey, who was going at racing speed. Diana knew that he was out of control, that she could not stop him if she tried, but she did not want to try, the faster the better. In time he would tire himself, but until then let him go as he pleased. She was fast putting miles between herself and the camp that had been a prison, between herself and the brute who had dared to do what he had done. At the thought of the Sheik a sick feeling of fear ran through her. If anything should happen? If he should catch her again? She shuddered, and a cry burst from her lips, but she gripped herself at once. She was idiotic, contemptible; it was impossible. It would be hours, perhaps even the next day, before the alarm was given; he would not know in what direction she had gone. She would have miles of start on one of the fleetest of his horses. She tried to put him out of her mind. She had escaped from him and his cruelty, it was a nightmare that was over. The effects would remain with her always, nothing would ever be the same again, but the daily dread, the daily contamination would be gone, the helpless tortured feeling, the shame of submission that had filled her with an acute self-loathing that was as intense as her passionate hatred of the man who had forced her to endure his will. The memory of it would live with her for ever. He had made her a vile thing. Her cheeks scorched with the thought and she shivered at the remembrance of all that she had gone through. She had been down into the depths and she would carry the scars all her life. The girl who had started out so triumphantly from Biskra had become a woman through bitter knowledge and humiliating experience.

The pace was less killing now. Silver Star had settled down into the steady tireless gallop for which Ahmed Ben Hassan's horses were famous. The little breeze had died away as quickly as it had sprung up, and it was very hot. Diana looked about her with glowing eyes. Everything seemed different. From the first she had loved the desert, but back of everything and mingled with everything had been the feeling of fear, the continual restraint, the perpetual subservience to the whims of her captor which had dominated everything. But now the whole aspect was changed. She loved the endless, undulating expanse stretching out before her, and as the grey topped each rise her interest grew keener. What might not be behind the next one? For an hour or more the ground rose and fell in monotonous succession, and then the desert grew level again and quite suddenly she could see for miles. About two miles away a few palm trees showed clustering together, and Diana turned in their direction. They probably meant a well, and it was time she rested her horse and herself. It was the tiniest little oasis, and she drew rein and dismounted with fears for the well she had hoped to find. But there was one, very much silted up, and she set to work to clear it as well as she could to procure enough for herself and Silver Star, who was frantically trying to get to the water. It was exhausting work, but she managed to satisfy the grey, and, having unloosed his girths, she flung herself down on the ground in a small patch of shade. She lit a cigarette and lay flat on her back with her helmet over her eyes.

For the first time since she had shaken off Gaston she began to think seriously. What she had done was madness. She had no food for herself or her horse, no water, and Heaven alone knew where the next well might be. She was alone in an uncivilised country among a savage people with no protection of any kind. She might fall in with friendly Arabs or she might not. She might come across an encampment, or she might wander for days and see no one, in which case death from hunger and thirst stared her in the face. What would she do when night came? With a sharp cry she leaped to her feet. What was she to do? She looked all around the little oasis with startled eyes, at the few palm trees and clumps of camel thorn, the broken well and the grey horse still snuffing about its mouth. She felt frightened for the first time; she was alone and about her was unending space, and she felt an atom, insignificant, the least of all things. She looked up into the clear sky and the blue vastness appalled her.

Then the sudden panic to which she had given way subsided and her courage rose with a bound. It was only midday, anything might happen between then and nightfall. Of one thing only she was sure, she did not repent of what she had done. Behind her was Ahmed Ben Hassan and before her was possibly death, and death was preferable. She was quite calm again and lay down in the patch of shade once more with a resolute determination to mind. Time to think of them when they came. For the next hour or two she must rest and escape the intense heat. She rolled over on her face with her head in her arms and tried to sleep, but she was too excited, and soon gave up the attempt. And in any case, she argued with herself, she might sleep too long and lose precious time. She stretched luxuriously on the soft ground, thankful for the shade from the burning sun. The grey, tired of nosing round the well and blowing disdainfully at the thorn bushes, wandered over to her side and nuzzled her gently. She caught at his velvety nose and drew it down beside her face. He was a very affectionate beast and gentler than most of the other horses, and he pressed close up to her, whinnying softly and looking at her with large expressive eyes. "I haven't anything to give you, poor old boy," she said regretfully, kissing his muzzle and then pushing him away from her. She looked up again into the sky, a dark speck sailed overhead, the slow heavy flight of a vulture. In a few hours he might be picking her bones! Merciful Heavens! Why did such thoughts come into her head? Had she nothing left of the courage that had once been second nature? If she let her nerves get the upper hand she might as well make no further effort, but lie down and die at once. With shaking fingers she took another cigarette; smoking would soothe her. Yet she hesitated before she lit it; there were only a few left and her need might still be greater. But with a reckless laugh she snapped the thin case to, and carefully scraped the evil-smelling sulphur match torn from a flat wood strip. She settled herself comfortably again full length. All around her were the innumerable tiny noises of the desert, the hum of countless insect life, the rustling of the sand and the occasional dry crackle of the camel thorns made by the slipping of a twig or the displacing of a branch, sounds that would have been incomprehensible some weeks before. For a few minutes a sand spider attracted her attention and she watched his hurried painstaking operations with wondering interest. Gradually a drowsy feeling stole over her and she realised suddenly that the air was impregnated with the scent of the tobacco that was always associated with the Sheik. It was one of his cigarettes that she was smoking. She had always been powerfully affected by the influence of smell, which induced recollection with her to an extraordinary degree, and now the uncommon penetrating odour of the Arab's cigarettes brought back all that she had been trying to put out of her mind. With a groan she flung it away and buried her face in her arms. The past rose up, and rushed, uncontrolled, through her brain. Incidents crowded into her recollection, memories of headlong gallops across the desert riding beside the man who, while she hated him, compelled her admiration, memories of him schooling the horses that he loved, sitting them like a centaur, memories of him amongst his men, memories more intimately connected with herself, of his varying moods, his swift changes from savage cruelty to amazing gentleness, from brutal intolerance to sudden consideration. There had even been times when he had interested her despite herself, and she had forgotten the relationship in which they stood towards each other in listening to his deep, slow voice, till a word or a gesture brought back the fact vividly. Memories of moments when she had struggled against his caresses, and he had mocked her helplessness with his great strength, when she had lain in his arms panting and exhausted, cold with fear and shrinking from his fierce kisses. She had feared him as she had never believed it possible to fear. His face rose before her clearly with all the expressions she had learned to know and dread. She tried to banish it, striving with all her might to put him from her mind, twisting this way and that, writhing on the soft sand as she struggled with the obsession that held her. She saw him all the time plainly, as though he were there before her. Would he pursue her always, phantom-like? Would the recollection of the handsome brown face haunt her for ever with its fierce eyes and cruel mouth? She buried her head deeper in her arms, but the vision persisted until with a scream she started up with heaving chest and wild eyes, standing rigid, staring towards the south with a desperate fixedness that made her eyeballs ache. The sense of his presence had been terribly real. She dropped on to the ground again with an hysterical laugh, and pushed the thick hair off her forehead wearily. Silver Star laying his muzzle suddenly on her shoulder made her start again violently with heavy, beating heart. A frightened look went across her face. "I'm nervous," she muttered, looking round with a little shiver. "I shall go mad if I stay here much longer." The little oasis that she had hailed so joyfully had become utterly repugnant and she was impatient to get away from it. She climbed eagerly into the saddle, and, with the rapid motion, she regained her calm and her spirits rose quickly.

She shook off the feeling of apprehension that had taken hold of her and her nervous fears died away. A reckless feeling, like the excitement of the morning, came over her, and she urged the grey on with coaxing words, and responding to her voice, and hardly feeling her light weight, he raced on untiringly. All around was silence and a solitude that was stupendous. The vast emptiness was awe-inspiring. The afternoon was wearing away; already it was growing cooler. Diana had seen no sign of human life since she had left Gaston hours before and a little feeling of anxiety stirred faintly deep down in her heart. Traces of caravans she passed several times, and from the whitening bones of dead camels she turned her head in aversion—they were too intimately suggestive. She had seen a few jackals, and once a hyena lumbered away clumsily among some rocks as she passed. She had got away from the level desert, and was threading her way in and out of some low hills, which she felt were taking her out of her right course. She was steering by the setting sun, which had turned the sky into a glory of golden crimson, but the intricate turnings amongst the rocky hills were bewildering. The low, narrow defile seemed hemming her in, menacing her on all sides, and she was beginning to despair of finding her way out of the labyrinth, when, on rounding a particularly sharp turn, the rocks fell away suddenly and she rode out into open country. She breathed a sigh of relief and called out cheerily to the grey, but, as she looked ahead, her voice died away, and she reined him in sharply with a quickening heart-beat. Across the desert about a mile away she saw a party of Arabs coming towards her. There were about fifty of them, the leader riding a big, black horse some little distance in front of his followers. In the clear atmosphere they seemed nearer than they were. It was not what she wished. She had hoped for an encampment, where there would be women or a caravan of traders whose constant communication with the towns would make them realise the importance of guiding her to civilisation unharmed. This band of fighting men, for she could see their rifles clearly, and their close and orderly formation was anything but peaceful, filled her with the greatest misgivings. Only the worst might be expected from the wild, lawless tribesmen towards a woman alone amongst them. She had fled from one hideousness to another which would be ten times more horrible. Her face blanched and she set her teeth in desperation. The human beings she had prayed for were now a deadly menace, and she prayed as fervently that they might pass on and not notice her. Perhaps it was not too late, perhaps they had not yet seen her and she might still slip away and hide in the twisting turnings of the defile. She backed Silver Star further into the shadow of the rock, but as she did so she saw that she had been seen. The leader turned in his saddle and raised his hand high above his head, and with a wild shout and a great cloud of dust and sand his men checked their horses, dragging them back on to their haunches, while he galloped towards her alone. And at the same moment an icy hand clutched at Diana's heart and a moan burst from her lips. There was no mistaking him or the big black horse he rode. For a moment she reeled with a sudden faintness, and then with a tremendous effort she pulled herself together, dragging her horse's head round and urged him back along the track which she had just left, and behind her raced Ahmed Ben Hassan, spurring the great, black stallion as he had never done before. With ashy face and wild, hunted eyes Diana crouched forward on the grey's neck, saving him all she could and riding as she had never ridden in her life. Utterly reckless, she urged the horse to his utmost pace, regardless of the rough, dangerous track. Perhaps she could still shake off her pursuer among the tortuous paths of the hills. Nothing mattered but that. Better even an ugly toss and a broken neck than that he should take her again. Panic-stricken she wanted to shriek and clenched her teeth on her lips to keep back the scream that rose in her throat. She dared not look behind, but straight ahead before her, riding with all her skill, hauling the grey round perilous corners and bending lower and lower in the saddle to aid him. In her terror she had forgotten what a little distance the hills stretched from where she had entered them, and blindly she turned into the track by which she had come, leaving the main hills on her right hand and emerging on to the open desert on the south side of the range. There was nothing now but the sheer speed of her horse to save her, and how long could she count on it? Then with a little glimmer of hope she remembered that the Sheik was riding The Hawk, own brother to the grey, and she knew that neither had ever outpaced the other. She had ridden hard all day, but it was probable that Ahmed Ben Hassan had ridden harder; he never spared his horses, and his weight was considerably greater than hers. Would it not be possible for Silver Star, carrying the lighter burden, to outdistance The Hawk? It was a chance. She would take it, but she would never give in. The perspiration was rolling down her face and her breath was coming laboriously. Suddenly, a few minutes after she had left the hills behind, the Sheik's deep voice came clearly across the space between them.

"If you do not stop I will shoot your horse. I give you one minute."

She swayed a little in the saddle, clutching the grey's neck to steady herself and for a moment she closed her eyes, but she did not falter for an instant. She would not stop; nothing on earth should make her stop now. Only, because she knew the man, she kicked her feet clear of the stirrups. He had said he would shoot and he would shoot, and if the grey shied or swerved a hair's breadth she would probably receive the bullet that was meant for him. Better that! Yes, even better that!

Silver Star tore on headlong and the minute seemed a lifetime. Then before even she heard the report he bounded in the air and fell with a crash. Diana was flung far forward and landed on some soft sand. For a moment she was stunned by the fall, then she staggered dizzily to her feet and stumbled back to the prostrate horse. He was lashing out wildly with his heels, making desperate efforts to rise. And as she reached him the black horse dashed up alongside, stopping suddenly, and rearing straight up. The Sheik leaped to the ground and ran towards her. He caught her wrist and flung her out of his way, and she lay where she had fallen, every nerve in her body quivering. She was beaten and with the extinguishing of her last hope all her courage failed her. She gave way to sheer, overwhelming terror, utterly cowed. Every faculty was suspended, swallowed up in the one dominating force, the dread of his voice and the dread of the touch of his hands. She heard a second report and knew that he had put Silver Star out of his misery, and then, in a few seconds, his voice beside her. She got up unsteadily, shrinking from him.

"Why are you here, and where is Gaston?"

In a stifled voice she told him everything. What did it matter? If she tried to be silent he would force her to speak.

He made no comment, and bringing The Hawk nearer tossed her up roughly into the saddle and swung up behind her, the black breaking at once into the usual headlong gallop. She made no kind of resistance, a complete apathy seemed to have come over her. She did not look at the body of Silver Star, she looked at nothing, clinging to the front of the saddle, and staring ahead of her unseeingly. She had dropped her helmet when she fell and she had left it, thankful to be relieved of the pressure on her aching head. Her mental collapse had affected her physically, and it needed a real effort of will-power to enable her to sit up right. Very soon they would join the horsemen, who were waiting for them, and for her pride's sake she must concentrate all her energy to avoid betraying her weakness.

Ahmed Ben Hassan did not go back through the defile, he turned into a little path that Diana had overlooked and which skirted the hills. In about half-an-hour the troop met them, riding slowly from the opposite direction. She did not raise her eyes as they approached, but she heard Yusef's clear tenor voice calling out to the Sheik, who answered shortly as the men fell in behind him. Back over the ground that she had traversed so differently. She knew that it had been madness from the first. She should have known that it could never succeed, that she could never reach civilisation alone. She had been a fool ever to imagine that she could win through. The chance that had thrown her again into the Sheik's power might just as easily have thrown her into the hands of any other Arab. Luck had helped Ahmed Ben Hassan even as she herself had unknowingly played into his hands when he had captured her first. Fate was with him. It was useless to try and struggle against him any more. Her brain was a confused medley of thoughts that she was too tired to unravel, strange, conflicting ideas chasing wildly through her mind. She did not understand them, she did not try. The effort of thinking made her head ache agonisingly. She was conscious of a great unrest, a dull aching in her heart and a terrible depression that was altogether apart from the fear she felt of the Sheik. She gave up trying to think; she was concerned only with trying to keep her balance.

She lifted her head for the first time and looked at the magnificent sky. The sun had almost set, going down in a ball of molten fire, and the heavens on either side were a riot of gold and crimson and palest green, shading off into vivid blue that grew blacker and blacker as the glory of the sunset died away. The scattered palm trees and the far-off hills stood out in strong relief. It was a country of marvellous beauty, and Diana's heart gave a sudden throb as she realised that she was going back to it all. She was drooping wearily, unable to sit upright any longer, and once or twice she jolted heavily against the man who rode behind her. His nearness had ceased to revolt her; she thought of it with a dull feeling of wonder. She had even a sense of relief at the thought of the strength so close to her. Her eyes rested on his hands, showing brown and muscular under the folds of his white robes. She knew the power of the long, lean fingers that could, when he liked, be gentle enough. Her eyes filled with sudden tears, but she blinked them back before they fell. She wanted desperately to cry. A wave of terrible loneliness went over her, a feeling of desolation, and a strange, incomprehensible yearning for what she did not know. As the sunset faded and it grew rapidly dusk a chill wind sprang up and she shivered from time to time, drooping more and more with fatigue, at times only half conscious. She had drifted into complete oblivion, when she was awakened with a jerk that threw her back violently against the Sheik, but she was too tired to more than barely understand that they had stopped for something, and that there were palm trees near her. She felt herself lifted down and a cloak wrapped round her, and then she remembered nothing more. She awoke slowly, shaking off a persistent drowsiness by degrees. She was still tired, but the desperate weariness was gone, and she was conscious of a feeling of well-being and security. The cool, night air blew in her face, dissipating her sleepiness. She became aware that night had fallen, and that they were still steadily galloping southward. In a few moments she was wide awake, and found that she was lying across the saddle in front of the Sheik, and that he was holding her in the crook of his arm. Her head was resting just over his heart, and she could feel the regular beat beneath her cheek. Wrapped warmly in the cloak and held securely by his strong arm at first she was content to give way only to the sensation of bodily rest. It was enough for the moment to lie with relaxed muscles, to have to make no effort of any kind, to feel the soothing rush of the wind against her face, and the swift, easy gallop of The Hawk as he carried them on through the night. Them! With a start of recollection she realised fully whose arm was round her, and whose breast her head was resting on. Her heart beat with sudden violence. What was the matter with her? Why did she not shrink from the pressure of his arm and the contact of his warm, strong body? What had happened to her? Quite suddenly she knew— knew that she loved him, that she had loved him for a long time, even when she thought she hated him and when she had fled from him. She knew now why his face had haunted her in the little oasis at midday—that it was love calling to her subconsciously. All the confusion of mind that had assailed her when they started on the homeward journey, the conflicting thoughts and contrary emotions, were explained. But she knew herself at last and knew the love that filled her, an overwhelming, passionate love that almost frightened her with its immensity and with the sudden hold it had laid upon her. Love had come to her at last who had scorned it so fiercely. The men who had loved her had not had the power to touch her, she had given love to no one, she had thought that she could not love, that she was devoid of all natural affection and that she would never know what love meant. But she knew now—a love of such complete surrender that she had never conceived. Her heart was given for all time to the fierce desert man who was so different from all other men whom she had met, a lawless savage who had taken her to satisfy a passing fancy and who had treated her with merciless cruelty. He was a brute, but she loved him, loved him for his very brutality and superb animal strength. And he was an Arab! A man of different race and colour, a native; Aubrey would indiscriminately class him as a "damned nigger." She did not care. It made no difference. A year ago, a few weeks even, she would have shuddered with repulsion at the bare idea, the thought that a native could even touch her had been revolting, but all that was swept away and was nothing in the face of the love that filled her heart so completely. She did not care if he was an Arab, she did not care what he was, he was the man she loved. She was deliriously, insanely happy. She was lying against his heart, and the clasp of his arm was joy unspeakable. She was utterly content; for the moment all life narrowed down to the immediate surroundings, and she wished childishly that they could ride so for ever through eternity. The night was brilliant. The stars blazed against the inky blackness of the sky, and the light of the full moon was startlingly clear and white. The discordant yelling of a pack of hunting jackals came from a little distance, breaking the perfect stillness. The men were riding in unusual silence, though a low exclamation or the subdued jingle of accoutrements was heard occasionally, once some one fired at a night creature that bounded out from almost under his horse's feet. But the Sheik flung a word of savage command over his shoulder and there were no more shots. Diana stirred slightly, moving her head so that she could see his face showing clearly in the bright moonlight, which threw some features into high relief and left the rest in dark shadow. She looked at him with quickening breath. He was peering intently ahead, his eyes flashing in the cold light, his brows drawn together in the characteristic heavy scowl, and the firm chin, so near her face, was pushed out more doggedly than usual.

He felt her move and glanced down. For a moment she looked straight into his eyes, and then with a low, inarticulate murmur she hid her face against him. He did not speak, but he shifted her weight a little, drawing her closer into the curve of his arm.

It was very late when they reached the camp. Lights flashed up in the big tent and on all sides, and they were surrounded by a crowd of excited tribesmen and servants. In spite of the hard day's work The Hawk started plunging and rearing, his invariable habit on stopping, which nothing could break, and at a word from the Sheik two men leaped to his head while he transferred Diana to Yusef's outstretched arms. She was stiff and giddy, and the young man helped her to the door of the tent, and then vanished again into the throng of men and horses.

Diana sank wearily on to the divan and covered her face with her hands. She was trembling with fatigue and apprehension. What would he do to her? She asked herself the question over and over again, with shaking, soundless lips, praying for courage, nerving herself to meet him. At last she heard his voice and, looking up, saw him standing in the doorway. His back was turned, and he was giving orders to a number of men who stood near him, for she could hear their several voices; and shortly afterwards half-a-dozen small bands of men rode quickly away in different directions. For a few moments he stood talking to Yusef and then came in. At the sight of him Diana shrank back among the soft cushions, but he took no notice of her, and, lighting a cigarette, began walking up and down the tent. She dared not speak to him, the expression on his face was terrible.

Two soft-footed Arab servants brought a hastily prepared supper. It was a ghastly meal. He never spoke or showed in any way that he was conscious of her presence. She had had nothing to eat all day, but the food nearly choked her and she could hardly swallow it, but she forced herself to eat a little. It seemed interminable until the servants finally withdrew, after bringing two little gold-cased cups of native coffee. She gulped it down with difficulty. The Sheik had resumed his restless pacing, smoking cigarette after cigarette in endless succession. The monotonous tramp to and fro worked on Diana's nerves until she winced each time he passed her, and, huddled on the divan, she watched him continually, fascinated, fearful.

He never looked at her. From time to time he glanced at the watch on his wrist and each time his face grew blacker. If he would only speak! His silence was worse than anything he could say. What was he going to do? He was capable of doing anything. The suspense was torture. Her hands grew clammy and she wrenched at the soft open collar of her riding-shirt with a feeling of suffocation.

Twice Yusef came to report, and the second time the Sheik came back slowly from the door where he had been speaking to him and stopped in front of Diana, looking at her strangely.

She flung out her hands instinctively, shrinking further back among the cushions, her eyes wavering under his. "What are you going to do to me?" she whispered involuntarily, with dry lips.

He looked at her without answering for a while, as if to prolong the torture she was enduring, and a cruel look crept into his eyes. "That depends on what happens to Gaston," he said at length slowly.

"Gaston?" she repeated stupidly. She had forgotten the valet, in all that had occurred since the morning she had forgotten his very existence.

"Yes—Gaston," he said sternly. "You do not seem to have thought of what might happen to him."

She sat up slowly, a puzzled look coming into her face. "What could happen to him?" she asked wonderingly.

He dragged back the flap of the tent and pointed out into the darkness. "Over there in the south-west, there is an old Sheik whose name is Ibraheim Omair. His tribe and mine have been at feud for generations. Lately I have learned that he has been venturing nearer than he has ever before dared. He hates me. To capture my personal servant would be more luck than he could have hoped for."

He dropped the flap and began walking up and down again. There was a sinister tone in his voice that made Diana suddenly comprehend the little Frenchman's peril. Ahmed Ben Hassan was not the man to be easily alarmed on any one's behalf. That he was anxious about Gaston was apparent, and with her knowledge of him she understood his anxiety argued a very real danger. She had heard tales before she left Biskra, and since then she had been living in an Arab camp, and she knew something of the fiendish cruelty and callous indifference to suffering of the Arabs. Ghastly mental pictures with appalling details crowded now into her mind. She shuddered.

"What would they do to him?" she asked shakily, with a look of horror.

The Sheik paused beside her. He looked at her curiously and the cruelty deepened in his eyes. "Shall I tell you what they would do to him?" he said meaningly, with a terrible smile.

She gave a cry and flung her arms over her head, hiding her face. "Oh, do not! Do not!" she wailed.

He jerked the ash from his cigarette. "Bah!" he said contemptuously. "You are squeamish."

She felt sick with the realisation of what could result to Gaston from her action. She had had no personal feeling with regard to him. On the contrary, she liked him—she had not thought of him, the man, when she had stampeded his horse and left him on foot so far from camp. She had looked upon him only as a jailer, his master's deputy.

The near presence of this hostile Sheik explained many things she had not understood: Gaston's evident desire daring their ride not to go beyond a certain distance, the special activity that had prevailed of late amongst the Sheik's immediate followers, and the speed and silence that had been maintained during the headlong gallop across the desert that evening. She had known all along the Arab's obvious affection for his French servant, and it was confirmed now by the anxiety that he did not take the trouble to conceal—so unlike his usual complete indifference to suffering or danger.

She looked at him thoughtfully. There were still depths that she had not fathomed in his strange character. Would she ever arrive at even a distant understanding of his complex nature? There was a misty yearning in her eyes as they followed his tall figure up and down the tent. His feet made no sound on the thick rugs, and he moved with the long, graceful stride that always reminded her of the walk of a wild animal. Her new-found love longed for expression as she watched him. If she could only tell him! If she had only the right to go to him and in his arms to kiss away the cruel lines from his mouth! But she had not. She must wait until she was called, until he should choose to notice the woman whom he had taken for his pleasure, until the baser part of him had need of her again. He was an Arab, and to him a woman was a slave, and as a slave she must give everything and ask for nothing.

And when he did turn to her again the joy she would feel in his embrace would be an agony for the love that was not there. His careless kisses would scorch her and the strength of his arms would be a mockery. But would he ever turn to her again? If anything happened to Gaston—if what he had suggested became a fact and the servant fell a victim to the blood feud between the two tribes? She knew he would be terribly avenged, and what would her part be? She wondered dully if he would kill her, and how. If the long, brown fingers with their steely strength would choke the life out of her. Her hands went up to her throat mechanically. He stopped near her to light a fresh cigarette, and she was trying to summon up courage to speak to him of Gaston when the covering of the doorway was flung open and Gaston himself stood in the entrance.

"Monseigneur—" he stammered, and with his two hands outstretched, palm uppermost, he made an appealing gesture.

The Sheik's hand shot out and gripped the man's shoulder. "Gaston! *Enfin, mon ami!*" he said slowly, but there was a ring in his low voice that Diana had never heard before.

For a moment the two men stared at each other, and then Ahmed Ben Hassan gave a little laugh of great relief. "Praise be to Allah, the Merciful, the Compassionate," he murmured.

"To his name praise!" rejoined Gaston softly, then his eyes roved around the tent towards Diana, and there was no resentment in them, but only anxiety.

"Madame is—" he hesitated, but the Sheik cut him short.

"Madame is quite safe," he said dryly, and pushed him gently towards the door with a few words in rapid Arabic. He stood some time after Gaston had gone to his own quarters looking out into the night, and when he came in, lingered unusually over closing the flap. Diana stood hesitating. She was worn out and her long riding-boots felt like lead. She was afraid to go and afraid to stay. He seemed purposely ignoring her. The relief of Gaston's return was enormous, but she had still to reckon with him for her attempted flight. That he said no word about it at the moment meant nothing; she knew him too well for that. And there was Silver Star, the finest of all his magnificent horses—she had yet to pay for his death. The strain that she had gone through since the morning was tremendous, she could not bear much more. His silence aggravated her breaking nerves until she felt that her nerves would go. He had moved over to the writing-table and was tearing the wrapping off a box of cartridges preparatory to refilling the magazine of his revolver. The little operation seemed to take centuries. She started at each separate click. She gripped her hands and passed her tongue over her dry lips. If he would not speak she must, she could endure it no longer.

"I am sorry about Silver Star," she faltered, and even to herself her voice sounded hoarse and strange. He did not answer, but only shrugged his shoulders as he dropped the last cartridge into its place.

The gesture and his uncompromising attitude exasperated her. "You had better have shot me," she said bitterly.

"Perhaps. You would have been easier replaced. There are plenty of women, but Silver Star was almost unique," he retorted quickly, and she winced at the cold brutality of his tone.

A little sad smile curved her lips. "Yet you shot your horse to get me back," she said in a barely audible voice.

He flung round with an oath. "You little fool! Do you know so little of me yet? Do you think that I will let anything stand between me and what I want? Do you think that by running away from me you will make me want you less? By Allah! I would have found you if you had got as far as France. What I have I keep, until I tire of it—and I have not tired of you yet." He jerked her to him, staring down at her passionately, and for a moment his face was the face of a devil. "How shall I punish you?" He felt the shudder he expected go through her and laughed as she shrank in his arms and hid her face. He forced her head up with merciless fingers. "What do you hate most?—my kisses?" and with another mocking laugh he crushed his mouth to hers in a long suffocating embrace.

Then he let her go suddenly, and, blind and dizzy, she reeled from him and staggered. He caught her as she swayed and swept her into his arms. Her head fell back against his shoulder and his face changed at the sight of her quivering features. He carried her into the adjoining room and laid her on the couch, his hands lingering as he drew them from her. For a moment he stood looking down with smouldering eyes on the slight, boyish figure lying on the bed, the ferocity dying out of his face. "Take care you do not wake the devil in me again, *ma belle,*" he said sombrely.

Alone Diana turned her face into the pillows with a moan of anguish. Back in the desert a few hours ago, under the shining stars, when the truth had first come to her, she had thought that she was happy, but she knew now that without his love she would never be happy. She had tasted the bitterness of his loveless kisses and she knew that a worse bitterness was to come, and she writhed at the thought of what her life with him would be.

"I love him! I love him! And I want his love more than anything in Heaven and earth."

CHAPTER VI

Diana was sitting on the divan in the living-room of the tent lingering over her *petit dejeuner*, a cup of coffee poised in one hand and her bright head bent over a magazine on her knee. It was a French periodical of fairly recent date, left a few days before by a Dutchman who was touring through the desert, and who had asked a night's hospitality. Diana had not seen him, and it was not until the traveller had been served with dinner in his own tent that the Sheik had sent the usual flowery message conveying what, though wrapped in honeyed words, amounted practically to a command that he should come to drink coffee and let himself be seen. Only native servants had been in attendance, and it was an Arab untinged by any Western influence who had received him, talking only Arabic, which the Dutchman spoke fluently, and placing at his disposal himself, his servants and all his belongings with the perfunctory Oriental insincerity which the traveller knew meant nothing and accepted at its own value, returning to the usual set phrases the customary answers that were expected of him. Once or twice as they talked a woman's subdued voice had reached the Dutchman's ears from behind the thick curtains, but he knew too much to let any expression betray him, and he smiled grimly to himself at the thought of the change that an indiscreet question would bring to the stern face of his grave and impassive host. He was an elderly man with a tender heart, and he wondered speculatively what the girl in the next room would have to pay for her own indiscretion in allowing her voice to be heard. He left the next morning early without seeing the Sheik again, escorted for some little distance by Yusef and a few men.

Diana read eagerly. Anything fresh to read was precious. She looked like a slender boy in the soft riding-shirt and smart-cut breeches, one slim foot in a long brown boot drawn up under her, and the other swinging idly against the side of the divan. She finished her coffee hastily, and, lighting a cigarette, leaned back with a sigh of content over the magazine.

Two months had slipped away since her mad flight, since her dash for freedom that had ended in tragedy for the beautiful Silver Star and so unexpectedly for herself. Weeks of vivid happiness that had been mixed with poignant suffering, for the perfect joy of being with him was marred by the passionate longing for his love. Even her surroundings had taken on a new aspect, her happiness coloured everything. The Eastern luxury of the tent and its appointments no longer seemed theatrical, but the natural setting of the magnificent specimen of manhood who surrounded himself by all the display dear to the heart of the native. How much was for his own pleasure and how much was for the sake of his followers she had never been able to determine. The beauties and attractions of the desert had multiplied a hundred times. The wild tribesmen, with their primitive ways and savagery, had ceased to disgust her, and the free life with its constant exercise and simple routine was becoming indefinitely dear to her. The camp had been moved several times—always towards the south—and each change had been a source of greater interest.

And since the night that he had carried her back in triumph he had been kind to her—kind beyond anything that she had expected. He had never made any reference to her fight or to the death of the horse that he had valued so highly; in that he had been generous. The episode over, he wished no further allusion to it. But there was nothing beyond kindness. The passion that smouldered in his dark eyes often was not the love she craved, it was only the desire that her uncommon type and her utter dissimilarity from all the other women who had passed through his hands had awakened in him. The perpetual remembrance of those other woman brought her a constant burning shame that grew stronger every day, a shame that was only less strong than her ardent love, and a wild jealousy that tortured her with doubts and fears, an ever-present demon of suggestion reminding her of the past when it was not she who lay in his arms, nor her lips that received his kisses. The knowledge that the embraces she panted for had been shared by *les autres* was an open wound that would not heal. She tried to shut her mind to the past. She knew that she was a fool to expect the abstinence of a monk in the strong, virile desert man. And she was afraid for the future. She wanted him for herself alone, wanted his undivided love, and that he was an Arab with Oriental instincts filled her with continual dread, dread of the real future about which she never dared to think, dread of the passing of his transient desire. She loved him so passionately, so completely, that beyond him was nothing. He was all the world. She gave herself to him gladly, triumphantly, as she would give her life for him if need be. But she had schooled herself to hide her love, to yield apathetically to his caresses, and to conceal the longing that possessed her. She was afraid that the knowledge that she loved him would bring about the disaster she dreaded. The words that he had once used remained continually in her mind: "If you loved me you would bore me, and I should have to let you go." And she hid her love closely in her heart. It was difficult, and it hurt her to hide it from him and to assume indifference. It was difficult to remember that she must make a show of reluctance when she was longing to give unreservedly. She dropped the end of the cigarette hissing into the dregs of the coffee and turned a page, and, as she did so, she looked up suddenly, the magazine dropping unheeded on the floor. Close outside the tent the same low, vibrating baritone was singing the Kashmiri love song that she had heard last the night before she left Biskra. She sat tense, her eyes growing puzzled.

"Pale hands I loved beside the Shalimar. Where are you now? Who lies beneath your spell?"

The voice came nearer and he swept in, still singing, and came to her. *"Pale hands, pink tipped,"* he sang, stopping in front of her and catching her fingers in his up to his lips, but she tore them away before he kissed them.

"You do know English?" she cried sharply, her eyes searching his.

He flung himself on the divan beside her with a laugh. "Because I sing an English song?" he replied in French. *"La! la!* I heard a Spanish boy singing in 'Carmen' once in Paris who did not know a word of French beside the score. He learned it parrot-like, as I learn your English songs," he added, smiling.

She watched him light a cigarette, and her forehead wrinkled thoughtfully. "It was you who sang outside the hotel in Biskra that night?" she asked at last, more statement than question.

"One is mad sometimes, especially when the moon is high," he replied teasingly.

"And was it you who came into my bedroom and put the blank cartridges in my revolver?"

His arm stole round her, drawing her to him, and he lifted her head up so that he could look into her eyes. "Do you think that—I would have allowed anybody else to go to your room at night?—I, an Arab, when I meant you for myself?"

"You were so sure?"

He laughed softly, as if the suggestion that any plan of his could be liable to miscarriage amused him infinitely, and the smouldering passion flamed up in his dark eyes. He strained her to him hungrily, as if her slim body lying against his had awakened the sleeping fires within him. She struggled against the pressure of his arm, averting her head.

"Always cold?" he chided. "Kiss me, little piece of ice."

She longed to, and it almost broke her heart to persevere in her efforts to repulse him. A wild desire seized her to tell him that she loved him, to make an end once and for all of the misery of doubt and fear that was sapping her strength from her, and abide by the issue. But the spark of hope that lived in her heart gave her courage, and she fought down the burning words that sought utterance, forcing indifference into her eyes and a mutinous pout to her lips.

His black brows drew together slowly. "Still disobedient? You said you would obey me. I loathe the English, but I thought their word—"

She interrupted him with a quick gesture, and, turning her face to his, for the first time kissed him voluntarily, brushing his tanned cheek with swift, cold lips.

He laughed disdainfully. *"Bon Dieu!* Has the hot sun of the desert taught you no better than that? Have you learned so little from me? Has the vile climate of your detestable country frozen you so thoroughly that nothing can melt you? Or is there some man in England who has the power to turn you from a statue to a woman?" he added, with an angry snarl.

She clenched her hands with the pain of his words. "There is no one," she muttered, "but I—I don't feel like that."

"You had better learn," he said thickly. "I am tired of holding an icicle in my arms," and sweeping her completely into his masterful grasp he covered her face with fierce, burning kisses.

And for the first time she surrendered to him wholly, clinging to him passionately, and giving him kiss for kiss with an absolute abandon of all resistance. At last he let her go, panting and breathless, and leaped up, drawing his hand across his eyes.

"You go to my head, Diane," he said, with a laugh that was half anger, and shrugging his shoulders moved across the tent to the chest where the spare arms were kept, and unlocking it took out a revolver and began to clean it.

She looked at him bewildered. What had he meant? How could she reconcile what he said with the advice that he had given her before? Was he totally inconsistent? Did he, after all, want the satisfaction of knowing that he had made her love him—of flattering himself on the power he exercised over her? Did he care that he was able to torture her heart with a refinement of cruelty that took all and gave nothing? Did he wish her to crawl abjectly to his feet to give him the pleasure of spurning her contemptuously, or was it only that he wanted her senses merely to respond to his ardent, Eastern temperament? Her face grew hot and shamed. She knew the fiery nature that was hidden under his impassive exterior and knew the control he exercised over himself, knew, too, that the strain he put upon himself was liable to be broken with unexpected suddenness. It was an easy thing to rule his wild followers, and she guessed that the relaxation that he looked for in the privacy of his own tent meant more to him than he would ever have admitted, than perhaps he even know. The hatred and defiance with which she had repelled him had provoked and amused him, but it had also at times angered him.

He was very human, and there must have been moments when he wanted a willing mate rather than a rebellious prisoner. She gave a quick sigh as she looked at him. He was so strong, so vigorous, so intensely alive. It was going to be very difficult to anticipate his moods and be subservient to his temper. She sighed again wearily. If she could but make him and keep him happy. She ruffled her loose curls, tugging them with a puzzled frown, a trick that was a survival of her nursery days, when she clutched frantically at her red-gold mop to help her settle any childish difficulty.

She knelt up suddenly on the cushions of the divan. "Why do you hate the English so bitterly, Monseigneur?" She had dropped almost unconsciously into Gaston's mode of address for some time; it was often awkward to give him no name, and she shrank from using his own; and the title fitted him.

He looked up from his work, and, gathering the materials together, brought them over to the divan. "Light me a cigarette, *cherie*, my hands are busy," he replied irrelevantly.

She complied with a little laugh. "You haven't answered my question."

He polished the gleaming little weapon in his hand for some time without speaking. *"Ma petite* Diane, your lips are of an adorable redness and your voice is music in my ears, but—I detest questions. They bore me to a point of exasperation," he said at last lightly, and started humming the Kashmiri song again.

She knew him well enough to know that all questions did not bore him, but that she must have touched some point connected with the past of which she was ignorant that affected him, and to prove her knowledge she asked another question. "Why do you sing? You have never sung before."

He looked at her with a smile of amusement at her pertinacity. "Inquisitive one! I sing because I am glad. Because my friend is coming."

"Your friend?"

"Yes, by Allah! The best friend a man ever had. Raoul de Saint Hubert."

She flashed a look at the bookcase with a jerk of her head, and he nodded. "Coming here?" she queried, and the dismay she felt sounded in her voice.

He frowned in quick annoyance at her tone. "Why not?" he said haughtily.

"No reason," she murmured, sinking down among the cushions again and picking up the magazine from the floor. The advent of a stranger—a European—was a shock, but she felt that the Sheik's eyes were on her and she determined to show no feeling in his presence. "What time will you be ready to ride?" she asked indifferently, with a simulated yawn, flirting over the pages.

"I can't ride with you today. I am going to meet Saint Hubert. His courier only came an hour ago. It is two years since I have seen him."

Diana slipped off the couch and went to the open doorway. A detachment of men were already waiting for him, and, close by the tent, Shaitan of the ugly temper was biting and fidgeting in the hands of the grooms. She scowled at the beautiful, wicked creature's flat-laid ears and rolling eyes. She would have backed him fearlessly herself if the Sheik had let her, but she was nervous for him every time he rode the vicious beast. No one but the Sheik could manage him, and though she knew that he had perfect mastery over the horse, she never lost the feeling of nervousness, a sensation the old Diana had never, never experienced, and she wished today that it had been any other horse but Shaitan waiting for him.

She went back to him slowly. "It makes my head ache, to stay in all day. May Gaston not ride with me?" she asked diffidently, her eyes anywhere but on his face. He had not allowed her to ride with any one except himself since her attempted escape, and to her tentative suggestions that the rides with the valet might be resumed he had given a prompt refusal. He hesitated now, and she was afraid he was going to refuse again, and she looked up wistfully. "Please, Monseigneur," she whispered humbly.

He looked at her for a moment with his chin squarer than usual. "Are you going to run away again?" he asked bluntly.

Her eyes filled slowly with tears, and she turned her head away to hide them. "No, I am not going to run away again," she said very low.

"Very well, I will tell him. He will be delighted, *le bon* Gaston. He is your very willing slave in spite of the trick you played him. He has a beautiful nature, *le pauvre diable*. He is not an Arab, eh, little Diane?" The mocking smile was back in his eyes as he turned her face up to his in the usual peremptory way. Then he held out the revolver he had been cleaning with sudden seriousness. "I want you to carry this always now when you ride. Ibraheim Omair is still in the neighbourhood."

She looked at it blankly.

"But—" she stammered.

He knew what was in her mind, and he stooped and kissed her lightly. "I trust you," he said quietly, and went out.

114

She followed him to the door, the revolver dangling from her hand, and watched him mount and ride away. His horsemanship was superb and her eyes glowed as they followed him. She went back into the tent and slipped the revolver into the holster he had left lying on a stool, and, tucking it and Saint Hubert's novel, which she took from the bookcase, under her arm, went into the bed-room and, calling to Zilah to pull off her riding-boots, threw herself on the bed to laze away the morning, and to try and picture the author from the book he had written.

She hated him in advance; she was jealous of him and of his coming. The Sheik's sudden new tenderness had given rise to a hope she hardly dared allow herself to dwell upon. Might not the power that she had exercised over other men be still extended to him in spite of the months that he had been indifferent to anything except the mere physical attraction she had for him? Was it not possible that out of that attraction might develop something finer and better than the primitive desire she had aroused? Oriental though he was, might he not be capable of a deep and lasting affection? He might have loved her if no outside influence had come to interrupt the routine that had become so intimately a part of his life. Those other episodes to which he had referred so lightly had been a matter of days or weeks, not months, as in her case. He might have cared but for the coming of this Frenchman. She hurled Saint Hubert's book across the room in a fit of girlish rage and buried her head in her arms. He would be odious—a smirking, conceited egotist! She had met several French writers and she visualised him contemptuously. His books were undoubtedly clever. So much the worse; he would be correspondingly inflated. His novel revealed a passionate, emotional temperament that promised to complicate the situation if he should be pleased to cast an eye of favour on her. She writhed at the very thought. And that he was to see her was evident; the Sheik had left no orders to the contrary. It was not to be the case of the Dutch traveller, when the fact that she belonged to an Arab had been brought home to her effectually by Ahmed Ben Hassan's peremptory commands, and she had experienced for the first time the sensation of a woman kept in seclusion.

The emotions of the morning and the disappointment of the intended ride, together with the dismay produced by the unexpected visitor, all combined to agitate her powerfully, and she worked herself up into a fever of self-torture and unhappiness. She ended by falling asleep and slept heavily for some hours. Zilah waked her with a shy hand on her arm and a soft announcement of lunch, and Diana sat up, rubbing her eyes, flushed and drowsy. She stared uncomprehendingly for a moment at the Arab girl, and then waved her away imperiously and buried her head in the pillows again. Lunch, when her heart was breaking!

Mindful of her lord's deputy, who was waiting in the next room, and whom she regarded with awe, Zilah held her ground with a timid insistence until Diana started up wrathfully and bade her go in tones that she had never used before to the little waiting-girl. Zilah fled precipitately, and, thoroughly awakened, Diana swung her heels to the ground and with her elbows on her knees rested her hot head in her hands. She felt giddy, her head ached and her mouth was parched and dry. She got up languidly, and going to the table studied her face in the mirror intently. She frowned at the reflection. She had never been proud of her own beauty; she had lived with it always and it had seemed to her a thing of no consequence, and now that it had failed to arouse the love she wanted in Ahmed Ben Hassan she almost hated it.

"Are you going to have fever or are you merely bad-tempered?" she asked out loud, and the sound of her own voice made her laugh in spite of her heavy heart. She went into the bathroom and soused her head in cold water. When she came back a frightened Zilah was putting a small tray on the brass-topped table by the bed.

"M'seiur Gaston," she stammered, almost crying.

Diana looked at the tray, arranged with all the dainty neatness dear to the valet's heart, and then at the travelling clock on the table beside it, and realised that it was an hour past her usual lunch-time and that she was extremely hungry, after all. A little piece of paper on the tray caught her eye, and, picking it up, she read in Gaston's clear though minute handwriting, "At what hour does Madame desire to ride?"

The servant clearly had no intention of giving up the programme for the afternoon without a struggle. She smiled as she added a figure to the end of the note, and went to the curtains that divided the rooms. "Gaston!"

"Madame!"

She passed the paper silently through the curtains and went back to her lunch. When she sent Zilah away with the empty tray she rescued the Vicomte de Saint Hubert's book from the floor where she had thrown it and tried to read it dispassionately. She turned to the title-page and studied the pencilled scrawl "Souvenir de Raoul" closely. It did not look like the handwriting of a small-minded man, but handwriting was nothing to go by, she argued obstinately. Aubrey, who was the essence of selfishness, wrote beautifully, and had once been told by an expert that his writing denoted a generous love of his fellow-men, which deduction had aroused no enthusiasm in the baronet, and had given his sister over to helpless mirth. She turned the pages, dipping here and there, finally forgetting the author altogether in the book. It was a wonderful story of a man's love and faithfulness, and Diana pushed it aside at last with a very bitter sigh. Things happened so in books. In real life they happened very differently. She looked round the room with pain-filled eyes, at the medley of her own and the Sheik's belongings, her ivory toilet appointments jostling indiscriminately among his brushes and his razors on the dressing-table, and then at the pillow beside her where his head rested every night. She stooped and kissed it with a little quivering breath. "Ahmed. Oh, Monseigneur!" she murmured longingly. Then, with an impatient jerk of the head, she sprang up and dragged on her boots. She pulled a soft felt hat down over her eyes and picked up the revolver the Sheik had given her. She paused a moment, looking at it with an odd smile before buckling it round her slim waist. Gaston's face lit up with genuine pleasure when she came out to the horses. She had felt a momentary embarrassment before she left the tent, thinking of the last time he had ridden with her, but she had known from the moment he came back that night that he bore no malice, and the look on his face and his stammered words to the Sheik had indicated that the fear he felt for her was not for what might have happened in the desert, but for what might yet happen to her at the hands of his master and hers.

The horse that she rode always now was pure white, not so fast as Silver Star and very tricky, called The Dancer, from a nervous habit of dancing on his hind-legs at starting and stopping, like a circus-horse. He was difficult to mount, and edged away shyly as Diana tried to get her foot into the stirrup. But she swung up at last, and by the time The Dancer had finished his display of *haute ecole*

Gaston was mounted. "After riding The Dancer I feel confident to enter for the *Concours Hippique*," she laughed over her shoulder, and touched the horse with her heel.

She wanted exercise primarily, hard physical exercise that would tire her out and keep her mind occupied and prevent her from thinking, and the horse she rode supplied both needs. He required watching all the time. She let him out to his full pace for his own sake and hers, and the air and the movement banished her headache, and a kind of exhilaration came over her, making her almost happy. After a while she reined in her horse and waved to Gaston to come alongside. "Tell me of this Vicomte de Saint Hubert who is coming. You know him, I suppose, as you have been so long with Monseigneur?"

Gaston smiled. "I knew him before Monseigneur did. I was born on the estate of Monsieur le Comte de Saint Hubert, the father of Monsieur le Vicomte. I and my twin brother Henri. We both went into Monsieur's le Comte's training stables, and then after our time in the Cavalry Henri became valet to Monsieur le Vicomte, and I came to Monseigneur."

Diana took off her hat and rubbed her forehead thoughtfully. Fifteen years ago Ahmed must have been about twenty. Why should an Arab chief of that age, or any age, indulge in such an anomaly as a French valet, or for that matter why should a French valet attach himself to an Arab Sheik and exile himself in the wilds of the desert? Whichever way she turned, the mystery of the man she loved seemed to crop up. She started arguing with herself in a circle—why should the Sheik have a European servant or why should he not, until she gave it up in hopeless confusion.

She turned to Gaston with the intention of asking further of the coming visitor, and, keeping The Dancer as still as she could, sat looking at the valet with great, questioning eyes, fanning her hot face with her hat. Gaston, whose own horse stood like a rock, was frankly mopping his forehead. Dianna decided against any more questions. Gaston would naturally be hopelessly biased, having been born and brought up in the shadow of the family, and after all she would rather judge for herself. One inquiry only she permitted herself: "The family of Saint Hubert, are they of the old or the new *noblesse?*"

"Of the old, Madame," replied Gaston quickly.

Diana coaxed her nervous mount close beside his steadier companion, and, thrusting his bridle and her hat into Gaston's hands, slipped to the ground and walked away a little distance to the top of a small mound. She sat down on the summit with her back to the horses and her arms clasped round her knees. All that the coming of this strange man meant to her rushed suddenly over her. He was a man, obviously, who moved in the world, her world, since he apparently travelled extensively and his father was wealthy enough to run a racing stable as a hobby and was a member of the dwindling class of *ancienne noblesse*. It was characteristic of her that she put first what she did. How could she bear to meet one of her own order in the position in which she was? She who had been proud Diana Mayo and now—the mistress of an Arab Sheik? She laid her face on her knees with a shudder. The ordeal before her cut like a knife into her heart. The pride that Ahmed Ben Hassan had not yet killed flamed up and racked her with humiliation and shame, the shame that still seared her soul like a hot iron, so that there were moments she could not bear even the presence of the man who had made her what she was, in spite of the love she bore him, and, pleading fever, prayed to be alone. Not that he ever granted her prayer, for he knew fever when he saw it, but would pull her down beside him with a mocking laugh that still had the power to hurt so much. The thought of what it would be to her to meet his friend had presumably never entered his mind, or if it had it had made no impression and been dismissed as negligible. It was the point of view, she supposed drearily; the standpoint from which he looked at things was fundamentally different from her own—racially and temperamentally they were poles apart. To him she was only the woman held in bondage, a thing of no account. She sat very still for a while with her face hidden, until a discreet cough from Gaston warned her that time was flying. She went back to the horses slowly with white face and compressed lips. There was the usual trouble in mounting, and her strained nerves made her impatient of The Dancer's idiosyncrasies, and she checked him sharply, making him rear dangerously.

"Careful, Madame," cried Gaston warningly.

"For whom—me or Monseigneur's horse?" she retorted bitterly, and ignoring her hat, which Gaston held out to her with reproachful eyes, she spurred the horse viciously, making him break into a headlong gallop. It had got to be gone through, so get it over as soon as possible. And behind her, Gaston, for the first time in all his long service, cursed the master he would cheerfully have died for.

The horse's nerves, like her own, were on edge, and he pulled badly, his smooth satiny neck growing dark and seamed with sweat; Diana needed all her knowledge to control him, and she began to wonder if when they came to the camp she would be able to stop him. She topped an undulation that was some little distance from the tents with misgivings, and wrapped the reins round her hands to prevent them slipping through her fingers. As they neared she saw the Sheik standing outside his tent, with a tall, thin man beside him. She had only a glimpse of dark, unruly hair and a close-cut beard as she shot past, unable to pull up The Dancer. But just beyond the tent, with the reins cutting into her hands, she managed to haul him round and bring him back. A couple of grooms jumped to his head, but, owing to his peculiar tactics, landed short, and he pranced to his own satisfaction and Diana's rage, until the amusement of it passed and he let himself be caught. Diana had done nothing to stop him once she had managed to turn him. If the horse chose to behave like a fool she was not going to be made to look foolish by fighting him when she knew that it was useless. In the hands of the men he sidled and snorted, and, dropping the reins, Diana pulled off her gloves and sat for a moment rubbing her sore hands. Then the Sheik came forward and she slid down. Before looking at him she turned and, catching at The Dancer's head, struck him angrily over the nose with her thick riding-gloves and watched him led away, plunging and protesting, pulling the gloves through her fingers nervously, until Ahmed Ben Hassan's voice made her turn.

"Diane, the Vicomte de Saint Hubert waits to be presented to you."

She drew herself up and the colour that had come into her face drained out of it again. Slowly she glanced up at the man standing before her, and looked straight into the most sympathetic eyes that her own sad, defiant ones had ever seen. Only for a moment, then he bowed with a conventional murmur that was barely audible.

His lack of words gave her courage. "Monsieur," she said coldly in response to his greeting, then turned to the Sheik without looking at him. "The Dancer has behaved abominably. Gaston, my hat, please! Thanks." And vanished into the tent without a further look at any one.

It was late, but she lingered over her bath and changed with slow reluctance into the green dress that the Sheik preferred—a concession that she despised herself for making. She had taken up the jade necklace when he joined her.

He turned her to him roughly, with his hands on her shoulders, and the merciless pressure of his fingers was indication enough without the black scowl on his face that he was angry. "You are not very cordial to my guest."

"Is it required of a slave to be cordial towards her master's friends?" she replied in a stifled voice.

"What is required is obedience to my wishes," he said harshly.

"And is it your wish that I should please this Frenchman?"

"It is my wish."

"If I were a woman of your own race—" she began bitterly, but he interrupted her.

"If you were a woman of my own race there would be no question of it," he said coldly. "You would be for the eyes of no other man than me. But since you are not—" He broke off with an enigmatical jerk of the head.

"Since I am not you are less merciful than if I was," she cried miserably. "I could wish that I was an Arab woman."

"I doubt it," he said grimly. "The life of an Arab woman would hardly be to your taste. We teach our women obedience with a whip."

"Why have you changed so since this morning," she whispered, "when you told me that you trusted no one to climb to my balcony in the hotel but yourself? Are you not an Arab now as then? Have I become of so little value to you that you are not even jealous any more?"

"I can trust my friend, and—I do not propose to share you with him," he said brutally.

She winced as if he had struck her, and hid her face in her hands with a low cry.

His fingers gripped her shoulder cruelly. "You will do as I wish?" The words were a question, but the intonation was a command.

"I have no choice," she murmured faintly.

His hands dropped to his sides and he turned to leave the room, but she caught his arm. "Monseigneur! Have you no pity? Will you not spare me this ordeal?"

He made a gesture of refusal. "You exaggerate," he said impatiently, brushing her hand from his arm.

"If you will be merciful this once——." she pleaded breathlessly, but he cut her short with a fierce oath. "If?" he echoed. "Do you make bargains with me? Have you so much yet to learn?"

She looked at him with a little weary sigh. The changing mood that she had set herself to watch for had come upon him suddenly and found her unprepared. The gentleness of the morning had vanished and he had reverted to the tyrannical, arbitrary despot of two months ago. She knew that it was her own fault. She knew him well enough to know that he was intolerant of any interference with his wishes. She had learned the futility of setting her determination against his. There was one master in his camp, whose orders, however difficult, must be obeyed.

His attention had concentrated on a broken fingernail, and he turned to the dressing-table for a knife. She followed him with her eyes and watched him carefully trimming the nail. She had often, amongst the many things that puzzled her, wondered at the fastidious care he took of his well-manicured hands. The light of the lamp fell full on his face, and there was a dull ache in her heart as she looked at him. He demanded implicit obedience, and only a few hours before she had made up her mind to unreserved submission, and she had broken down at the first test. The proof of her obedience was a hard one, from which she shrank, but it was harder far to see the look of anger she had provoked on the face of the man she loved. For two months of wild happiness it had been absent, the black scowl she had learned to dread had not been directed at her, and the fierce eyes had looked at her with only kindness or amusement shining in their dark depths. Anything could be borne but a continuance of his displeasure. No sacrifice was too great to gain his forgiveness. She could not bear his anger. She longed so desperately for happiness, and she loved him so passionately, so utterly, that she was content to give up everything to his will. If she could only get back the man of the last few weeks, if she had not angered him too far. She was at his feet, tamed thoroughly at last, all her proud, angry self-will swamped in the love that was consuming her with an intensity that was an agony. Love was a bitter pain, a torment that was almost unendurable, a happiness that mocked her with its hollowness, a misery that tortured her with visions of what might have been. She went to him slowly, and he turned to her abruptly.

"Well?" His voice was hard and uncompromising, and the flash of his eyes was like the tiger's in the Indian jungle.

She set her teeth to keep down the old paralysing fear.

"I will do what you want. I will do anything you want, only be kind to me, Ahmed," she whispered unsteadily. She had never called him by his name before; she did not even know that she had done so now, but at the sound of it a curious look crossed his face, and he drew her into his arms with hands that were as gentle as they had been cruel before. She let him lift her face to his, and met his searching gaze bravely. Holding her look with the mesmerism that he could exert when he chose, he read in her face her final surrender, and knew that while it pleased him to keep her he had broken her utterly to his hand. A strange expression grew in his eyes as they travelled slowly over her. She was like a fragile reed in his strong grasp that he could crush without an effort, and yet for four months she had fought him, matching his determination with a courage that had won his admiration even while it had exasperated him. He knew she feared him, he had seen terror leap into her flickering eyes when she had defied him most. Her defiance and her hatred, which had piqued him by contrast with the fawning adulation to which he had been accustomed and which had wearied him infinitely, had provoked in him a fixed resolve to master her. Before he tired of her she must yield her will to him absolutely. And tonight he knew that the last struggle had been made, that she would never oppose him again, that she was clay in his hands to do with as he would. And the knowledge that he had won gave him no feeling of exultation, instead a vague, indefinite sense of irritation swept over him and made him swear softly under his breath. The satisfaction he had expected in his triumph was lacking and the unaccountable dissatisfaction that filled him seemed inexplicable. He did not understand himself, and he looked down at her again with a touch of impatience. She was very lovely, he thought, with a strange new appreciation of the beauty he had appropriated, and very womanly in the soft, clinging green dress. The slim, boyish figure that rode with him had a charm all its own, but it was the woman in her that sent the hot blood racing through his veins and made his heart beat as it was beating now. His eyes lingered a moment on her bright curls, on her dark-fringed, pleading eyes and on her bare neck, startlingly white against the jade green of her gown, then he put her from him.

"*Va*," he said gently, "*depeche-toi*."

She looked after him as he went through the curtains with a long, sobbing sigh. She was paying a heavy price for her happiness, but she would have paid a heavier one willingly. Nothing mattered now that he was not angry any more. She knew what her total submission meant: it was an end to all individualism, a complete self-abnegation, an absolute surrender to his wishes, his moods and his temper. And she was content that it should be so, her love was prepared to endure whatever he might put upon her. Nothing that he could do could alter that, and nothing should make her own her love. She had hidden it from him, and she would hide it from him—cost what it might. Though he did not love her he wanted her still; she had read that in his eyes five minutes ago, and she was happy even for that.

She turned to the glass suddenly and wrenched the silk folds off her shoulder. She looked at the marks of his fingers on the delicate skin with a twist of the lips, then shut her eyes with a little gasp and hid her bruised arm hastily, her mouth quivering. But she did not blame him, she had brought it on herself; she knew his mood, and he did not know his own strength.

"If he killed me he could not kill my love," she murmured, with a little pitiful smile.

The men were waiting for her, and with a murmured apology for her lateness she took her place. The Sheik and his guest resumed the conversation that her entrance had interrupted. Diana's thoughts were in confusion. She felt as if she were in some wild, improbable dream. An Arab Sheik, a French explorer, and herself playing the conventional hostess in the midst of lawless unconventionalism. She looked around the tent that had become so familiar, so dear. It seemed different tonight, as if the advent of the stranger had introduced a foreign atmosphere. She had grown so accustomed to the routine that had been imposed upon her that even the

Vicomte's servant standing behind his master seemed strange. The man's likeness to his twin brother was striking, the only difference being that while Gaston's face was clean-shaven, Henri's upper lip was hidden by a neat, dark moustache. The service was, as always, perfect, silent and quick.

She glanced at the Sheik covertly. There was a look on his face that she had never seen and a ring in his voice that was different even from the tone she had heard when Gaston had come back on the night of her flight. That had been relief and the affection of a man for a valued servant, this was the deep affection of a man for the one chosen friend, the love passing the love of women. And the jealousy she had felt in the morning welled up uncontrollably. She looked from the Sheik to the man who was absorbing all his attention, but in his pale, clever face, half hidden by the close beard, she saw no trace of the conceited, smirking egotist she had imagined, and his voice, as low as the Sheik's, but more animated, was not the voice of a man unduly elated or conscious of himself. And as she looked her eyes met his. A smile that was extraordinarily sweet and half-sad lit up his face.

"Is it permitted to admire Madame's horsemanship?" he asked, with a little bow.

Diana coloured faintly and twisted the jade necklace round her fingers nervously. "It is nothing," she said, with a shy smile that his sympathetic personality evoked in spite of herself. "With The Dancer it is all foolishness and not vice. One has to hold on very tightly. It would have been humiliating to precipitate myself at the feet of a stranger. Monseigneur would not have approved of the concession to The Dancer's peculiarities. It is an education to ride his horses, Monsieur."

"It is a strain to the nerves to ride *beside* some of them," replied the Vicomte pointedly.

Diana laughed with pure amusement. The man whose coming she had loathed was making the dreadful ordeal very easy for her. "I sympathise, Monsieur. Was Shaitan very vile?"

"If Monsieur de Saint Hubert is trying to suggest to you that he suffers from nerves, Diane," broke in the Sheik, with a laugh, "disabuse yourself at once. He has none."

Saint Hubert turned to him with a quick smile. "*Et toi,* Ahmed, eh? Do you remember—?" and he plunged into a flood of reminiscences that lasted until the end of dinner.

125

The Vicomte had brought with him a pile of newspapers and magazines, and Diana curled up on the divan with an armful, hungry for news, but, somehow, as she dipped into the batch of papers her interest waned. After four months of complete isolation it was difficult to pick up the threads of current events, allusions were incomprehensible, and controversies seemed pointless. The happenings of the world appeared tame beside the great adventure that was carrying her on irresistibly and whose end she could not see and dared not think of. She pushed them aside carelessly and kept only on her knee a magazine that served as a pretext for her silence.

When Gaston brought coffee the Vicomte hailed him with a gay laugh. *"Enfin,* Gaston, after two years the nectar of the gods again! There is a new machine for you amongst my things, *mon ami,* providing it has survived Henri's packing."

He brought a cup to Diana and set it on a stool beside her. "Ahmed flatters himself I come to see him, Madame. I do not. I come to drink Gaston's coffee. It has become proverbial, the coffee of Gaston. I propitiate him every time I come with a new apparatus for making it. The last is a marvel of ingenuity. Excuse me, I go to drink it with the reverence it inspires. It is a rite, Madame, not a gastronomic indulgence."

Once more the sympathetic eyes looked straight into hers, and the quick blood rushed into her face as she bent her head again hurriedly over the magazine. She knew instinctively that he was trying to help her, talking nonsense with a tact that ignored her equivocal position. She was grateful to him, but even his chivalry hurt. She watched him under her thick lashes as he went back to the Sheik and sat down beside him, refusing his host's proffered cigarettes with a wry face of disgust and a laughing reference to a "perverted palate," as he searched for his own. The hatred she had been prepared to give him had died away during dinner—only the jealousy remained, and even that had changed from its first intensity to an envy that brought a sob into her throat. She envied him the light that shone in the Arab's dark eyes, she envied him the intonation of the soft slow voice she loved. Her eyes turned to the Sheik. He was leaning back with his hands clasped behind his head, talking with a cigarette between his teeth. His attitude towards his European friend was that of an equal, the haughty, peremptory accent that was noticeable when he spoke to his followers was gone, and a flat contradiction from Saint Hubert provoked only a laugh and a gesture of acceptance.

As they sat talking the contrast between the two men was strongly marked. Beside the Frenchman's thin, spare frame and pale face, which gave him an air of delicacy, the Sheik looked like a magnificent animal in superb condition, and his quiet repose accentuated the Vicomte's quick, nervous manner. Under the screen of her thick lashes Diana watched them unheeded. Their voices rose and fell continuously; they seemed to have a great deal to say to each other, and they talked indiscriminately French and Arabic so that much that they said was incomprehensible to her. She was glad that it should be so, she did not want to know what they were saying. It seemed as if they had forgotten her presence with the accumulated conversation of two years. She was thankful to be left alone, happy for the rare chance of studying the beloved face unnoticed. It was seldom she had the opportunity, for when they were alone she was afraid to look at him much lest her secret should be betrayed in her eyes. But she looked at him now unobserved, with passionate longing. She was so intent that she did not notice Gaston come in until he seemed suddenly to appear from nowhere beside his master. He murmured something softly and the Sheik got up. He turned to Saint Hubert.

"Trouble with one of the horses. Will you come? It may interest you."

They went out together, leaving her alone, and she slipped away to the inner room. In half-an-hour they came back, and for a few minutes longer stayed chatting, then the Vicomte yawned and held out his watch with a laugh. The Sheik went with him to his tent and sat down on the side of his guest's camp-bed. Saint Hubert dismissed the waiting Henri with a nod and started to undress silently. The flow of talk and ready laugh seemed to have deserted him, and he frowned as he wrenched his things off with nervous irritability.

The Sheik watched him for a while, and then took the cigarette out of his mouth with a faint smile. *"Eh, bien!* Raoul, say it," he said quietly.

Saint Hubert swung round. "You might have spared her," he cried.

"What?"

"What? Good God, man! Me!"

The Sheik flicked the ash from his cigarette with a gesture of indifference. "Your courier was delayed, he only came this morning. It was too late then to make other arrangements."

Saint Hubert took a hasty turn up and down the tent and stopped in front of the Sheik with his hands thrust deep in his pockets and his shoulders hunched up about his ears. "It is abominable," he burst out. "You go too far, Ahmed."

The Sheik laughed cynically. "What do you expect of a savage? When an Arab sees a woman that he wants he takes her. I only follow the customs of my people."

Saint Hubert clicked his tongue impatiently. "Your people!—which people?" he asked in a low voice.

The Sheik sprang to his feet with flashing eyes, his hand dropping heavily on Saint Hubert's shoulder.

"Stop, Raoul! Not even from you—!" he cried passionately, and then broke off abruptly, and the anger died out of his face. He sat down again quietly, with a little amused laugh. "Why this sudden access of morality, *mon ami?* You know me and the life I lead. You have seen women in my camp before now."

Saint Hubert dismissed the remark with a contemptuous wave of the hand. "There is to comparison. You know it as well as I," he said succinctly. He moved over slowly to the camp table, where his toilet things had been laid out, and began removing the links from the cuffs of his shirt. "She is English, surely that is reason enough," he flung over his shoulder.

"You ask me, *me* to spare a woman because she is English? My good Raoul, you amuse me," replied the Sheik, with an ugly sneer.

"Where did you see her?" asked Saint Hubert curiously.

"In the streets of Biskra, for five minutes, four months ago."

The Vicomte turned quickly. "You love her?" he shot out, with all the suddenness of an American third degree.

The Sheik exhaled a long, thin cloud of blue smoke and watched it eddying towards the top of the tent. "Have I ever loved a woman? And this woman is English," he said in a voice as hard as steel.

"If you loved her you would not care for her nationality."

The Sheik spat the end of his cigarette on to the floor contemptuously. "By Allah! Her cursed race sticks in my throat. But for that—" He shrugged his shoulders impatiently and got up from the bed on which he was sitting.

"Let her go then," said Saint Hubert quickly. "I can take her back to Biskra."

The Sheik turned to him slowly, a sudden flame of fierce jealousy leaping into his eyes. "Has she bewitched you, too? Do you want her for yourself, Raoul?" His voice was as low as ever, but there was a dangerous ring in it.

Saint Hubert flung his hands out in a gesture of despair. "Ahmed! Are you mad? Are you going to quarrel with me after all these years on such a pretext? *Bon Dieu!* What do you take me for? There has been too much in our lives together ever to let a woman come between us. What is a woman or any one to me where you are concerned? It is for quite a different reason that I ask you, that I beg you to let this girl go."

"Forgive me, Raoul. You know my devilish temper," muttered the Sheik, and for a moment his hand rested on Saint Hubert's arm.

"You have not answered me, Ahmed."

The Sheik turned away. "She is content," he said evasively.

"She has courage," amended the Vicomte significantly.

"As you say, she has courage," agreed the Sheik, without a particle of expression in his voice.

"Bon sang—" quoted Saint Hubert softly.

The Sheik swung round quickly. "How do you know she has good blood in her?"

"It is very evident," replied Saint Hubert drily.

"That is not what you mean. What do you know?"

The Vicomte shrugged his shoulders, and, going to his suit-case, took from it an English illustrated paper, and opening it at the central page handed it to the Sheik silently.

Ahmed Ben Hassan moved closer to the hanging lamp so that the light fell directly on the paper in his hands. There were two large full-length photographs of Diana, one in evening dress and the other as the Vicomte had first seen her, in riding breeches and short jacket, her hat and whip lying at her feet, and the bridle of the horse that was standing beside her over her arm.

Under the photographs was written: "Miss Diana Mayo, whose protracted journey in the desert is causing anxiety to a large circle of friends. Miss Mayo left Biskra under the guidance of a reputable caravan-leader four months ago, with the intention of journeying for four weeks in the desert and returning to Oran. Since the first camp nothing has been heard of Miss Mayo or her caravan. Further anxiety is occasioned by the fact that considerable unrest is reported amongst the tribes in the locality towards which Miss Mayo was travelling. Her brother, Sir Aubrey Mayo, who is detained in America as the result of an accident, is in constant cable communication with the French authorities. Miss Mayo is a well-known sports-woman and has travelled widely."

For a long time the Sheik studied the photographs silently, then with slow deliberation he tore the page out of the paper and rolled it up. "With your permission," he said coolly, and held it over the flame of the little lamp by the bedside. He held it until the burning paper charred to nothing in his hand and then flicked the ashes from his long fingers. "Henri has seen this?"

"Unquestionably. Henri reads all my papers," replied Saint Hubert, with a touch of impatience.

"Then Henri can hold his tongue," said the Sheik nonchalantly, searching in the folds of his waist-cloth for his case and lighting another cigarette with elaborate carelessness.

"What are you going to do?" asked Saint Hubert pointedly.

"I? Nothing! The French authorities have too many affairs on hand and too high an appreciation of Ahmed Ben Hassan's horses to prosecute inquiries in my direction. Besides, they are not responsible. Mademoiselle Mayo was warned of the risks she ran before she left Biskra. She chose to take the risks, *et voila!*"

"Will nothing make you change your mind?"

"I am not given to changing my mind. You know that. And, besides, why should I? As I told you before, she is content."

Saint Hubert looked him full in the face. "Content! Cowed is the better word, Ahmed."

The Sheik laughed softly. "You flatter me, Raoul. Do not let us speak any more about it. It is an unfortunate contretemps, and I regret that it distresses you," he said lightly; then with a sudden change of manner he laid his hands on the Vicomte's shoulders. "But this can make no difference to our friendship, *mon ami;* that is too big a thing to break down over a difference of opinion. You are a French nobleman, and I—!" He gave a little bitter laugh. "I am an uncivilised Arab. We cannot see things in the same way."

"You could, but you will not, Ahmed," replied the Vicomte, with an accent of regret. "It is not worthy of you." He paused and then looked up again with a little crooked smile and a shrug of defeat. "Nothing can ever make any difference with us, Ahmed. I can disagree with you, but I can't wipe out the recollection of the last twenty years."

A few minutes later the Sheik left him and went out into the night. He traversed the short distance between the tents slowly, stopping to speak to a sentry, and then pausing outside his own tent to look up at the stars. The Persian hound that always slept across the entrance uncurled himself and got up, thrusting a wet nose into his hand. The Sheik fondled the huge creature absently, stroking the dog's shaggy head mechanically, hardly conscious of what he was doing. A great restlessness that was utterly foreign to his nature had taken possession of him. He had been aware of it growing within him for some time, becoming stronger daily, and now the coming of Raoul de Saint Hubert seemed to have put the crowning touch to a state of mind that he was unable to understand. He had never been given to thinking of himself, or criticising or analysing his passing whims and fancies. All his life he had taken what he wanted; nothing on which he had ever laid eyes of desire had been denied him. His wealth had brought him everything he had ever wished. His passionate temper had been characteristic even when he was a child, but these strange fits of unreasonable irritability were new, and he searched for a cause vainly. His keen eyes looked through the darkness towards the south. Was it the nearness of his hereditary enemy, who had presumed to come closer than he had ever done before to the border of the country that Ahmed Ben Hassan regarded as his own, that was causing this great unrest? He laughed contemptuously. Nothing would give him greater pleasure than coming into actual collision with the man whom he had been trained from boyhood to hate. As long as Ibraheim Omair remained within his own territory Ahmed Ben Hassan held his hand and kept in check his fierce followers, whose eyes were turned longingly towards the debatable land, but once let the robber Sheik step an inch over the border, and it was war, and war until one or both of the chiefs were dead. And if he died who had no son to succeed him; the huge tribe would split up in numerous little families for want of a leader to keep them together, and it would be left to the French Government to take over, if they could, the vast district that he had governed despotically. And at the thought he laughed again. No, it was not Ibraheim Omair who was troubling him. He pushed the hound aside and went into the tent. The divan where Diana had been sitting was strewn with magazines and papers, the imprint of her slender body still showed in the soft, heaped-up cushions, and a tiny, lace-edged handkerchief peeped out under one of them. He picked it up and looked at it curiously, and his forehead contracted slowly in the heavy black scowl. He turned his burning eyes toward the curtains that divided the rooms. Saint Hubert's words rang in his ears. "English!" he muttered with a terrible oath. "And I have made her suffer as I swore any of that damned race should if they fell into my hands. Merciful Allah! Why does it give me so little pleasure?"

CHAPTER VII

Diana came into the living-room one morning about a week after the arrival of the Vicomte de Saint Hubert. She had expected to find the room empty, for the Sheik had risen at dawn and ridden away on one of the distant expeditions that had become so frequent, and she thought his friend had accompanied him, but as she parted the curtains between the two rooms she saw the Frenchman sitting at the little writing-table surrounded by papers and writing quickly, loose sheets of manuscript littering the floor around him. It was the first time that they had chanced to be alone, and she hesitated with a sudden shyness. But Saint Hubert had heard the rustle of the curtain, and he sprang to his feet with the courteous bow that proclaimed his nationality.

"Your pardon, Madame. Do I disturb you? Tell me if I am in the way. I am afraid I have been very untidy," he added, laughing apologetically, and looking at the heap of closely-written sheets strewing the rug.

Diana came forward slowly, a faint colour rising in her face. "I thought you had gone with Monseigneur."

"I had some work to do—some notes that I wanted to transcribe before I forgot myself what they meant; I write vilely. I have had a hard week, too, so I begged a day off. I may stay? You are sure I do not disturb you?"

His sympathetic eyes and the deference in his voice brought an unexpected lump into her throat. She signed to him to resume his work and passed out under the awning. Behind the tent the usual camp hubbub filled the air. A knot of Arabs at a little distance were watching one of the rough-riders schooling a young horse, noisily critical and offering advice freely, undeterred by the indifference with which it was received. Others lounged past engaged on the various duties connected with the camp, with the Eastern disregard for time that relegated till tomorrow everything that could possibly be neglected today. Near her one of the older men, more rigid in his observances than the generality of Ahmed Ben Hassan's followers, was placidly absorbed in his devotions, prostrating himself and fulfilling his ritual with the sublime lack of self-consciousness of the Mohammedan devotee.

Outside his own tent the valet and Henri were sitting in the sun, Gaston on an upturned bucket, cleaning a rifle, and his brother stretched full length on the ground, idly flapping at the flies with the duster with which he had been polishing the Vicomte's riding-boots. Both men were talking rapidly with frequent little bursts of gay laughter. The Persian hound was lying at their feet. He raised his head as Diana appeared, and, rising, went to her slowly, rearing up against her with a paw on each shoulder, making clumsy efforts to lick her face, and she pushed him down with difficulty, stooping to kiss his shaggy head.

She looked away across the desert beyond the last palms of the oasis. A haze hung round about, shimmering in the heat and blurring the outline of the distant hills. A tiny breeze brought the acrid smell of camels closer to her, and the creaking whine of the tackling over the well sounded not very far away. Diana gave a little sigh. It had all grown so familiar. She seemed to have lived no other life beside this nomad existence. The years that had gone before faded into a kind of dim remembrance, the time when she had travelled ceaselessly round the world with her brother seemed very remote. She had existed then, filling her life with sport, unconscious of the something that was lacking in her nature, and now she was alive at last, and the heart whose existence she had doubted was burning and throbbing with a passion that was consuming her. Her eyes swept lingeringly around the camp with a very tender light in them. Everything she saw was connected with and bound up in the man who was lord of it all. She was very proud of him, proud of his magnificent physical abilities, proud of his hold over his wild turbulent followers, proud with the pride of primeval woman in the dominant man ruling his fellow-men by force and fear.

The old Arab had finished his prayers and rose leisurely from his knees, salaaming with a broad smile. All the tribesmen smiled on her, and would go out of their way to win a nod of recognition from her. She faltered a few words in stumbling Arabic in reply to his long, flowery speech, and with a little laugh beat a hasty retreat into the tent.

She paused beside the Vicomte. "Is it another novel?" she asked shyly, indicating the steadily increasing pile of manuscript.

He turned on his chair, resting his arms on the rail, twirling a fountain pen between his fingers, and smiled at her as she curled up on the divan with Kopec, who had followed her into the tent. "No, Madame, Something more serious this time. It is a history of this very curious tribe of Ahmed's. They are different in so many ways from ordinary Arabs. They have been a race apart for generations. They have beliefs and customs peculiarly their own. You may, for instance, have noticed the singular absence among them of the strict religious practices that hold among other Mohammedans. Ahmed Ben Hassan's tribe worship first and foremost their Sheik, then the famous horses for which they are renowned, and then and then only—Allah."

"Is Monseigneur a Mohammedan?"

Saint Hubert shrugged. "He believes in a God," he said evasively, turning back to his writing.

Diana studied him curiously as he bent over his work. She smiled when she thought of the mental picture she had drawn of Saint Hubert before he came, and contrasted it with the real man under her eyes. During the week that he had been in the camp he had forced her liking and compelled her confidence by the sympathetic charm of his manner. He had carried off a difficult position with a delicacy and *savoir-faire* that had earned him her gratitude. He had saved her a hundred humiliations with a tact that had been as spontaneous as it had been unobtrusive. And they had the bond between them of the common love they had for this strange leader of a strange tribe. What had been the origin of the friendship between these utterly dissimilar men—a friendship that seemed to go back to the days of their boyhood? The question intrigued her and she pondered over it, lying quietly on the divan, smoothing the hound's huge head resting on her knee.

The Vicomte wrote rapidly for some time and then flung down his pen with an exclamation of relief, gathered up the loose sheets from the floor and, stacking them in an orderly heap on the table, swung round on his chair again. He looked at the girl's slender little figure lying with the unconsciously graceful attitude of a child against the heaped-up cushions, her face bent over the dog's rough, grey head, and he felt an unwonted emotion stirring in him. The quick sympathy that she had aroused from the first moment of seeing her had given place to a deeper feeling that moved him profoundly, and with it a chivalrous desire to protect, a longing to stand between her and the irremediable disaster that loomed inevitably ahead of her.

She felt his concentrated gaze and looked up. "You have done your work?"

"All I can do at the moment. Henri must unravel the rest; he has a passion for hieroglyphics. He is an invaluable person; I could never get on without him. He bullied me when we were boys together—at least that is what I called it. He called it 'amusing Monsieur le Vicomte,' and for the last fifteen years he has tyrannised over me wholeheartedly." He laughed and snapped his fingers at Kopec, who whined and rolled his eyes in his direction, but did not lift his head from Diana's knee.

There was a pause, and Diana continued fondling the hound absently. "I have read your books, Monsieur—all that Monseigneur has here," she said at last, looking up gravely.

He gave a little bow with a few murmured words that she did not catch.

"Your novel interested me," she went on, still stroking the hound, as if the nearness of the great beast helped her.

"As a rule novels bore me, the subjects they deal with have been of no interest to me, but this one gripped me. It is unusual, it is wonderful, but—is it real?" She had spoken dispassionately with the boyish candour that was characteristic, not complimenting an author on a masterpiece, but stating a fact simply, as it appeared to her.

Saint Hubert leaned forward over the back of his chair. "In what way—real?" he asked.

She looked at him squarely. "Do you think there really exists such a man as you have drawn—a man who could be as tender, as unselfish, as faithful as your hero?"

Saint Hubert looked away, and, picking up his pen, stabbed idly at the blotting-pad, drawing meaningless circles and dots, with a slow shrug. The scorn in her voice and the sudden pain in her eyes hurt him.

"Do you know such a man, Monsieur, or is he wholly a creature of your imagination?" she persisted.

He completed a complicated diagram on the sheet of blotting-paper before answering. "I do know a man who, given certain circumstances, has the ability to develop into such a character," he said eventually in a low voice.

She laughed bitterly. "Then you are luckier than I. I am not very old, but during the last five years I have met many men of many nationalities, and I have never known one who in any degree resembles the *preux chevalier* of your book. The men who have most intimately touched my life have not known the meaning of the word tenderness, and have never had a thought for any one beyond themselves. You have been more fortunate in your acquaintances, Monsieur."

A dull red crept into the Vicomte's face, and he continued looking at the pen in his fingers. "Beautiful women, Madame," he said slowly, "unfortunately provoke in some men all that is basest and vilest in their natures. No man knows to what depths of infamy he may stoop under the stress of a sudden temptation."

"And the woman pays," cried Diana vehemently. "Pays for the beauty God curses her with—the beauty she may hate herself; pays until the beauty fades. How much—" She pulled herself up short, biting her lips. Moved by the sense of the sympathy that had unconsciously been influencing her during the past week and which had shaken the self-suppression that she had imposed upon herself, her tongue had run away with her. She was afraid of the confidence that his manner was almost demanding of her. Her pride restrained her from the compassion that her loneliness had nearly yielded to.

"Excuse me," she said coldly, "my ideas cannot possibly interest you."

"On the contrary, you interest me profoundly," he corrected quickly.

She noticed the slight difference in his words and laughed more bitterly than before. "As what?—a subject for vivisection? Get on your operating coat and bring your instruments without delay. The victim is all ready for you. It will be 'copy' for your next book!"

"Madame!"

He had sprung to his feet, and she looked up at him miserably, her hand held out in swift contrition. "Oh, forgive me! I shouldn't have said that. You haven't deserved it. You have been—kind. I am grateful. Forgive me and my rudeness. It must be the heat, it makes one very irritable, don't you think?"

He ignored her pitiful little subterfuge and raised her outstretched, quivering fingers to his lips. "If you will honour me with your friendship," he said, with a touch of the old-world chivalry that was often noticeable in him, "my life is at your service."

But as he spoke his voice changed. The touch of her cold fingers sent a rush of feeling through him that for an instant overpowered him.

She let her hand lie in his, and for a few moments she avoided his eyes and looked down at the rough head in her lap. Then she met his gaze frankly. "Your offer is too rare a thing to put on one side. If you will be my friend, as you are Monseigneur's friend—" she faltered, turning her head away, and her fingers lying in his trembled slightly.

He started and crushed the hand he was holding unknowingly, as the thought was forced on him. Monseigneur's friend! He realized that in the last few moments he had forgotten the Sheik, had forgotten everything, swept off his feet by an intense emotion that staggered him with its unexpectedness, except the loveliness and helplessness of the girl beside him. His head was reeling; his calmness, his loyalty, his earlier feelings of dispassionate pity had given way to an extreme agitation that was rushing him headlong and threatening to overwhelm him. His heart beat furiously and he clenched his teeth, fighting to regain his usual *sang-froid*. The emotional temperament that Diana had divined from his novel had sprung uppermost with a bound, overthrowing the rigid repression of years. The blood beat in his ears as he strove to master himself, to crush the madness that had come upon him.

He had closed his eyes with the shock of self-revelation, he opened them now and looked down at her hesitatingly, almost fearfully, clasping her hand closer in his and leaning nearer to her, drawn irresistibly by the intoxication of her nearness. He saw her through a mist that cleared gradually, saw that she was ignorant of the emotion she had awakened in him, and, conscious only of his sympathy, had left her hand in his as she would have left it in her brother's. She was bent low over the hound, her face almost touching his big head, and as Saint Hubert looked a glistening tear dropped on Kopec's rough, grey neck. She had forgotten him, forgotten even that he was standing beside her, in the one predominant thought that filled her mind. With an immense effort he got command of himself. Somehow he must conquer this sudden insanity. The loyalty that had hung trembling in the balance reasserted itself and a self-disgust seized him. He had been within an ace of betraying the man who had been for twenty years nearer to him than a brother. She belonged to his friend, and now he had not even the right to question the ethics of the Sheik's possession of her. The calm that he had lost came back to him. The wound would heal though it might always throb, but he was strong enough to hide its existence even from the jealous eyes that had watched him ceaselessly since his outburst on the night of his arrival. He had been conscious of them daily. Even this morning the Sheik had made every effort short of a direct command to induce him to go with him on the expedition that had taken him away so early. Sure of himself now, he lifted her fingers to his lips again reverently with a kind of renunciation in his kiss, and laid her hand down gently. He turned away with a smothered sigh and a little pang at her complete absorption, and, as he did so, Henri came in quickly.

"Monsieur le Vicomte! Will you come? There has been an accident."

With a cry that Saint Hubert never forgot Diana leaped to her feet, her face colourless, and her lips framed the word "Ahmed," though no sound came from them. She was shaking all over, and the Vicomte put his arm round her instinctively. She clung to him, and he knew with a bitter certainty that the support of a table or a chair would have meant no less to her.

"What is it, Henri?" he said sharply, with a slight movement that interposed himself between Diana and his servant.

"One of the men, Monsieur le Vicomte. His gun burst, and his hand is shattered."

Saint Hubert nodded curtly towards the door and turned his attention to Diana. She sank down on the divan and, gathering the hound's head in her arm, buried her face in his neck. "Forgive me," she murmured, her voice muffled in the rough, grey hair. "It is stupid of me, but he is riding that brute Shaitan today. I am always nervous. Please go. I will come in a minute."

He went without a word. "I am always nervous." The tales he had heard of Diana Mayo as he passed through Biskra did not include nerves. His face was set as he ran hurriedly across the camp.

Diana sat quite still after he had gone until the nervous shuddering ceased, until Kopec twisted his head free of her arms and licked her face with an uneasy whine. She brushed her hand across her eyes with a gasp of relief, and went out into the bright sunlight with the hound at her heels.

The noisy clamour of excited voices guided her to the scene of the accident, and the surrounding crowd opened to let her pass through. The wounded man was sitting holding up his hand stoically for Saint Hubert's ministrations with a look of mild interest on his face. In response to Diana's smile and cheery word he grinned sheepishly with a roll of his fine eyes. Saint Hubert looked up quickly. "It is not a pleasant sight," he said doubtfully.

"I don't mind. Let me hold that," she said quietly, rolling up her sleeves and taking a crimson-spattered basin from Henri. Saint Hubert flashed another look at her, marvelling at her steady voice and even colour when he thought of the white-faced girl who had clung trembling to him ten minutes earlier. Outside of Ahmed Ben Hassan she still retained the fearless courage that she had always had; it was only when anything touched him nearly that the new Diana, with the coward anxiety of love, rose paramount.

She watched the Vicomte's skilful treatment of the maimed hand with interest. There was a precision in his movement and a deft touch that indicated both knowledge and practise. "You are a doctor?"

"Yes," he said, without looking up from his work, "I studied when I was a young man and passed all the necessary examinations. It is indispensable when one travels as I do. I have found it invaluable."

He took up some dressing that Henri held ready for him, and Diana handed the now unwanted bowl to Gaston. She looked again at the Arab, whose impassive face showed no sign of any feeling. "Does he feel it very much, do you think?" she asked the valet.

He laughed and shrugged his shoulders. "Less than I should, Madame. What is really troubling him is the thought of what Monseigneur will say when he hears that Selim was fool enough to buy a worthless gun from one of the servants of the Dutchman who passed here last week," and he added a few teasing words in Arabic which made Selim look up with a grimace.

Saint Hubert finished adjusting the bandages and stood up, wiping the perspiration from his forehead.

"Will he do all right now?" asked Diana anxiously.

"I think so. The thumb is gone, as you saw, but I think I can save the rest of the hand. I will watch him carefully, but these men of Ahmed's are in such excellent condition that I do not think there will be any trouble."

"I am going to ride," said Diana, turning away. "It is rather late, but there is just time. Will you come?"

It was a temptation and he hesitated, gathering together the instruments he had been using, but prudence prevailed.

"I should like to, but I ought to keep an eye on Selim," he said quietly, snatching at the plausible excuse that offered. He found her later before the big tent as she was ready to start, and waited while she mounted.

"If I am late don't wait for me. Tell Henri to give you your lunch," she called out between The Dancer's idiotic prancings.

He watched her ride away, with Gaston a few paces behind and followed by the escort of six men that the Sheik had lately insisted upon. The continual presence of these six men riding at her heels irked her considerably. The wild, free gallops that she had loved became quite different with the thought of the armed guard behind her. They seemed to hamper her and put a period to her enjoyment. The loneliness of her rides had been to her half their charm; she had grown accustomed to and oblivious of Gaston, but she was acutely conscious of the six pairs of eyes watching her every movement. She did not see the necessity for them. She had never been aware of anything any time when she was riding that seemed to justify the Sheik's order. The oasis was not on a caravan route, and if she ever saw Arabs at any distance from the camp they always proved to be Ahmed Ben Hassan's own men. She had thought of remonstrating with him, but her courage had failed her. His mood, since the coming of Saint Hubert, had been of the coldest—almost repellant. The weeks of happiness that had gone before had developed the intimacy between them almost into a feeling of camaraderie. He had been more humane, more Western, more considerate than he had ever been, and the fear that she had of him had lain quiescent. She could have asked him then. But since the morning of Raoul's arrival, when the unexpected fervour of his embrace had given new birth to the hope that had almost died within her, he had changed completely into a cold reserve that chilled her. His caresses had been careless and infrequent, and his indifference so great that she had wondered miserably if the flame of his passion for her was burning out and if this was the end. And yet throughout his indifference she had been conscious, like Saint Hubert, of the surveillance of constant jealous eyes that watched them both with a fierce scrutiny that was felt rather than actually seen. But the spark of hope that the knowledge of this jealousy still fanned was not great enough to overcome the barrier that his new mood had raised between them. She dared ask no favour of him now. Her heart tightened at the thought of his indifference. It hurt so. This morning he had left her without a word when he had gone out into the early dawn, and she was hungry for the kisses he withheld. She was used to his taciturn fits, but her starved heart ached perpetually for tangible recognition. Love, the capacity for which she had so long denied, had become a force that, predominating everything, held her irresistibly. The accumulated affection that, for want of an outlet, had been stemmed within her, had burst all restraint, and the love that she gave to the man to whom she had surrendered her proud heart was immeasurable—a love of infinite tenderness and complete unselfishness, a love that had made her strangely humble. She had yielded up everything to him, he dominated her wholly. Her imperious will had bent before his greater determination, and his mastery over her had provoked a love that craved for recompense. She only lived for him and for the hope of his love, engulfed in the passion that enthralled her. Her surrender had been no common one. The feminine weakness that she had despised and fought against had triumphed over her unexpectedly without humiliating thoroughness. Sex had supervened to overthrow all her preconceived notions. The womanly instincts that under Aubrey's training had been suppressed and undeveloped had, in contact with the Sheik's vivid masculinity and compelling personality, risen to the surface with startling completeness.

Today she was almost desperate. His callousness of the morning had wounded her deeply, and a wave of rebellion welled up in her. She would not be thrown aside without making any effort to fight for his love. She would use every art that her beauty and her woman's instinct gave her. Her cheek burned as she thought of the role she was setting herself. She would be no better than "those others" whose remembrance still made her shiver. But she crushed down the repugnant feeling resolutely, flinging up her head with the old haughty gesture and drawing herself straighter in the saddle with compressed lips. She had endured so much already that she could even bear this further outrage to her feelings. At no matter what cost she must make him care for her. Though she loathed the means she would make him love her. But even as she planned the doubt of her ability to succeed crept into her mind, torturing her with insidious recollections.

Ahmed Ben Hassan was no ordinary man to succumb to the fascinations of a woman. She had experienced his obstinacy, and knew the inflexibility of his nature. His determination was a rock against which she had been broken too many times not to know its strength. For a moment she despaired, then courage came to her again, thrusting away the doubts that crowded in upon her and leaving the hope that still lingered in her heart. A faint tremulous smile curved her lips, and she looked up, forcing her thoughts back to the present with an effort.

At the beginning of the ride they had passed several vedettes sitting motionless on their impatient horses. The men had swung their rifles high in the air in salute as she passed, and once or twice Gaston had shouted a question as he galloped after her. But for the last hour they had seen no one. The desert was undulating here, rising and falling in short, sharp declivities that made a wide outlook impossible.

Gaston spurred to Diana's side. "Will Madame please to turn?" he said respectfully. "It is late, and it is not safe riding amongst these slopes. One cannot see what is coming and I am afraid."

"Afraid, Gaston?" she rallied laughingly.

"For you, Madame," he answered gravely.

She reined in The Dancer as she spoke; but it was too late. Even as she turned her horse's head innumerable Arabs seemed to spring up on all sides of them. Before she realised what was happening her escort flashed past and wheeled in behind her, shooting steadily at the horde of men who poured in upon them, and, with a groan, Gaston seized her bridle and urged the horses back in the direction from which they had come. The noise was deafening, the raucous shouting of the Arabs and the continuous sharp crack of the rifles. Bullets began to whizz past her.

Gaston tucked his reins under his knee, and with one hand grasping The Dancer's bridle and his revolver in the other, rode looking back over his shoulder. Diana, too, glanced behind her, and mechanically her fingers closed over the shining little weapon that the Sheik had given her the previous week. She saw with a sudden sickening the six men who had formed her escort beaten back by the superior numbers that enclosed them on every side. Already two were down and the rest were on foot, and, as she watched, they were swallowed up in the mass of men that poured over them, and, at the same time, a party of about twenty horsemen detached themselves from the main body and galloped towards her and Gaston.

She seized his arm. "Can't we do something? Can't we help them? We can't leave them like that," she gasped, wrenching the revolver from the holster at her waist.

"No, no, Madame, it is impossible. It is a hundred to six. You must think of yourself. Go on, Madame. For God's sake, ride on. We may have a chance." He loosed her bridle and dropped behind her, interposing himself between her and the pursuing Arabs. A fierce yelling and a hail of bullets that went wide made Diana turn her head as she crouched low in the saddle. She realised the meaning of Gaston's tactics and checked her horse deliberately.

"I won't go first. You must ride with me," she cried, wincing as a bullet went close by her.

"Mon Dieu! What are you stopping for? Do you think I can face Monseigneur if anything happens to you, Madame?" replied Gaston fiercely. "Do as I tell you. Go on!" Deference was gone in the fear that roughened his voice.

He looked back and his face grew grey. For himself he had no fear, but for the girl beside him he dared not even think. They were Ibraheim Omair's men who had trapped them, and he cursed his folly in allowing Diana to come so far. Yet it had seemed safe enough. The scout's reports had lately proved that the robber Sheik had up to now respected the boundary line between the two territories. This must be a sudden tentative raid which had met with unlooked-for success. The bait would be too tempting to allow of any slackening on the part of the raiders. The white woman, who was Ahmed Ben Hassan's latest toy, and his servant, whom he was known to value so highly, would be a prize that would not be lightly let go. For himself it would be probably torture, certainly death, and for her—! He set his teeth as he looked at her and the perspiration poured down his face. He would kill her himself before it came to that. And as he looked she turned her head, and met his agonised eyes for a moment, smiling bravely. He had refrained up till now from shooting, trying to reserve his ammunition for a last resource, but he saw that he must delay no longer. He fired slowly and steadily, picking his men with careful precision. It was a forlorn hope, but by checking the leaders even for a few moments he might gain time. The accuracy of his aim, that every time proved effectual, might keep back the onrush until they got clear of the undulating country, until they got out into the open where the sounds of the firing might reach some of the outpost sentinels, until they got too near to the Sheik's camp for pursuit to be possible. The bullets pattered continuously round them, but the men who fired them were not Ahmed Ben Hassan's carefully trained marksmen. But still Gaston knew that their position was almost hopeless. Any moment a bullet might reach one of them.

Their pursuers, too, seemed to guess his thoughts and opened out into an irregular, extended line, swerving and manoeuvring continually, making accurate shooting impossible, while they urged their horses to a terrific pace trying to outflank them. Diana was shooting now. The thought of her escort's annihilation and her own and Gaston's peril had overcome the reluctance she had had at first, and she had even a moment to wonder at her coolness. She did not feel afraid, the death of Ahmed's men had made her angry, a fierce revengeful anger that made her see red and filled her with a desire to retaliate in kind. She fired rapidly, emptying her revolver, and she had just reloaded with steady fingers when The Dancer stumbled, recovering himself for a few steps, and then lurched slowly over on to his side, blood pouring from his mouth. Diana sprang clear, and in a moment Gaston was beside her, thrusting her behind him, shielding her with his own body, and firing steadily at the oncoming Arabs.

The same feeling of unreality that she had experienced once before the first day in the Sheik's camp came over her. The intense stillness—for the Arabs had ceased shouting—the hot, dry sand with the shimmering heat haze rising like mist from its whispering surface, the cloudless deep blue sky overhead, the band of menacing horsemen circling nearer and nearer, the dead Dancer, with Gaston's horse standing quietly beside his prostrate companion, and lastly, the man beside her, brave and devoted to the end, all seemed fantastic and unreal. She viewed it dispassionately, as if she were a spectator rather than a participant in the scene. But for a moment only, then the reality of the situation came clearly to her again. Any minute might mean death for one or other or both of them, and with an instinctive movement she pressed closer to Gaston. They were both silent, there seemed nothing to say. The valet's left hand clenched over hers at the involuntary appeal for companionship that she made, and she felt it contract as a bullet gashed his forehead, blinding him for a moment with the blood that dripped into his eyes. He let go her hand to brush his arm across his face, and as he did so the Arabs with suddenly renewed shouting bore down upon them.

Gaston turned sharply and Diana read his purpose in the horror in his eyes. She held up her head with a little nod and the same brave smile on her white lips. "Please," she whispered, "quickly!" A spasm crossed his face, "Turn your head," he muttered desperately. "I cannot do it if you—"

There was a rattle of shots, and with a gasp he crumpled up against her. For a moment it was pandemonium. Standing over Gaston's body she fired her last shot and flung the empty revolver in the face of a man who sprang forward to seize her. She turned with a desperate hope of reaching Gaston's horse, but she was hemmed in, and for a second she stood at bay, hands clenched and teeth set, braving the wild faces that surrounded her, and were closing in upon her, with flashing defiant eyes. Then she was conscious of a crashing blow on her head, the ground heaved up under her feet, everything went black before her eyes, and without a sound she fell senseless.

Late in the afternoon Saint Hubert was still writing in the big tent. Henri had deciphered the notes that had baffled his master in the morning, and the Vicomte had taken advantage of the solitude to do some long-neglected work. He had forgotten the time, forgotten to be surprised at Diana's continued absence, immersed in the interesting subject he was dealing with, and not realising the significance of her delayed return. Ahmed had spoken of the proximity of his hereditary enemy, but Saint Hubert had not grasped how near the robber Sheik had ventured.

He was too engrossed to notice the usual noise in the camp that heralded the Sheik's arrival, and he looked up with a start when Ahmed Ben Hassan swept in. The Sheik's dark eyes glanced sombrely around the tent and without a word he went through into the inner room. In a moment he came back.

"Where is Diane?"

Saint Hubert got up, puzzled at his tone. He looked at his watch. "She went for a ride this morning. *Dieu!* I had no idea it was so late."

"This morning!—and not back yet?" repeated the Sheik slowly. "What time this morning?"

"About ten, I think," replied Saint Hubert uneasily. "I'm not sure. I didn't look. There was an accident, and she delayed to watch me tie up one of your foolish children who had been playing with a worthless gun."

The Sheik moved over to the doorway. "She had an escort?" he asked curtly.

"Yes."

Ahmed Ben Hassan's face hardened and the heavy scowl contracted his black brows. Had she all these weeks been tricking him—feigning a content she did not feel, lulling his suspicions to enable her to seize another opportunity to attempt to get away? For a moment his face grew dark, then he put the thought from him. He trusted her. Only a week before she had given him her word, and he knew she would not lie to him. And, besides, the thing was impossible. Gaston would never be caught napping a second time, and there were also the six men who formed her guard. She would never be able to escape the vigilance of seven men. But it was the trust he had in her that weighed most with him. He had never trusted a woman before, but this woman had been different. The others who had come and gone so lightly had not even left a recollection behind them; they had faded into one concrete cause of utter boredom. There had never been any reason to trust or mistrust them, or to care if they came or went. Satiety had come with possession and with it indifference. But the emotion that this girl's uncommon beauty and slender boyishness had aroused in him had not diminished during the months she had been living in his camp. Her varying moods, her antagonism, her fits of furious rage, and, lastly, her unexpected surrender, had kept his interest alive. He had grown accustomed to her. He had come to looking forward with a vague, indefinite pleasure, on returning from his long expeditions, to seeing the dainty little figure curled up among the cushions on the big divan. Her presence seemed to pervade the atmosphere of the whole tent, changing it utterly. She had become necessary to him as he had never believed it possible that a woman could be. And with the change that she had made in his camp there had come a change in himself also.

For the first time a shadow had risen between him and the man whose friendship had meant everything to him since, as a lad of fifteen, he had come under the influence of the young Frenchman, who was three years his senior. He realized that since the night of Raoul's arrival he had been seething with insensate jealousy. He had relied on the Western tendencies that prompted him to carry off the difficult situation, but his ingrained Orientalism had broken through the superficial veneer. He was jealous of every word, every look she gave Saint Hubert. Pride had prevented an open rupture with the Vicomte this morning, but he had ridden away filled with a cold rage that had augmented every hour and finally driven him back earlier than he had intended, riding with a recklessness that had been apparent even to his men. The sight of Raoul sitting alone absorbed in his work had in part allayed his suspicions, and he had gone on into the other room with a feeling of new expectancy that had changed to a sudden chill at its emptiness. The vacant room had brought home to him abruptly all that the girl meant to him. A latent anxiety crept into his eyes.

He went out under the awning and clapped his hands, and a servant answered the summons almost immediately. He gave an order and waited, his hands thrust into the folds of his waist-cloth and his teeth clenched on a cigarette that he had forgotten to light.

Saint Hubert joined him. "What do you think?" he asked, with a touch of diffidence.

"I don't know what to think," replied the Sheik shortly.

"But is there any real danger?"

"There is always danger in the desert, particularly when that devil is abroad." He motioned to the south with an impatient jerk of his head.

Saint Hubert's breath whistled sharply through his teeth. "My God! You don't imagine—"

But the Sheik only shrugged his shoulders and turned to Yusef, who had come up with half-a-dozen men. There was a rapid interchange of questions and answers, some brief orders, and the men hurried away in different directions, while Ahmed Ben Hassan turned again to Saint Hubert.

"They were seen by three of the southern patrols this morning, but of course it was nobody's business to find out if they had come back or not. I will start at once—in about ten minutes. You will come with me? Good! I have sent for reinforcements, who are to follow us if we are not back in twelve hours." His voice was expressionless, and only Raoul de Saint Hubert, who had known him since boyhood, could and did appreciate the significance of a fleeting look that crossed his face as he went back into the tent.

For a moment the Vicomte hesitated, but he knew that not even he was wanted inside that empty tent, and a half-bitter, half-sad feeling that the perfect friendship and confidence that had existed between them for twenty years would never again be the same came to them, the regretful sense of inevitable change, the consciousness of personal relegation. Then fear for Diana drove out every other consideration, and he went to his own quarters with a heavy heart.

When he came back in a few minutes with Henri following him the camp had undergone a transformation. With the promptness of perfect discipline the hundred men who had been chosen to go on the expedition were already waiting, each man standing by his horse, and the Sheik, quiet and impassive as usual, was superintending the distribution of extra ammunition. A groom was walking The Hawk slowly up and down, and Yusef, whose gloomy eyes had been fixed reproachfully on his chief, chafing against the order to remain behind to take command of the reinforcements should they be needed, went to him and took the horse's bridle from him and brought him to the Sheik. Even as he held the stirrup Saint Hubert could see that he was expostulating with an unusual insistence, begging for permission to accompany them. But the Sheik shook his head, and the young man stood sullenly aside to avoid The Hawk's hoofs as he reared impatiently.

Ahmed Ben Hassan motioned Saint Hubert to his side and in silence the cavalcade started at the usual swift gallop. The silence impressed Raoul, who was accustomed to the Arab's usual clamour. It affected his sensitive temperaments, filling him with a sinister foreboding. The silent band of stern-faced horsemen riding in close and orderly formation behind them suggested something more than a mere relief party. The tradition of reckless courage and organised fighting efficiency that had made the tribe known and feared for generations had been always maintained, and under the leadership of the last two holders of the hereditary name to so high a degree that the respect in which it was held was such that no other tribe had ventured to dispute its supremacy, and for many years its serious fighting capacities had not been tested.

Even Ibraheim Omair had inherited a feud that was largely traditional. Only once during the lifetime of the last Ahmed Ben Hassan had he dared to come into open conflict, and the memory of it had lasted until now. Skirmishes there had been and would always be inevitably sufficient to keep the tribesmen in a state of perpetual expectancy, and for this Ahmed Ben Hassan preserved the rigid discipline that prevailed in his tribe, insisting on the high standard that had kept them famous. The life-work that his predecessor had taken over from his father the present Ahmed Ben Hassan had carried on and developed with autocratic perseverance. The inborn love of fighting had been carefully fostered in the tribe, the weapons with which they were armed were of the newest pattern. Raoul knew with perfect certainty that to the picked men following them this hasty expedition meant only one thing—war, the war that they had looked forward to all their lives, precipitated now by an accident that gave to a handful of them the chance that hundreds of their fellow-tribesmen were longing for, a chance that sent them joyfully behind their chief, careless whether the reinforcements that had been sent for arrived in time or not. The smallness of their numbers was a source of pleasure rather than otherwise; if they won through to them would be the glory of victory; if they were annihilated with them would rest the honour of dying with the leader whom they worshipped, for not one of them doubted that Ahmed Ben Hassan would not survive his bodyguard, the flower of his tribe, the carefully chosen men from whose ranks his personal escort was always drawn. With them he would crush his hereditary enemy or with them he would die.

The short twilight had gone and a brilliant moon shone high in the heavens, illuminating the surrounding country with a clear white light. At any other time the beauty of the scene, the glamour of the Eastern night, the head-long gallop in company with this band of fierce fighting men would have stirred Saint Hubert profoundly. His artistic temperament and his own absolute fearlessness and love of adventure would have combined to make the expedition an exciting experience that he would not willingly have foregone. But the reason for it all, the peril of the girl whom he loved so unexpectedly, changed the whole colour of the affair, tinging it with a gravity and a suspense that left a cold fear in his heart. And if to him, what then to the man beside him? The question that Ahmed Ben Hassan had negatived so scornfully a week before had been answered differently in the swift look that had crossed his face this evening. He had not spoken since they started, and Saint Hubert had not felt able to break the silence. They had left the level country and were in amongst the long, successive ranges of undulating ground, the summits standing out silver white in the gleaming moonlight, the hollows filled with dark shadow, like black pools of deep, still water. And at the bottom of one of the slopes the Sheik pulled up suddenly with a low, hissing exclamation. A white shape was lying face downwards, spread-eagled on the sand, almost under The Hawk's feet, and at their approach two lean, slinking forms cantered away into the night. The Sheik and Henri reached the still figure simultaneously and Saint Hubert almost as quickly. He made a hurried examination. The bullet that had stunned Gaston had glanced off, leaving an ugly cut, and others that had hit him at the same time had ploughed through his shoulder, breaking the bone and causing besides wounds that had bled freely. He had staggered more than a mile before he had fainted again from loss of blood. He came to under Saint Hubert's handling, and lifted his heavy eyes to the Sheik, who was kneeling beside him.

"Monseigneur—Madame—Ibraheim Omair," he whispered weakly, and relapsed into unconsciousness.

For a moment the Sheik's eyes met Raoul's across his body, and then Ahmed Ben Hassan rose to his feet. "Be as quick as you can," he said, and went back to his horse. He leaned against The Hawk, his fingers mechanically searching for and lighting a cigarette, his eyes fixed unseeingly on the group around Gaston. The valet's broken words had confirmed the fear that he had striven to crush since he discovered Diana's absence.

He had only seen Ibraheim Omair once when, ten years before, he had gone with the elder Ahmed Ben Hassan to a meeting of the more powerful chiefs at Algiers, arranged under the auspices of the French Government, to confer on a complicated boundary question that had threatened an upheaval amongst the tribes which the nominal protectors of the country were afraid would be prejudicial to their own prestige, as it would have been beyond their power to quell. He had chafed at having to meet his hereditary enemy on equal terms, and only the restraining influence of the old Sheik, who exacted an unquestioning obedience that extended even to his heir, had prevented a catastrophe that might have nullified the meeting and caused infinitely more complications than the original boundary dispute. But the memory of the robber Sheik remained with him always, and the recollection of his bloated, vicious face and gross, unwieldy body rose clearly before him now.

Ibraheim Omair and the slender daintiness that he had prized so lightly. Diane! His teeth met through the cigarette in his mouth. His senseless jealousy and the rage provoked by Raoul's outspoken criticism had recoiled on the innocent cause. She, not Saint Hubert, had felt the brunt of his anger. In the innate cruelty of his nature it had given him a subtle pleasure to watch the bewilderment, alternating with flickering fear, that had come back into the deep blue eyes that for two months had looked into his with frank confidence. He had made her acutely conscious of his displeasure. Only last night, when his lack of consideration and his unwonted irritability had made her wince several times during the evening and after Saint Hubert had gone to his own tent, he, had looked up to find her eyes fixed on him with an expression that, in his dangerous mood, had excited all the brutality of which he was capable, and had filled him with a desire to torture her. The dumb reproach in her eyes had exasperated him, rousing the fiendish temper that had been hardly kept in check all the previous week. And yet, when he held her helpless in his arms, quivering and shrinking from the embrace that was no caress, but merely the medium of his anger, and the reproach in her wavering eyes changed to mute entreaty, the pleasure he had anticipated in her fear had failed him as it had before, and had irritated him further. The wild beating of her heart, the sobbing intake of her breath, the knowledge of his power over her, gave him no gratification, and he had flung her from him cursing her savagely, till she had fled into the other room with her hands over her ears to shut out the sound of his slow, deliberate voice. And this morning he had left her without a sign of any kind, no word or gesture that might have effaced the memory of the previous night. He had not meant to, he had intended to go back to her before he finally rode away, but Saint Hubert's refusal to accompany him had killed the softer feelings that prompted him, and his rage had flamed up again.

And now? The longing to hold her in his arms, to kiss the tears from her eyes and the colour into her pale lips, was almost unbearable. He would give his life to keep even a shadow from her path, and she was in the hands of Ibraheim Omair! The thought and all that it implied was torture, but no sign escaped him of the hell he was enduring. The unavoidable delay seemed interminable, and he swung into the saddle, hoping that the waiting would seem less with The Hawk's restless, nervous body gripped between his knees, for though the horse would stand quietly with his master beside him, he fretted continually at waiting once the Sheik was mounted, and the necessity for soothing him was preferable to complete inaction.

Saint Hubert rose to his feet at last, and, leaving behind Henri and two Arabs, who were detailed to take the wounded man back to the camp, the swift gallop southward was resumed. On, over the rising and falling ground along which Gaston had stumbled, blind and faint with loss of blood and the pain of his wounds, past the dead body of The Dancer, ghostly white in the moonlight, lying a little apart from the semicircle of Arabs that proved the efficiency of Gaston's shooting where Diana and he had made their last stand. The Sheik made no sign and did not check the headlong gallop, but continued on, The Hawk taking the fallen bodies that lay in his path in his stride, with only a quiver of repugnance and a snort of disgust. Still on, past the huddled bundles of tumbled draperies that marked the way significantly, avoiding them where the moonlight illuminated brightly, and riding over them in the deep hollows, where once Raoul's horse stumbled badly and nearly fell, recovering himself with a wild scramble, and the Vicomte heard the dead man's skull crack under the horse's slipping hoof.

The distant howling of jackals came closer and closer until, topping one long rise and descending into a hollow that was long enough and wide enough to be fully lit by the moon, they came to the place where the ambush had been laid. Instinctively Ahmed Ben Hassan knew that amongst the jostling heaps of corpses and dead horses lay the bodies of his own men. Perhaps amongst the still forms from which the jackals, whose hideous yelling they had heard, had slunk away, there might be one left with life enough to give some news. One of his own men who would speak willingly, or one of Ibraheim Omair's who would be made to speak. His lips curled back from his white teeth in a grin of pure cruelty.

The silence that had prevailed amongst his men broke suddenly as they searched quickly among the dead. The Sheik waited impassively, silent amidst the muttered imprecations and threats of vengeance of his followers as they laid beside him the six remains of what had been Diana's escort, slashed and mutilated almost beyond recognition. But it was he who noticed that the last terrible figure stirred slightly as it was laid down, and it was into his face, grown suddenly strangely gentle, that the dying Arab looked with fast-filming eyes. The man smiled, the happy smile of a child that had obtained an unexpected reward, and raised his hand painfully in salute, then pointed mutely to the south.

The Sheik caught his follower's nerveless fingers as they fell in his own strong grasp, and with a last effort the Arab drew his chief's hand to his forehead and fell back dead.

CHAPTER VIII

Slowly and painfully, through waves of deadly nausea and with the surging of deep waters in her ears, Diana struggled back to consciousness. The agony in her head was excruciating, and her limbs felt cramped and bruised. Recollection was dulled in bodily pain, and, at first, thought was merged in physical suffering. But gradually the fog cleared from her brain and memory supervened hesitatingly. She remembered fragmentary incidents of what had gone before the oblivion from which she had just emerged. Gaston, and the horror and resolution in his eyes, the convulsive working of his mouth as he faced her at the last moment. Her own dread—not of the death that was imminent, but lest the mercy it offered should be snatched from her. Then before the valet could effect his supreme devotion had come the hail of bullets, and he had fallen against her, the blood that poured from his wounds saturating her linen coat, and rolled over across her feet. She remembered vaguely the wild figures hemming her in, but nothing more.

Her eyes were still shut; a leaden weight seemed fixed on them, and the effort to open them was beyond her strength. "Gaston," she whispered feebly, and stretched out her hand. But instead of his body or the dry hot sand her fingers had expected to encounter they closed over soft cushions, and with the shock she sat up with a jerk, her eyes staring wide, but, sick and faint, she fell back again, her arm flung across her face, shielding the light that pierced like daggers through her throbbing eye-balls. For a while she lay still, fighting against the weakness that overpowered her, and by degrees the horrible nausea passed and the agony in her head abated, leaving only a dull ache. The desire to know where she was and what had happened made her forget her bruised body. She moved her arm slightly from before her eyes so that she could see, and looked cautiously from under thick lashes, screened by the sleeve of her coat. She was lying on a pile of cushions in one corner of a small-tented apartment which was otherwise bare, except for the rug that covered the floor. In the opposite corner of the tent an Arab woman crouched over a little brazier, and the smell of native coffee was heavy in the air. She closed her eyes again with a shudder. The attempted devotion of Gaston had been useless. This must be the camp of the robber Sheik, Ibraheim Omair.

She lay still, pressing closely down amongst the cushions, and clenching the sleeve of her jacket between her teeth to stifle the groan that rose to her lips. A lump came into her throat as she thought of Gaston. In those last moments all inequality of rank had been swept away in their common peril—they had been only a white man and a white woman together in their extremity. She remembered how, when she had pressed close to him, his hand had sought and gripped hers, conveying courage and sympathy. All that he could do he had done, he had shielded her body with his own, it must have been over his lifeless body that they had taken her. He had proved his faithfulness, sacrificing his life for his master's play-thing. Gaston was in all probability dead, but she was alive, and she must husband her strength for her own needs. She forced the threatening emotion down, and, with an effort, controlled the violent shivering in her limbs, and sat up slowly, looking at the Arab woman, who, hearing her move, turned to gaze at her. Instantly Diana realised that there was no help or compassion to be expected from her. She was a handsome woman, who must have been pretty as a girl, but there was no sign of softness in her sullen face and vindictive eyes. Instinctively Diana felt that the glowing menace of the woman's expression was inspired by personal hatred, and that her presence in the lent was objectionable to her. And the feeling gave a necessary spur to the courage that was fast coming back to her. She stared with all the haughtiness she could summon to her aid; she had learned her own power among the natives of India the previous year, and here in the desert there was only one Arab whose eyes did not fall beneath hers, and presently with a muttered word the woman turned back to her coffee-making.

Diana's muscles relaxed and she sat back easily on the cushions, the little passage of wills had restored her confidence in herself. She moved her hand and it brushed against her jacket, coming away stained and sticky, and she noticed for the first time that all one side and sleeve were soaked with blood. She ripped it off with a shudder and flung it from her, rubbing the red smear from her hands with a kind of horror.

The little tent was intensely hot, and there was a close, pungent smell that was eminently *native* that she never experienced in the cool airiness and scrupulous cleanliness of Ahmed Ben Hassan's tents. Her sensitive lip curled with disgust, all her innate fastidiousness in revolt. The heat aggravated a burning thirst that was parching her throat. She got up on to her feet slowly, and with infinite caution, to prevent any jar that might start again the throbbing in her head; but the effects of the blow were wearing off, and, though her head continued to ache, it did no more than that, and the sick, giddy feeling had gone completely. She crossed the tent to the side of the Arab woman.

"Give me some water," she said in French, but the woman shook her head without looking up. Diana repeated the request in Arabic, one of the few sentences she knew without stumbling. This time the woman rose up hastily and held out a cup of the coffee she had been making.

Diana hated the sweet, thick stuff, but it would do until she could get the water she wanted, and she put out her hand to take the little cup. But her eyes met the other's fixed on her, and something in their malignant stare made her pause. A sudden suspicion shot through her mind. The coffee was drugged. What beyond the woman's expression made her think so she did not know, but she was sure of it. She put the cup aside impatiently.

"No. Not coffee. Water," she said firmly.

Before she realised what was happening the woman thrust a strong arm round her and forced the cup to her lips. That confirmed Diana's suspicions and rage lent her additional strength. The woman was strong, but Diana was stronger, younger and more active. She dashed the cup to the floor, spilling its contents, and, with an effort, tore the clinging hands from her and sent the woman crashing on to the ground, rolling against the brazier, oversetting it, and scattering brass pots and cups over the rug. The woman scrambled to her knees and beat out the glowing embers, uttering scream after scream in a shrill, piercing voice. And, in answer to her cries, a curtain at the side of the tent, that Diana had not noticed, slid aside and a gigantic Nubian came in. With outstretched hand shaking with rage, pointing at Diana, she burst into voluble abuse, punctuating every few words with the shrieks that had brought the negro.

Diana could understand nothing of what she said, but her expressive gestures told the story of the struggle plainly enough. The Nubian listened with white teeth flashing in a broad grin, and shook his head in response to some request urged with denunciatory fist. He picked up the last remaining embers that had scattered on the rug, rubbing the smouldering patches till they were extinguished, and then turned to leave the room. But Diana called him back. She went a step forward, her head high, and looked him straight in the face.

"Fetch me water!" she said imperiously. He pointed to the coffee that the woman had recommenced to make, her back turned to them, but Diana stamped her foot. "Water! Bring me water!" she said again, more imperiously than before. With a wider grin the negro made a gesture of acquiescence and went out, returning in a few moments with a water-skin.

The thought of its condition made her hesitate for a moment, but only for a moment. Her thirst was too great to allow niceties to interfere with it. She picked up one of the clean coffee-cups that had rolled to her feet, rinsed it several times, and then drank. The water was warm and slightly brackish, but she needed it too much to mind. In spite of being tepid it relieved the dry, suffocating feeling in her throat and refreshed her. The Nubian went away again, leaving the woman still crouching over the brazier.

Diana walked back to the cushions and dropped down on to them gladly. The events of the last few moments had tried her more than she realised, her legs were shaking under her, and she was thankful to sit down. But her courage had risen with a bound; the fact that she was physically stronger than the woman who had been put to guard her, and also that she had gained her point with the burly negro, had a great moral effect on her, further restoring her confidence in herself.

Her position was an appalling one, but hope was strong within her. The fact that since she had regained consciousness she had seen only the woman and the Nubian seemed to argue that Ibraheim Omair must be absent from his camp; the thought that he might purposely be delaying the moment of inspecting his captive with a view to prolonging her mental torture she put from her as improbable. She did not credit him with so much acumen. And from his absence her courage gained strength. If it could only be prolonged until Ahmed reached her. That the Sheik would come she knew, her faith in him was unbounded. If he only came in time! Hours had passed since the ambuscade had surprised them. It had been early afternoon then. Now the lighted lamp told her it was night. How late she did not know. Her watch had been broken some months before, and she had no means of even guessing the hour, but it must be well on in the evening. By now the absence of herself and Gaston and their escort would be discovered. He would know her peril and he would come to her. Of that she had no doubt. Although he had changed so strangely in the last few days, though the wonderful gentleness of the last two months had merged again into indifference and cruelty, still she never doubted. Even if desire had passed and indifference had become so great that she was no longer necessary to him, still the Oriental jealousy with which he was so deeply imbued would never allow him to let her pass so lightly from his keeping. He might discard her at his own pleasure, but no one would take her from him with impunity. Her woman's intuition had sensed the jealousy that had actuated him during the unhappy days since Saint Hubert had come. An inconsistent jealousy that had been unprovoked and unjustified, but for which she had suffered. She had known last night, when she winced under his sarcastic tongue, and later, when Saint Hubert had left them and his temper had suddenly boiled over, that she was paying for the unaccustomed strain that he was putting on his own feelings. His curses had eaten into her heart, and she had fled from him to stifle the coward instinct that urged her to confess her love and beg his mercy. She had lain awake with shivering apprehension waiting for him, but when, after nearly two hours, he had sauntered in, the usual cigarette between his lips, indifference had taken the place of rage, and he had ignored her, as she had grown used to being ignored. And long after she knew from his even breathing that he was asleep she had lain wide-eyed beside him, grasping at what happiness she could, living for the moment as she had schooled herself to live, trying to be content with just the fact of his nearness. And the indifference of the night had been maintained when he had left her at dawn, his persistent silence pointing the continuance of his displeasure. But he would come, if for no other reason than the same jealousy which held him in its inexorable grip. He would come! He would come! She whispered it over to herself as if merely the sound of the words gave her courage. He would not let anything happen to her. Every moment that Ibraheim Omair stayed away was so much gained, every moment he would be coming nearer. The reversal of the role he played in her life brought a quivering smile to her lips. For the advent of the man who a few weeks before she had loathed for his brutal abduction of herself she now prayed with the desperation of despair. He represented safety, salvation, everything that made life worth living.

A sudden noise and men's voices in the adjoining room sent her to her feet with heaving breast and clenched hands. But the sharp, guttural voice predominating over the other voices killed the wild hope that had sprung up in her by its utter dissimilarity to the soft low tones for which she longed. Ibraheim Omair! He had come first! She set her teeth with a long, shuddering breath, bracing herself to meet what was coming.

The Arab woman turned to look at her again with a sneering smile that was full of significance, but beyond a fleeting glance of disdain Diana paid no attention to her. She stood rigid, one foot beating nervously into the soft rug. She noticed irrelevantly at the moment that both her spurs and the empty holster had been removed whilst she was unconscious, and with the odd detachment that transfers a train of thought from the centre of importance even at a supreme moment, she wondered, with an annoyance that seemed curiously futile, why it had been done.

The voices in the next room continued, until Diana almost prayed for the moment she was waiting for would come; suspense was worse than the ordeal for which she was nerving herself, It came at last. The curtain slid aside again, and the same huge negro she had seen before entered. He came towards her, and her breath hissed in suddenly between her set teeth, but before he reached her the Arab woman intercepted him, blocking his way, and with wild eyes and passionate gestures poured out a stream of low, frenzied words. The Nubian turned on her impatiently and thrust her roughly out of his way, and, coming to Diana, put out his hand as if to grasp her arm, but she stepped back with flashing eyes and a gesture that he obeyed.

Her heart was pounding, but she had herself under control. Only her hands twitched, her long fingers curling and uncurling spasmodically, and she buried them deep in her breeches' pockets to hide them. She walked slowly to the curtain and nodded to the Nubian to draw it aside, and slower still she passed into the other room. Only a little larger than the one she had left, almost as bare, but her mind took in these things uncomprehendingly, for all her attention was focussed on the central figure in the room.

Ibraheim Omair, the robber Sheik, lolling his great bulk on a pile of cushions, a little inlaid stool with coffee beside him, and behind him, standing motionless as if formed of bronze, two other negroes, so like the one that had summoned her that they seemed like statues that had been cast from one mould.

Diana paused for a moment framed in the entrance, then, with head thrown back and swaggering, boyish stride, she moved across the thick rugs leisurely and halted in front of the chief, looking straight at him with haughty, curling lips and insolent, half-closed eyes. The hold she was exercising over herself was tremendous, her body was rigid with the effort, and her hands deep down in her pockets clenched till the nails bit into the palms. Every instinct was rebelling against the calm she forced upon herself. She longed to scream and make a dash for the opening that she guessed was behind her, and to take her chance in the darkness outside. But she knew that such a chance was impossible; if she ever reached the open air she would never be allowed to get more than a few steps from the tent. Her only course lay in the bravado that alone kept her from collapse. She must convey the impression of fearlessness, though cold terror was knocking at her heart. Masked with indifference her veiled eyes were watching the robber chief closely. This was, indeed, the Arab of her imaginings, this gross, unwieldy figure lying among the tawdry cushions, his swollen, ferocious face seamed and lined with every mark of vice, his full, sensual lips parted and showing broken, blackened teeth, his deep-set, bloodshot eyes with a look in them that it took all her resolution to sustain, a look of such bestial evilness that the horror of it bathed her in perspiration. His appearance was slovenly, his robes, originally rich, were stained and tumbled, the fat hands lying spread out on his knees were engrained with dirt, showing even against his dark skin. His heavy face lit up with a gleam of malicious satisfaction as Diana came towards him, his loose mouth broadened in a wicked smile. He leaned forward a little, weighing heavily on the hands that were on his knees, his eyes roving slowly over her till they rested on her face again.

"So! the white woman of my brother Ahmed Ben Hassan," he said slowly, in villainous French, with a sudden, snarling intonation as he uttered his enemy's name. "Ahmed Ben Hassan! May Allah burn his soul in hell!" he added with relish, and spat contemptuously.

He leaned back on the cushions with a grunt, and drank some coffee noisily.

Diana kept her eyes fixed on him, and under their unwavering stare he seemed to be uneasy, his own inflamed eyes wandering ceaselessly over her, one hand fumbling at the curved hilt of a knife stuck in his belt, and at last he grew exasperated, hitching himself forward once more and beckoning her to come nearer to him. She hesitated, and as she paused uncertainly, there was a flutter of draperies behind her, and the Arab woman from the inner room, evading the negro who stepped forward to stop her, flung herself at the feet of Ibraheim Omair, clinging to his knees with a low wailing cry. In a flash Diana realised the meaning of the hatred that had gleamed in the woman's eyes earlier in the evening. To her she was a rival, whose coming to share the favours of her lord had aroused all the jealousy of the reigning favourite. A wave of disgust mingled with the fear that was torturing her. She jerked her head angrily, fighting against the terror that was growing on her, and for a moment her lashes drooped and hid her eyes. When she looked up again the woman was still crouched at the old Arab's feet, imploring and distraught.

Ibraheim Omair looked down on her curiously, his lips drawn back from his blackened teeth in an evil grin, and then shook her off violently with a swift blow in the mouth, but the woman clung closer, with upturned, desperate face, a thin trickle of blood oozing from her lips, and with a hoarse growl that was like the dull roar of a savage beast the robber chief caught her by the throat and held her for a moment, her frantic, clutching hands powerless against his strong grasp, then slowly drew the long knife from the ample folds of his waist-cloth, and as slowly drove it home into the strangling woman's breast. With savage callousness, before he released his hold of her, he wiped the stained knife carefully on her clothing and replaced it, and then flung the dead body from him. It rolled over on the rug midway between him and Diana.

There was a momentary silence in the room, and Diana became conscious of a muffled, rhythmical beat near her, like the ticking of a great clock, and realised with dull wonder that it was her own heart beating. She seemed turned to stone, petrified with the horror of the last few moments. Her eyes were glued to the still figure on the rug before her with the gaping wound in the breast, from which the blood was welling, staining the dark draperies of the woman's clothes, and creeping slowly down to the rug on which the body lay. She was dazed, and odd thoughts flitted through her mind. It was a pity, she thought stupidly, that the blood should spoil the rug. It was a lovely rug. She wondered what it would have cost in Biskra—less, probably, than it would in London. Then she forgot the rug as her eyes travelled upward to the woman's face. The mouth was open and the streak of blood was drying, but it was the eyes, protruding, agonised, that brought Diana abruptly to herself. She seemed to wake suddenly to the full realisation of what had happened and to her own peril. She felt physically sick for a moment, but she fought it down. Very slowly she raised her head, and, meeting Ibraheim Omair's eyes fixed on her, she looked full at him across the dead woman's body and laughed! It was that or shriek. The curls were clinging drenched on her forehead, and she wondered if her clenched hands would ever unclose. She must make no sign, she must not scream or faint, she must keep her nerve until Ahmed came. Oh, dear God, send him quickly! The laugh wavered hysterically, and she caught her lip between her teeth. She must do something to distract her attention from that awful still shape at her feet. Almost unconsciously she grasped the cigarette case in her pocket and took it out, dragging her eyes from the horrible sight on which they were fixed, and chose and lit a cigarette with slow care, flicking the still-burning match on to the carpet between the feet of the negro who stood near her. He had not moved since he had failed to stop the woman's entrance, and the two stationed behind the pile of cushions had stood motionless, their eyes hardly following the tragedy enacted before them. At a nod from the chief they came now and carried away the body of the woman. One returned in a moment, bringing fresh coffee, and then vanished noiselessly.

Then Ibraheim Omair leaned forward with a horrible leer and beckoned to Diana, patting the cushions beside him. Mastering the loathing that filled her she sat down with all the unconcern she could assume. The proximity of the man nauseated her. He reeked of sweat and grease and ill-kept horses, the pungent stench of the native. Her thoughts went back to the other Arab, of whose habits she had been forced into such an intimate knowledge. Remembering all that she had heard of the desert people she had been surprised at the fastidious care he took of himself, the frequent bathing, the spotless cleanliness of his robes, the fresh wholesomeness that clung about him, the faint, clean smell of shaving-soap mingling with the perfume of the Turkish tobacco that was always associated with him.

The contrast was hideous.

She refused the coffee he offered her with a shake of her head, paying no attention to his growl of protest, not even understanding it, for he spoke in Arabic. As she laid down the end of her cigarette with almost the feeling of letting go a sheet anchor—for it had at least kept her lips from trembling—his fat hand closed about her wrist and he jerked her towards him.

"How many rifles did the Frenchman bring to that son of darkness?" he said harshly.

She turned her head, surprised at the question, and met his bloodshot eyes fixed on hers, half-menacing, half-admiring, and looked away again hastily. "I do not know."

His fingers tightened on her wrist. "How many men had Ahmed Ben Hassan in the camp in which he kept you?"

"I do not know."

"I do not know! I do not know!" he echoed with a sudden savage laugh. "You will know when I have done with you." He crushed her wrist until she winced with pain, and turned her head away further that she might not see his face. Question after question relating to the Sheik and his tribe followed in rapid succession, but to all of them Diana remained silent, with averted head and compressed lips. He should not learn anything from her that might injure the man she loved, though he tortured her, though her life paid the price of her silence, as it probably would. She shivered involuntarily. "Shall I tell you what they would do to him?" She could hear the Sheik's voice plainly as on the night when she had asked him what Gaston's fate would be at the hands of Ibraheim Omair. She could hear the horrible meaning he had put into the words, she could see the terrible smile that had accompanied them. Her breath came faster, but her courage still held. She clung desperately to the hope that was sustaining her. Ahmed must come in time. She forced down the torturing doubts that whispered that he might never find her, that he might come too late, that when he came she might be beyond a man's desire.

Ibraheim Omair ceased his questioning. "Later you will speak," he said significantly, and drank more coffee. And his words revived the agonising thoughts she had crushed down. Her vivid imagination conjured up the same ghastly mental pictures that had appalled her when she had applied them to Gaston, but now it was herself who was the central figure in all the horrors she imagined, until the shuddering she tried to suppress shook her from head to foot, and she clenched her teeth to stop them chattering.

Ibraheim Omair kept his hold upon her, and presently, with a horrible loathing, she felt his hand passing over her arm, her neck, and down the soft curves of her slim young body, then with a muttered ejaculation he forced her to face him.

"What are you listening for? You think that Ahmed Ben Hassan will come? Little fool! He has forgotten you already. There are plenty more white women in Algiers and Oran that he can buy with his gold and his devil face. The loves of Ahmed Ben Hassan are as the stars in number. They come and go like the swift wind in the desert, a hot breath—and it's finished. He will not come, and if he does, he will not find you, for in an hour we shall be gone."

Diana writhed in his grasp. The hateful words in the guttural voice, pronounced in vile French, the leering, vicious face with the light of admiration growing in the bloodshot eyes, were all a ghastly nightmare. With a sudden desperate wrench she freed herself and fled across the tent—panic-stricken at last. But in her blind rush she tripped, and with a swiftness that seemed incompatible with his unwieldiness Ibraheim Omair followed her and caught her in his arms. Struggling he carried her to the divan. For a moment he paused, and instinctively Diana lay still, reserving her strength for the final struggle.

"One hour, my little gazelle, one hour—" he said hoarsely, and bent his face to hers.

With a cry Diana flung her head aside and strained away from him, fighting with the strength of madness. She fought like a boy with a swift thought of gratitude for Aubrey's training, and twisting and writhing she managed to slip through his grasp until her feet rested on the ground. But his grip on her never relaxed; he dragged her back to him, resisting fiercely, ripping the thin shirt from her shoulders, baring her white, heaving bosom. Gasping, she struggled, until, little by little, his arms closed round her again. She braced her hands against his chest, fending him from her till she felt the muscles in her arms must crack, but the crushing force of his whole weight was bearing her steadily backwards, and downwards on to the soft cushions beside them. His hot breath was on her face, the sickening reek of his clothes was in her nostrils. She felt her resistance growing weaker, her heart was labouring, beating with wild bounds that suffocated her, the strength was going from her arms, only a moment more and her force would be exhausted. Her brain was growing numbed, as it had been when the man who held her had murdered the woman before her eyes. If he would only kill her now. Death would be easy compared with this. The faint hope that still lingered was almost extinguished. Ahmed had not come, and in her agony the thought of him was a further torture. The sneering words of Ibraheim Omair had not shaken her faith. He would come, but he would come too late. He would never know now that she loved him. Oh, God! How she loved him! Ahmed! Ahmed! And with the soundless cry the last remnant of her strength went all at once, and she fell weakly against the chief. He forced her to her knees, and, with his hand twined brutally in her curls, thrust her head back. There was a mad light in his eyes and a foam on his lips as he dragged the knife from his waistbelt and laid the keen edge against her throat. She did not flinch, and after a moment he dropped it with a horrible laugh.

"No, afterwards," he said, and picked her up unresistingly. He flung her on the cushions and for one awful moment she felt his hands on her. Then from outside came a sudden uproar and the sharp crack of rifles. Then in a lull in the firing the Sheik's powerful voice: "Diane! Diane!"

His voice and the knowledge of his nearness gave her new strength. She leaped up in spite of Ibraheim Omair's gripping hands. "Ahmed!" she screamed once, then the chief's hand dashed against her mouth, but, frantic, she caught it in her teeth, biting it to the bone, and as he wrenched it away, shrieked again, "Ahmed! Ahmed!"

But it seemed impossible that her voice could be heard above the demoniacal noise outside the tent, and she could not call again, for, with a snarl of rage, the chief caught her by the throat as he had caught the Arab woman. And like the Arab woman her hands tore at his gripping fingers vainly. Choking, stifling with the agony in her throat, her lungs seemed bursting, the blood was beating in her ears like the deafening roar of waves, and the room was darkening with the film that was creeping over her eyes. Her hands fell powerless to her sides and her knees gave way limply. He was holding her upright only by the clutch on her throat. The drumming in her ears grew louder, the tent was fading away into blackness. Dimly, with no kind of emotion, she realised that he was squeezing the life out of her and she heard his voice coming, as it were, from a great distance: "You will not languish long in Hawiyat without your lover. I will send him quickly to you."

She was almost unconscious, but she heard the sneering voice break suddenly and the deadly pressure on her throat relaxed as the chief's hands rapidly transferred their grip to her aching shoulders, swinging her away from him and in front of him. To lift her head was agony, and the effort brought back the black mist that had lessened with the slackening of Ibraheim Omair's fingers round her neck, but it cleared again sufficiently for her to see, through a blurring haze, the outline of the tall figure that was facing her, standing by the ripped-back doorway.

There was a pause, a silence that contrasted oddly with the tumult outside, and Diana wondered numbly why the Sheik did nothing, why he did not use the revolver that was clenched in his hand Then slowly she understood that he dared not fire, that the chief was holding her, a living shield, before him, sheltering himself behind the only thing that would deter Ahmed Ben Hassan's unerring shots. Cautiously Ibraheim Omair moved backward, still holding her before him, hoping to gain the inner room. But in the shock of his enemy's sudden appearance he miscalculated the position of the divan and stumbled against it, losing his balance for only a moment, but long enough to give the man whose revolver covered him the chance he wanted. With the cold ring of steel pressing against his forehead the robber chief's hands dropped from Diana, and she slid weak and trembling on to the rug, clasping her pulsating throat, moaning with the effort that it was to breathe.

For a moment the two men looked into each other's eyes and the knowledge of death leaped into Ibraheim Omair's. With the fatalism of his creed he made no resistance, as, with a slow, terrible smile, the Sheik's left hand reached out and fastened on his throat. It would be quicker to shoot, but as Diana had suffered so should her torturer die. All the savagery in his nature rose uppermost. Beside the pitiful, gasping little figure on the rug at his feet there was the memory of six mutilated bodies, his faithful followers, men of his own age who had grown to manhood with him, picked men of his personal bodyguard who had been intimately connected with him all his life, and who had served him with devotion and unwavering obedience. They and others who had from time to time fallen victims to Ibraheim Omair's hatred of his more powerful enemy. The man who was responsible for their deaths was in his power at last, the man whose existence was a menace and whose life was an offence, of whose subtleties he had been trained from a boy to beware by the elder Ahmed Ben Hassan, who had bequeathed to him the tribal hatred of the race of whom Ibraheim Omair was head, and whose dying words had been the wish that his successor might himself exterminate the hereditary enemy. But far beyond the feelings inspired by tribal hatred or the remembrance of the vow made five years ago beside the old Sheik's deathbed, or even the death of his own followers, was the desire to kill, with his bare hands, the man who had tortured the woman he loved. The knowledge of her peril, that had driven him headlong through the night to her aid, the sight of her helpless, agonised, in the robber chief's hands, had filled him with a madness that only the fierce joy of killing would cure. Before he could listen to the clamouring of the new love in his heart, before he could gather up into his arms the beloved little body that he was yearning for, he had to destroy the man whose murders were countless and who had at last fallen into his hands.

The smile on his face deepened and his fingers tightened slowly on their hold. But with the strangling clasp of Ahmed Ben Hassan's hands upon him the love of life waked again in Ibraheim Omair and he struggled fiercely. Crouched on the floor Diana watched the two big figures swaying in mortal combat with wide, fearful eyes, her hands still holding her aching throat. Ibraheim Omair wrestled for his life, conscious of his own strength, but conscious also of the greater strength that was opposed to him. The Sheik let go the hold upon his throat and with both arms locked about him manoeuvred to get the position he required, back to the divan. Then, with a wrestler's trick, he swept Ibraheim's feet from under him and sent his huge body sprawling on to the cushions, his knee on his enemy's chest, his hands on his throat. With all his weight crushing into the chief's breast, with the terrible smile always on his lips, he choked him slowly to death, till the dying man's body arched and writhed in his last agony, till the blood burst from his nose and mouth, pouring over the hands that held him like a vice.

Diana's eyes never left the Sheik's face, she felt the old paralysing fear of him rushing over her, irresistibly drowning for the moment even the love she had for him. She had seen him in cruel, even savage moods, but nothing that had ever approached the look of horrible pleasure that was on his face now. It was a revelation of the real man with the thin layer of civilisation stripped from him, leaving only the primitive savage drunk with the lust of blood. And she was afraid, with a shuddering horror, of the merciless, crimson-stained hands that would touch her, of the smiling, cruel mouth that would be pressed on hers, and of the murderous light shining in his fierce eyes. But for the dying wretch expiating his crimes so hideously she felt no pity, he was beyond all sympathy. She had seen him murder wantonly, and she knew what her own fate would have been if Ahmed Ben Hassan had not come. And the retribution was swift. The Sheik was being more merciful to him than the robber chief had been to many, a few moments of agony instead of hours of lingering torture.

The noise outside the tent was growing louder as the fighting rolled back in its direction, and once or twice a bullet ripped through the hangings. One that came closer than the others made Diana turn her head and she saw what Ahmed Ben Hassan, absorbed in the fulfilment of his horrible task, had not even thought of—the three big negroes and a dozen Arabs who had stolen in silently from the inner room. For once, in the intoxication of the moment, the Sheik was careless and caught off his guard. Agony leaped into her eyes. The fear of him was wiped out in the fear for him. She tried to warn him, but no sound would come from her throbbing throat, and she crawled nearer to him and touched him. He dropped the dead chief back into the tumbled cushions and looked up swiftly, and at the same moment Ibraheim Omair's men made a rush. Without a word he thrust her behind the divan and turned to meet them. Before his revolver they gave way for a moment, but the burly Nubians behind swept the Arabs forward. Three times he fired and one of the negroes and two Arabs fell, but the rest hurled themselves on him, and Diana saw him surrounded. His strength was abnormal, and for some minutes the struggling mass of men strained and heaved about him. Diana was on her feet, swaying giddily, powerless to help him, cold with dread. Then above the clamour that was raging inside and out she heard Saint Hubert's voice shouting, and with a shriek that seemed to rip her tortured throat she called to him. The Sheik, too, heard, and with a desperate effort for a moment won clear, but one of the Nubians was behind him, and, as Saint Hubert and a crowd of the Sheik's own men poured in through the opening, he brought down a heavy club with crashing force on Ahmed Ben Hassan's head, and as he fell another drove a broad knife deep into his back. For a few minutes more the tramping feet surged backward and forward over the Sheik's prostrate body. Diana tried to get to him, faint and stumbling, flung here and there by the fighting, struggling men, until a strong hand caught her and drew her aside. She strained against the detaining arm, but it was one of Ahmed's men, and she gave in as a growing faintness came over her. Mistily she saw Saint Hubert clear a way to his friend's side, and then she fainted, but only for a few moments. Saint Hubert was still on his knees beside the Sheik when she opened her eyes, and the tent was quite quiet, filled with tribesmen waiting in stoical silence. The camp of Ibraheim Omair had been wiped out, but Ahmed Ben Hassan's men looked only at the unconscious figure of their leader.

Saint Hubert glanced up hastily as Diana came to his side. "You are all right?" he asked anxiously, but she did not answer. What did it matter about her?

"Is he going to die?" she said huskily, for speaking still hurt horribly.

"I don't know—but we must get away from here. I need more appliances than I have with me, and we are too few to stay and risk a possible attack if there are others of Ibraheim Omair's men in the neighbourhood."

Diana looked down on the wounded man fearfully. "But the ride—the jolting," she gasped.

"It has got to be risked," replied Saint Hubert abruptly.

Of the long, terrible journey back to Ahmed Ben Hassan's camp Diana never remembered very much. It was an agony of dread and apprehension, of momentary waiting for some word or exclamation from the powerful Arab who was holding him, or from Saint Hubert, who was riding beside him, that would mean his death, and of momentary respites from fear and faint glimmerings of hope as the minutes dragged past and the word she was dreading did not come. Once a sudden halt seemed to stop her heart beating, but it was only to give a moment's rest to the Arab whose strength was taxed to the uttermost with the Sheik's inert weight, but who refused to surrender his privilege to any other. Moments of semi-unconsciousness, when she swayed against the arm of the watchful tribesman riding beside her, and his muttered ejaculation of "Allah! Allah!" sent a whispered supplication to her own lips to the God they both worshipped so differently. He must not die. God would not be so cruel.

From time to time Saint Hubert spoke to her, and the quiet courage of his voice steadied her breaking nerves. As they passed the scene of the ambuscade he told her of Gaston. It was there that the first band of waiting men met them, warned already of their coming by a couple of Arabs whom the Vicomte had sent on in advance with the news.

The dawn was breaking when they reached the camp. Diana had a glimpse of rows of unusually silent men grouped beside the tent, but all her mind was concentrated on the long, limp figure that was being carefully lifted down from the sweating horse. They carried him into the tent and laid him on the divan, beside which Henri had already put out all the implements that his master would need.

While Saint Hubert, with difficulty, cleared the tent of the Sheik's men Diana stood beside the divan and looked at him. He was soaked in blood that had burst through the temporary bandages, and his whole body bore evidence of the terrible struggle that had gone before the blow that had felled him. One blood-covered hand hung down almost touching the rug. Diana lifted it in her own, and the touch of the nerveless fingers sent a sob into her throat. She caught her lip between her teeth to stop it trembling as she laid his hand down on the cushions. Saint Hubert came to her, rolling up his shirt-sleeves significantly.

"Diane, you have been through enough," he said gently. "Go and rest while I do what I can for Ahmed. I will come and tell you as soon as I am finished."

She looked up fiercely. "It's no good telling me to go away, because I won't. I must help you. I can help you. I shall go mad if you don't let me do something. See! My hands are quite steady." She held them out as she spoke, and Saint Hubert gave in without opposition.

The weakness that had sent her trembling into his arms the day before had been the fear of danger to the man she loved, but in the face of actual need the courage that was so much a part of her nature did not fail her. He made no more remonstrances, but set about his work quickly. And all through the horrible time that followed she did not falter. Her face was deadly pale, and dark lines showed below her eyes, but her hands did not shake, and her voice was low and even. She suffered horribly. The terrible wound that the Nubian's knife had made was like a wound in her own heart. She winced as if the hurt had been her own when Saint Hubert's gentle, dexterous fingers touched the Sheik's bruised head. And when it was over and Raoul had turned aside to wash his hands, she slipped on to her knees beside him. Would he live? The courage that had kept her up so far had not extended to asking Saint Hubert again, and a few muttered words from Henri, to which the Vicomte had responded with only a shrug, had killed the words that were hovering on her lips. She looked at him with anguished eyes.

Only a few hours before he had come to her in all the magnificence of his strength. She looked at the long limbs lying now so still, so terribly, suggestively still, and her lips trembled again, but her pain-filled eyes were dry. She could not cry, only her throat ached and throbbed perpetually. She leaned over him whispering his name, and a sudden hunger came to her to touch him, to convince herself that he was not dead. She glanced back over her shoulder at Saint Hubert, but he had gone to the open doorway to speak to Yusef, and was standing out under the awning. She bent lower over the unconscious man; his lips were parted slightly, and the usual sternness of his mouth was relaxed.

"Ahmed, oh, my dear!" she whispered unsteadily, and kissed him with lips that quivered against the stillness of his. Then for a moment she dropped her bright head beside the bandaged one on the pillow, but when the Vicomte came back she was kneeling where he had left her, her hands clasped over one of the Sheik's and her face hidden against the cushions.

Saint Hubert put his hand on her shoulder. "Diane, you are torturing yourself unnecessarily. We cannot know for some time how it will go with him. Try and get some sleep for a few hours. You can do no good by staying here. Henri and I will watch. I will call you if there is any change, my word of honour."

She shook her head without looking up. "I can't go. I couldn't sleep."

Saint Hubert did not press it. "Very well," he said quietly, "but if you are going to stay you must take off your riding-boots and put on something more comfortable than those clothes."

She realised the sense of what he was saying, and obeyed him without a word. She even had to admit to herself a certain sensation of relief after she had bathed her aching head and throat, and substituted a thin, silk wrap for the torn, stained riding-suit.

Henri was pouring out coffee when she came back, and Saint Hubert turned to her with a cup in his outstretched hand. "Please take it. It will do you good," he said, with a little smile that was not reflected in his anxious eyes.

She took it unheeding, and, swallowing it hastily, went to the side of the divan again. She slid down on to the rug where she had knelt before. The Sheik was lying as she had left him. For a few moments she looked at him, then drowsily her eyes closed and her head fell forward on the cushions, and with a half-sad smile of satisfaction Saint Hubert gathered her up into his arms.

He carried her into the bedroom, hesitating beside the couch before he put her down. Surely one moment out of a lifetime might be granted to him. He would never have the torturing happiness of holding her in his arms again, would never again clasp her against the heart that was crying out for her with the same mad passion that had swept over him yesterday. He looked down longingly on the pale face lying against his arm, and his features contracted at the sight of the cruel marks marring the whiteness of her delicate throat. The love that all his life he had longed for, that he had sought vainly through many countries, had come to him at last, and it had come too late. The helpless loveliness lying in his arms was not for him. It was Ahmed whom she loved, Ahmed who had waked to such a tardy recognition of the priceless gift that she had given him, Ahmed whom he must wrest from the grim spectre that was hovering near him lest the light that shone in her violet eyes should go out in the blackness of despair. And yet as he looked at her with eyes filled with hopeless misery a demon of suggestion whispered within him, tempting him. He knew his friend as no one else did. What chance of happiness had any woman with a man like Ahmed Ben Hassan, at the mercy of his savage nature and passionate changeable moods? What reason to suppose that the love that had flamed up so suddenly at the thought that he had lost her would survive the knowledge of repossession? To him, all his life, a thing desired had upon possession become valueless. With the fulfilment of acquisition had come always disinterest. The pleasure of pursuit faded with ownership. Would this hapless girl who had poured out such a wealth of love at the feet of the man who had treated her brutally fare any better at his hands? Her chance was slight, if any. Ahmed in the full power of his strength again would be the man he had always been, implacable, cruel, merciless. Saint Hubert's own longing, his passionate, Gallic temperament, were driving him as they had driven him the day before. The longing to save her from misery was acute, that, and his own love, prompted by the urging of the desire within him. Then he trembled, and a great fear of himself came over him. Ahmed was his friend. Who was he that he should judge him? He could at least be honest with himself, he could own the truth. He coveted what was not his, and masked his envy with a hypocrisy that now appeared contemptible. The clasp of his arms around her seemed suddenly a profanation, and he laid her down very gently on the low couch, drawing the thin coverlet over her, and went back slowly to the other room.

He sent Henri away and sat down beside the divan to watch with a feeling of weariness that was not bodily. The great tent was very still, a pregnant silence seemed to hang in the air, a brooding hush that strained Saint Hubert's already overstrained nerves. He had need of all his calm, and he gripped himself resolutely. For a time Ahmed Ben Hassan lay motionless, and then, as the day crept on and the early rays of the warm sun filled the tent, he moved uneasily, and began to mutter feverishly in confused Arabic and French. At first the words that came were almost unintelligible, pouring out with rapid indistinctness, then by degrees his voice slowed, and hesitating, interrupted sentences came clearly from his lips. And beside him, with his face buried in his hands, Raoul de Saint Hubert thanked God fervently that he had saved Diana the added torture of listening to the revelations of the past four months.

The first words were in Arabic, then the slow, soft voice lapsed into French, pure as the Vicomte's own.

"Two hours south of the oasis with the three broken palm trees by the well . . . Lie still, you little fool, it is useless to struggle. You cannot get away, I shall not let you go . . . Why have I brought you here? You ask me why? *Mon Dieu!* Are you not woman enough to know? No! I will not spare you. Give me what I want willingly and I will be kind to you, but fight me, and by Allah! you shall pay the cost! . . . I know you hate me, you have told me so already. Shall I make you love me? . . . Still disobedient? When will you learn that I am master? . . . I have not tired of you yet, you lovely little wild thing, *garçon manqué* . . . You say she is cowed; I say she is content— content to give me everything I ask of her . . . For four months she has fought me. Why does it give me no pleasure to have broken her at last? Why do I want her still? She is English and I have made her pay for my hatred of her cursed race. I have tortured her to keep my vow, and still I want her . . . Diane, Diane, how beautiful you are! . . . What devil makes me hate Raoul after twenty years? Last night she only spoke to him, and when he went I cursed her till I saw the terror in her eyes. She fears me. Why should I care if she loves him . . . I knew she was not asleep when I went to her. I felt her quivering beside me . . . I wanted to kill Raoul when he would not come with me, but for that I would have gone back to her . . . Allah! how long the day has been . . . Has it been long to her? Will she smile or tremble when I come? . . . Where is Diane? . . . Diane, Diane, how could I know how much you meant to me? How could I know that I should love you? . . . Diane, Diane, my sunshine. The tent is cold and dark without you . . . Ibraheim Omair! That devil and Diane! Oh, Allah! Grant me time to get to her . . . How the jackals are howling . . . See, Raoul, there are the tents . . . Diane, where are you? . . . Grand Dieu! He has been torturing her! . . . You knew that I would come, *ma bien aimee*, only a few moments while I kill him, then I can hold you in my arms. *Dieu!* If you knew how much I loved you . . . Diane, Diane, it is all black. I cannot see you, Diane, Diane . . ."

And hour after hour with weary hopelessness the tired voice went on—"Diane, Diane . . ."

CHAPTER IX

It was evening when Diana opened drowsy and heavy eyes, a bitter taste in her mouth from the effects of the drug that Saint Hubert had given her. Everything had been laid out in readiness for her waking with the little touches that were characteristic of Zilah's handiwork, but the Arab girl herself was not visible. The lamp was lighted, and Diana turned her head languidly, still half confused, to look at the clock beside her. The tiny chime sounded seven times, and with a rush of recollection she leaped up. More than twelve hours since she had knelt beside him after drinking the coffee that Raoul had given her. She guessed what he had done and tried to be grateful, but the thought of what might have happened during the twelve hours she had lain like a log was horrible. She dressed with feverish haste and went into the outer room. It was filled with Arabs, many of whom she did not recognise, and she knew that they must belong to the reinforcements that Ahmed Ben Hassan had sent for. Two, who seemed from their appearance to be petty chiefs, were talking in low tones to Saint Hubert, who looked worn and tired. The rest were grouped silently about the divan, looking at the still-unconscious Sheik. The restlessness and delirium of the morning had passed and been succeeded by a death-like stupor. Nearest to him stood Yusef, his usual swaggering self-assurance changed into an attitude of deepest dejection, and his eyes, that were fixed on Ahmed Ben Hassan's face, were like those of a whipped dog.

Gradually the tent emptied until only Yusef was left, and at last, reluctantly, he too went, stopping at the entrance to speak to Saint Hubert, who had just taken leave of the two headmen.

The Vicomte came back, bringing a chair for Diana, and put her into it with gentle masterfulness. "Sit down," he said almost gruffly. "You look like a ghost."

She looked up at him reproachfully. "You drugged that coffee, Raoul. If he had died today while I was asleep I don't think I could ever have forgiven you."

"My dear child," he said gravely, "you don't know how near you were to collapse. If I had not made you sleep I should have had three patients on my hands instead of two."

"I am very ungrateful," she murmured, with a tremulous little smile.

Saint Hubert brought a chair for himself and dropped into it wearily. He felt very tired, the strain of the past twenty-four hours had been tremendous. He had a very real fear that was fast growing into a conviction that his skill was going to prove unequal to save his friend's life, and beside that anxiety and his physical fatigue he had fought a bitter fight with himself all day, tearing out of his heart the envy and jealousy that filled it, and locking away his love as a secret treasure to be hidden for always. His devotion to Ahmed Ben Hassan had survived the greatest test that could be imposed upon it, and had emerged from the trial strengthened and refined, with every trace of self obliterated. It had been the hardest struggle of his life, but it was over now, and all the bitterness had passed, leaving only a passionate desire for Diana's happiness that outweighed every other thought. One spark of comfort remained. He would not be quite useless. His help and sympathy would be necessary to her, and even for that he was grateful.

He looked across the divan at her, and the change that the last few hours had made in her struck him painfully. The alert, vigorous boyishness that had been so characteristic was gone. Her slim figure drooping listlessly in the big chair, her white face with the new marks of suffering on it, and her wide eyes burning with dumb misery, were all purely womanly. And yet though he resented the change he wished it could have gone further. The restraint she was putting on herself was unnatural. She asked no questions and she shed no tears. He could have borne them both easier than the silent anguish of her face. He feared the results of the emotion she was repressing so rigidly.

There was a long silence.

Henri came in once and Diana roused herself to ask for Gaston, and then relapsed into silent watchfulness again. She sighed once, a long quivering sigh that nearly broke Saint Hubert's heart. He rose and bent over the Sheik with his fingers on his wrist, and as he laid the nerveless hand down again she leaned nearer and covered it with her own.

"His hand is so big for an Arab's," she said softly, like a thought spoken aloud unconsciously.

"He is not an Arab," replied Saint Hubert with sudden, impatient vehemence. "He is English."

Diana looked up at him swiftly with utter bewilderment in her startled eyes. "I don't understand," she faltered. "He hates the English."

"Quand-même, he is the son of one of your English peers. His mother was a Spanish lady; many of the old noble Spanish families have Moorish blood in their veins, the characteristics crop up even after centuries. It is so with Ahmed, and his life in the desert has accentuated it. Has he never told you anything about himself?"

She shook her head. "Sometimes I have wondered—" she said reflectively. "He seemed different from the others, and there has been so much that I could never understand. But then again there were times when he seemed pure Arab," she added in a lower voice and with an involuntary shiver.

"You ought to know," said Saint Hubert. "Yes!" he went on firmly, as she tried to interrupt him. "It is due to you. It will explain so many things. I will take the responsibility. His father is the Earl of Glencaryll."

"But I know him," said Diana wonderingly. "He was a friend of my father. I saw him only a few months ago when Aubrey and I passed through Paris. He is such a magnificent-looking old man, so fierce and sad. Oh, now I know why that awful frown of Ahmed's has always seemed so familiar. Lord Glencaryll frowns like that. It is the famous Caryll scowl. But I still don't understand." She looked from Saint Hubert to the unconscious man on the divan and back to Saint Hubert with a new trouble growing in her eyes.

"I had better tell you the whole story," said Raoul, dropping back into his chair.

"Thirty-six years ago my father, who was as great a wanderer as I am, was staying here in the desert with his friend the Sheik Ahmed Ben Hassan. A chance acquaintance some years before over the purchase of some horses had ripened into a very intimate friendship that was unusual between a Frenchman and an Arab.

The Sheik was a wonderful man, very enlightened, with strong European tendencies. As a matter of pure fact he was not too much in sympathy with the French form of administration as carried on in Algeria, but he was not affected sufficiently by it to make any real difficulty. The territory that he regarded as his own lay too much to the south, and he kept his large and scattered tribe in too good order for any interference to be possible. He was unmarried, and the women of his own race seemed to have no attraction for him. He was wrapped up in his tribe and his horses. My father had come for a stay of some months. My mother had recently died and he wanted to get away from everything that reminded him of her. One evening, shortly after his arrival at the camp, a party of the Sheik's men who had been absent for some days in the north on the chief's affairs arrived, bringing with them a woman whom they had found wandering in the desert. How she had got there, or from what direction she had come, they did not know. They were nearer civilisation than Ahmed Ben Hassan's camp at the time, but with true native tendency to avoid responsibility they thought that the disposal of her was a matter more for their Sheik than themselves. She could give no account of herself, as, owing to the effects of the sun or other causes, she was temporarily out of her mind. Arabs are very gentle with any one who is mad—'Allah has touched them!' She was taken to the tent of one of the headmen, whose wife looked after her. For some days it was doubtful whether she would recover, and her condition was aggravated by the fact that she was shortly to become a mother. She did regain her senses after a time, however, but nothing could make her say anything about herself, and questions reduced her to terrible fits of hysterical crying which were prejudicial in her state of health. She seemed calmest when she was left quite alone, but even then she started at the slightest sound, and the headman's wife reported that she would lie for hours on her bed crying quietly to herself. She was quite young—seemingly not more than nineteen or twenty. From her accents my father decided that she was Spanish, but she would admit nothing, not even her nationality. In due course of time the child was born, a boy."

Saint Hubert paused a moment and nodded towards the Sheik. "Even after the child's birth she refused to give any account of herself. In that she was as firm as a rock; in everything else she was the frailest, gentlest little creature imaginable. She was very small and slender, with quantities of soft dark hair and beautiful great dark eyes that looked like a frightened fawn's. I have heard my father describe her many times, and I have seen the water-colour sketch he made of her—he was quite an amateur. Ahmed has it locked away somewhere. She nearly died when the baby was born, and she never recovered her strength. She made no complaint and never spoke of herself, and seemed quite content as long as the child was with her. She was a child herself in a great number of ways. It never seemed to occur to her that there was anything odd in her continued residence in the Sheik's camp. She had a tent and servants of her own, and the headman's wife was devoted to her. So were the rest of the camp for that matter. There was an element of the mysterious in her advent that had taken hold of the superstitious Arabs, and the baby was looked upon as something more than human and was adored by all the tribe. The Sheik himself, who had never looked twice at a woman before in his life, became passionately attached to her. My father says that he has never seen a man so madly in love as Ahmed Ben Hassan was with the strange white girl who had come so oddly into his life. He repeatedly implored her to marry him, and even my father, who has a horror of mixed marriages, was impelled to admit that any woman might have been happy with Ahmed Ben Hassan. She would not consent, though she would give no reason for her refusal, and the mystery that surrounded her remained as insolvable during the two years that she lived after the baby's birth as it had been on the day of her arrival. And her refusal made no difference with the Sheik. His devotion was wonderful. When she died my father was again visiting the camp. She knew that she was dying, and a few days before the end she told them her pitiful little history. She was the only daughter of one of the oldest noble houses in Spain, as poor as they were noble, and she had been married when she was seventeen to Lord Glencaryll, who had seen her with her parents in Nice. She had been married without any regard to her own wishes, and though she grew to love her husband she was always afraid of him. He had a terrible temper that was very easily roused, and, in those days, he also periodically drank a great deal more than was good for him, and when under the influence of drink behaved more like a devil than a man. She was very young and *gauche*, failing often to do what was required of her from mere nervousness. He was exigent and made no allowance for her youth and inexperience, and her life was one long torture. And yet in spite of it all she loved him. Even in speaking of it she insisted that the fault was hers, that the trouble was due to her stupidity, glossing over his brutality; in fact, it was not from her, but from inquiries that he made after her death, that my father learned most of what her life had been. It seems that Lord Glencaryll had taken her to Algiers and had wished to make a trip into the desert. He had been drinking heavily, and she did not dare to upset his plans by refusing to go with him or even by telling him how soon her child was going to be born. So she went with him, and one night something happened—what she would not say, but my father says he has never seen such a look of terror on any woman's face as she hurried over that part of her story. Whatever it was she waited until the camp was asleep and then slipped out into the desert, mad with fear, with no thought beyond a blind instinct of flight that drove her panic-stricken to face any danger rather than remain and undergo the misery she was flying from. She remembered hurrying onward, terrified by every sound and every shadow, frightened even by the blazing stars that seemed to be watching her and pointing out the way she had taken, until her mind was numb from utter weariness and she remembered nothing more until she awoke in the headman's tent. She had been afraid to say who she was lest she should be sent back to her husband. And with the birth of the child she became more than ever determined to preserve her secret. The boy should be spared the suffering she had herself endured, he should not be allowed to fall into the hands of his father to be at his mercy when the periodical drinking fits made him a very fiend of cruelty. She made my father and the Sheik swear that not until the boy grew to manhood should Lord Glencaryll be told of his existence. She wrote a letter for her husband which she gave into my father's keeping, together with her wedding ring, which had an inscription inside of it, and a miniature of Glencaryll which she had worn always hidden away from sight. She was very contrite with the Sheik, begging his forgiveness for the sorrow she had caused him and for keeping from his knowledge the fact that she was not free. She loved her husband loyally to the end, but the last few days that she lived the Sheik's devotion seemed to wake an answering tenderness in her heart. She was happiest when he was with her, and she died in his arms with his kisses on her lips. She left her boy in his keeping, and Ahmed Ben Hassan adopted him formally and made him his heir, giving him his own name—the hereditary name that the Sheik of the tribe has borne for generations. His word was law amongst his people, and there was no thought of any opposition to his wishes; further, the child was considered lucky, and his choice of successor was received with unanimous delight. All the passionate love that the Sheik had for the mother was transferred to the son. He idolised him, and the boy grew up believing that Ahmed Ben Hassan was his own father. With the traits he had inherited from his mother's people and with his desert upbringing he looked, as he does now, pure Arab. When he was fifteen my father induced the Sheik to send him to Paris to be educated. With his own European tendencies the Sheik had wished it also, but he could not bring himself to part with the boy before, and it was a tremendous wrench to let him go when he did. It was then that I first saw him. I was eighteen at the time, and had just begun my military training, but as my regiment was stationed in Paris I was able to be at home a good deal. He was such a handsome, high-spirited lad. Men mature very young in the desert and in many ways he was a great deal older than I was, in spite of my three years' seniority. But, of course, in other ways he was a perfect child. He had a fiendish temper and resented any check on his natural lawless inclinations. He loathed the restrictions that had to be put upon him and he hated the restraint of town life. He had been accustomed to having his own way in nearly everything, and to the constant adulation of the tribesmen, and he was not prepared to give to anybody else the obedience that he gave willingly to the Sheik. There were some very stormy times, and I never admired my father in anything so much as his handling of that young savage. His escapades were nerve-racking and his *beaux yeux* led him into endless scrapes. The only threat that reduced him to order was that of sending him home to the Sheik in disgrace. He would promise amendment and take himself off to the Bois to work off his superfluous energy on my father's horses—until he broke out again. But in spite of his temper and his *diableries* he was very lovable and everybody liked him.

"After a year with us in Paris my father, always mindful of his real nationality, sent him for two years to a tutor in England, where I had myself been. The tutor was an exceptional man, used to dealing with exceptional boys, and Ahmed did very well with him. I don't mean that he did much work—that he evaded skilfully and spent most of his time hunting and shooting. The only thing that he studied at all seriously was veterinary surgery, which he knew would be useful to him with his own horses, and in which his tutor was level-headed enough to encourage him. Then at the end of two years he came back to us for another year. He had gone to the desert every summer for his holidays, and on each occasion the Sheik let him return with greater reluctance. He was always afraid that the call of civilisation would be too much for his adopted son, especially as he grew older, but although Ahmed had changed very much from the wild desert lad who had first come to us, and had developed into a polished man of the world, speaking French and English as fluently as Arabic, with plenty of means to amuse himself in any way that he wished—for the Sheik was very rich and kept him lavishly supplied with money—and though in that last year he was with us he was courted and feted in a way that would have turned most people's heads, he was always secretly longing for the time when he would go back to the desert. It was the desert, not civilisation that called loudest to him. He loved the life and he adored the man whom he thought was his father. To be the son and heir of Ahmed Ben Hassan seemed to him to be the highest pinnacle that any man's ambition could reach. He was perfectly indifferent to the flattery and attention that his money and his good looks brought him. My father entertained very largely and Ahmed became the fashion—'*Le bel Arabe*' he was called, and he enjoyed a *succes fou* which bored him to extinction—and at the end of the year, having written to the Sheik for permission to go home, he shook the dust of Paris off his feet and went back to the desert. I went with him. It was my first visit and the first time that I had experienced Ahmed *en prince*. I had never seen him in anything but European clothes, and I got quite a shock when I came up on deck the morning that we arrived at Oran and found an Arab of the Arabs waiting for me. The robes and a complete change of carriage and expression that seemed to go with them altered him curiously and I hardly recognised him. Some of his men were waiting for him on the quay and their excitement was extraordinary. I realised from the deference and attention that the French officials paid to Ahmed the position that the old Sheik had made for himself and the high esteem in which he was held. We spent the rest of the day in arranging for the considerable baggage that he had brought with him to be forwarded by the camel caravan that had been sent for the purpose, and also in business for the Sheik in Oran. We spent the night in a villa on the outskirts of the town belonging to an old Arab who entertained us lavishly, and who spent the evening congratulating Ahmed heartily on having escaped from the clutches of the odious French, by no means abashed when Ahmed pointed out that there was an odious Frenchman present, for he dismissed me with a gesture that conveyed that my nationality was my misfortune and not my fault, and in impressing on him the necessity of immediately acquiring a wife or two and settling down for the good of the tribe—all this in the intervals of drinking coffee, listening to the most monotonous native music and watching barbaric dances. There was one particularly well-made dancing girl that the old man tried to induce Ahmed to buy, and he made a show of bargaining for her—not from any real interest he took in her, but merely to see the effect that it would have on me. But I refused to be drawn, and as my head was reeling with the atmosphere I escaped to bed and left him still bargaining. We started early next morning, and were joined a few miles out of the town by a big detachment of followers. The excitement of the day before was repeated on a very much larger scale. It was a novel experience for me, and I can hardly describe my feelings in the midst of that yelling horde of men, galloping wildly round us and firing their rifles until it seemed hardly possible that some accident would not happen. It was Ahmed's attitude that impressed me most. He took it all quietly as his due, and when he had had enough of it stopped it with a peremptory authority that was instantly obeyed, and apologised for the exuberant behaviour of his children. It was a new Ahmed to me; the boy I had known for four years seemed suddenly transformed into a man who made me feel very young. In France I had naturally always rather played elder brother, but here Ahmed was on his own ground and the roles seemed likely to be reversed. The arrival at the Sheik's camp was everything that the most lavish scenic producer could have wished. Though I had heard of it both from my father and Ahmed I was not quite prepared for the splendour with which the Sheik surrounded himself. With Eastern luxury was mingled many European adjuncts that added much to the comfort of camp life. The meeting between the Sheik and Ahmed was most touching. I had a very happy time and left with regret. The charm of the desert took hold of me then and has never left me since. But I had to return to my medical studies. I left Ahmed absorbed in his life and happier than I had ever seen him in Paris. He was nineteen then, and when he was twenty-one my father had the unpleasant task of carrying out Lady Glencaryll's dying wishes. He wrote to Lord Glencaryll asking him to come to Paris on business connected with his late wife, and, during the course of a very painful interview, put the whole facts before him. With the letter that the poor girl had written to her husband, with the wedding-ring and the locket, together with the sketch that my father had made of her, the proofs of the genuineness of the whole affair were conclusive. Glencaryll broke down completely. He admitted that his wife had every justification for leaving him, he spared himself nothing. He referred quite frankly to the curse of which he had been the slave and which had made him irresponsible for his actions when he was under its influence. He had never known himself what had happened that terrible night, but the tragedy of his wife's disappearance had cured him. He had made every effort to find her and it was many years before he gave up all hope. He mourned her bitterly, and worshipped her memory. It was impossible not to pity him, for he had expiated his fault with agony that few men can have experienced. The thought that he had a son and that son her child almost overwhelmed him. He had ardently desired an heir, and, thinking himself childless, the fact that his title and his old name, of which he was very proud, would die with him had been a great grief. His happiness in the knowledge of Ahmed's existence was pathetic, he was consumed with impatience for his son's arrival. Nothing had been said to Ahmed in case Lord Glencaryll should prove difficult to convince and thereby complicate matters, but his ready acceptance of the affair and his eagerness to see his son made further delay unnecessary, and my father sent for Ahmed. The old Sheik let him go in ignorance of what was coming. He had always dreaded the time when his adopted son would have to be told of his real parentage, fearful of losing him, jealous of sharing his affection and resenting anybody's claim to him over his own. And so, with the only instance he ever gave of want of moral courage, he sent Ahmed to Paris with no explanation, and left to my father the task of breaking to him the news. I shall never forget that day. It had been arranged that Ahmed should be told first and that afterwards father and son should meet. Ahmed arrived in the morning in time for *dejeuner*, and afterwards we went to my father's study, and there he told him the whole story as gently and as carefully as he could. Ahmed was standing by the window. He never said a word the whole time my father was speaking, and when he finished he stood quite still for a few moments, his face almost grey under the deep tan, his eyes fixed passionately on my father's—and then his fiendish temper broke out suddenly. It was a terrible scene. He cursed his father in a steady stream of mingled Arabic and French blasphemy that made one's blood run cold. He cursed all English people impartially. He cursed my father because he had dared to send him to England. He cursed me because I had been a party to the affair. The only person whom he spared was the Sheik; who after all was as much implicated as we were, but he never once mentioned him. He refused to see his father, refused to recognise that he was his father, and he left the house that afternoon and Paris that night, going straight back to the desert, taking with him Gaston, who had arranged some time before to enter his service as soon as his time in the cavalry was up. A letter that Lord Glencaryll wrote to him, addressed to Viscount Caryll, which is, of course, his courtesy title, begging for at least an interview, and which he gave to us to forward, was returned unopened, and scrawled across the envelope: '*Inconnu*. Ahmed Ben Hassan.' And since that day his hatred of the English had been a monomania, and he has never spoken a word of English. Later on, when we used to travel together, his obvious avoidance of English people was at times both awkward and embarrassing, and I have often had to go through the farce of translating into French or Arabic remarks made to him by English fellow-travellers, that is, when he condescended to notice the remarks, which was not often. From the day he learned the truth about himself for two years we saw nothing of him. Then the old Sheik asked us to visit him. We went with some misgivings as to what Ahmed's reception of us would be, but he met us as if nothing had happened. He ignored the whole episode and has never referred to it. It is a closed incident. The Sheik warned us that Ahmed had told him that any reference to it would mean the breaking off of all relations with us. But

Ahmed himself had changed indescribably. All the lovable qualities that had made him so popular in Paris were gone, and he had become the cruel, merciless man he has been ever since. The only love left in him was given to his adopted father, whom he worshipped. Later I was allowed back on the old footing, and he has always been good to Gaston, but with those three exceptions he has spared nobody and nothing. He is my friend, I love him, and I am not telling you more than you know already."

Saint Hubert broke off and looked anxiously at Diana, but she did not move or meet his gaze. She was sitting with her hand still clasped over the Sheik's and the other one shading her face, and the Vicomte went on speaking: "It is so easy to judge, so difficult to understand another person's temptations. Ahmed's position has always been a curious one. He has had unique temptations with always the means of gratifying them."

There was a longer pause, but still Diana did not move or speak.

"The curse of Ishmael had taken hold of me by then and I wandered continually. Sometimes Ahmed came with me; we have shot big game together in most parts of the globe. A few times he stayed with us in Paris, but never for long; he always wearied to get back to the desert. Five years ago the old Sheik died; he was an exceptionally strong man, and should have lived for years but for an accident which crippled him hopelessly and from which he died a few months afterwards. Ahmed's devotion during his illness was wonderful. He never left him, and since he succeeded to the leadership of the tribe he has lived continuously amongst his people, absorbed in them and his horses, carrying on the traditions handed down to him by his predecessor and devoting his life to the tribe. They are like children, excitable, passionate and headstrong, and he has never dared to risk leaving them alone too long, particularly with the menace of Ibraheim Omair always in the background. He has never been able to seek relaxation further afield than Algiers or Oran—" Saint Hubert stopped abruptly, cursing himself for a tactless fool. She could not fail to realise the significance of those visits to the gay, vicious little towns. The inference was obvious. His thoughtless words would only add to her misery. Her sensitive mind would shrink from the contamination they implied. If Ahmed was going to die, she would be desolate enough without forcing on her knowledge the unworthiness of the man she loved. He pushed his chair back impatiently and went to the open doorway. He felt that she wanted to be alone. She watched him go, then slipped to her knees beside the couch.

She had realised the meaning of Raoul's carelessly uttered words and they had hurt her poignantly, but it was no new sorrow. He had told her himself months ago, callously, brutally, sparing her nothing, extenuating nothing. She pressed her cheek against the hand she was holding. She did not blame him, she could only love him, no matter what his life had been. It was Ahmed as he was she loved, his faults, his vices were as much a part of him as his superb physique and the alternating moods that had been so hard to meet. She had never known him otherwise. He seemed to stand alone, outside the prescribed conventions that applied to ordinary men. The standards of common usage did not appear compatible with the wild desert man who was his own law and followed only his own precedent, defiant of social essentials and scornful of criticism. The proud, fierce nature and passionate temper that he had inherited, the position of despotic leadership in which he had been reared, the adulation of his followers and the savage life in the desert, free from all restraint, had combined to produce the haughty unconventionalism that would not submit to the ordinary rules of life. She could not think of him as an Englishman. The mere accident of his parentage was a factor that weighed nothing. He was and always would be an Arab of the wilderness. If he lived! He *must* live! He could not go out like that, his magnificent strength and fearless courage extinguished by a treacherous blow that had not dared to meet him face to face—in spite of the overwhelming numbers—but had struck him down from behind, a coward stroke. He must live, even if his life meant death to her hopes of happiness; that was nothing compared with his life. She loved him well enough to sacrifice anything for him. If he only lived she could bear even to be put out of his life. It was only he that mattered, his life was everything. He was so young, so strong, so made to live. He had so much to live for. He was essential to his people. They needed him. If she could only die for him. In the days when the world was young the gods were kind, they listened to the prayers of hapless lovers and accepted the life that was offered in place of the beloved whose life was claimed. If God would but listen to her now. If He would but accept her life in exchange for his. If—! if—!

Her fingers crept up lightly across his breast, fearful lest even their tender touch should injure his battered body, and she looked long and earnestly at him. His crisp brown hair was hidden by the bandages that, dead white against his tanned face, swathed his bruised head. His closed eyes with the thick dark lashes curling on his cheek, hiding the usual fierce expression that gleamed in them, and the relaxation of the hard lines of his face made him look singularly young. That youthful look had been noticeable often when he was asleep, and she had watched it wondering what Ahmed the boy had been like before he grew into the merciless man at whose hands she had suffered so much.

And now the knowledge of his boyhood seemed to make him even dearer than he had been before. What sort of man would he have been if the little dark-eyed mother had lived to sway him with her gentleness? Poor little mother, helpless and fragile!—yet strong enough to save her boy from the danger that she feared for him, but paying the price of that strength with her life, content that her child was safe.

Diana thought of her own mother dying in the arms of a husband who adored her, and then of the little Spanish girl slipping away from life, a stranger in a strange land, her heart crying out for the husband whom she still loved, turning in ignorance of his love for consolation in the agony of death to the lover she had denied, and seeking comfort in his arms. A sudden jealousy of the two dead women shook her. They had been loved. Why could not she be loved? Wherein did she fail that he would not love her? Other men had loved her, and his love was all she longed for in the world. To feel his arms around her only once with love in their touch, to see his passionate eyes kindle only once with the light she prayed for. She drew a long sobbing breath. "Ahmed, *mon bel Arabe*," she murmured yearningly.

She rose to her feet. She was afraid of breaking down, of giving way to the fear and anxiety that racked her. She turned instinctively to the help and sympathy that offered and went to Saint Hubert, joining him under the awning. Usually at night the vicinity of the Sheik's tent was avoided by the tribesmen, even the sentry on guard was posted at some little distance. Kopec curled up outside the doorway kept ample watch. But tonight the open space was swarming with men, some squatting on the ground in circles, others clustered together in earnest conversation, and far off through the palm trees she caught an occasional glimpse of mounted men. Yusef and the headmen acting under him were taking no risks, there was to be no chance of a surprise attack.

"You must be very tired, Raoul," she said, slipping her hand through his arm, for her need was almost as much for physical as mental support. The frank touch of her hand sent a quiver through him, but he suppressed it, and laid his own hand over her cold fingers.

"I must not think of that yet. Later on, perhaps, I can rest a little. Henri can watch; he is almost as good a doctor as I am, the incomparable Henri! Ahmed and I have always quarrelled over the respective merits of our servants."

He felt her hand tighten on his arm at the mention of the Sheik's name and heard the smothered sigh that she choked back. They stood in silence for a while watching the shifting groups of tribesmen. A little knot of low-voiced men near them opened up, and one of their number came to Saint Hubert with an inquiry.

"The men are restless." Raoul said when the Arab had gone back to his fellows with all the consolation the Vicomte could give him. "Their devotion is very strong. Ahmed is a god to them. Their anxiety takes them in a variety of ways. Yusef, who has been occupied with his duties most of the day, has turned to religion for the first time in his life, he has gone to say his prayers with the pious Abdul, as he thinks that Allah is more likely to listen if his petitions go heavenward in company with the holy man's."

Diana's thoughts strayed back to the story that Saint Hubert had told her. "Does Lord Glencaryll know that you see Ahmed?" she asked.

"Oh yes. He and my father became great friends. He often stays with us in Paris. We are a link between him and Ahmed. He is always hungry for any news of him, and still clings to the hope that one day he will relent. He has never made any further effort to open up relations with him because he knows it would be useless. If there is to be any *rapprochement* between them it must come from Ahmed. They have almost met accidentally once or twice, and Glencaryll has once seen him. It was at the opera. He was staying in Paris for some months and had a box. I had gone across from our own box on the other side of the house to speak to him. There were several people with him. I was standing beside him, talking. Ahmed had just come into our box opposite and was standing right in the front looking over the theatre. Something had annoyed him and he was scowling. The likeness was unmistakable. Glencaryll gave a kind of groan and staggered back against me. 'Good God! Who is that?' he said, and I don't think he knew he was speaking out loud.

"A man next him looked in the direction he was looking and laughed. 'That's the Saint Huberts' wild man of the desert. Looks fierce, doesn't he? The women call him *"le bel Arabe."* He certainly wears European clothes with better grace than most natives. He is said to have a peculiar hatred of the English, so you'd better give him a wide berth, Glencaryll, if you don't want to be bow-stringed or have your throat cut, or whatever fancy form of death the fellow cultivates in his native habitat. Raoul can tell you all about him.'

"There was not any need for me to tell him. Fortunately the opera began and the lights went down, and I persuaded him to go away before the thing was over."

Diana gave a little shiver. She felt a great sympathy coming over her for the lonely old man, hoping against hope for the impossible, that she had not felt earlier in the evening. He, too, was wearing his heart out against the inflexible will of Ahmed Ben Hassan.

She shivered again and turned back into the tent with Saint Hubert. They halted by the couch and stood for a long time in silence. Then Diana slowly raised her head and looked up into Raoul's face, and he read the agonised question in her eyes.

"I don't know," he said gently. "All things are with Allah."

CHAPTER X

The night grew hotter and the atmosphere more oppressive. Wrapped in a thin silk kimono Diana lay very still on the outside of the wide couch in the inner room, propped high with pillows that the shaded light of the little reading-lamp beside her might fall on the book she held, but she was not reading.

It was Raoul's latest book, that he had brought with him, but she could not concentrate her mind on it, and it lay idle on her knee—while her thoughts were far away. It was three months since the night that Saint Hubert had almost given up hope of being able to save the Sheik's life—a night that had been followed by days of suspense that had reduced Diana to a weary-eyed shadow of her former vigorous self, and had left marks on Raoul that would never be effaced. But thanks to his great strength and splendid constitution the Sheik had rallied and after the first few weeks convalescence had been rapid. When the terrible fear that he might die was past it had been a wonderful happiness to wait on him. With the determination to live for the moment, to which she had forced herself, she had banished everything from her mind but the joy of being near him and of being necessary to him. It had been a very silent service, for he would lie for hours with closed eyes without speaking, and something that she could not master kept her tongue-tied in his presence when they were alone. Only once he had referred to the raid. As she bent over him to do some small office his fingers closed feebly round her wrist and his eyes, with a searching apprehension in them, looked into hers for the first time since the night when she had fled from his curses.

"Was it—in time?" he whispered slowly, and as she nodded with crimson cheeks and lowered eyes he turned his head away without another word, but a shudder that he was too weak to control shook him.

But the happiness of ministering to him passed very swiftly. As he grew stronger he managed so that she was rarely alone with him, and he insisted on her riding twice every day, sometimes with Saint Hubert, sometimes with Henri, coolly avowing a preference for his own society or that of Gaston, who was beginning to get about again. Later, too, he was much occupied with headmen who came in from the different camps, and as the days passed she found herself more and more excluded from the intimacy that had been so precious. She was thrown much into the society of Raoul de Saint Hubert. All that they had gone through together had drawn them very closely to each other, and Diana often wondered what her girlhood would have been like if it had been spent under his guardianship instead of that of Sir Aubrey Mayo. The sisterly affection she had never given her own brother she gave to him, and, with the firm hold over himself that he had never again slackened, the Vicomte accepted the role of elder brother which she unconsciously imposed on him.

It was hard work sometimes, and there were days when he dreaded the daily rides, when the strain seemed almost more than he could bear, and he began to make tentative suggestions about resuming his wanderings, but always the Sheik pressed him to stay.

Ahmed Ben Hassan's final recovery was quick, and the camp soon settled down into normal conditions. The reinforcements were gone back to the different camps from which they had been drawn. There was no further need of them. Ibraheim Omair's tribe, with their leader dead, had broken up and scattered far to the south; there was no chief to keep them together and no headman strong enough to draw them round a new chieftain, for Ibraheim had allowed no member of his tribe to attain any degree of wealth or power that might prove him a rival; so they had split up into numerous small bands lacking cohesion. In fulfilling the vow made to his predecessor Ahmed Ben Hassan had cleared the desert of a menace that had hung over it for many years.

The relations between the Sheik and Saint Hubert had gone back to what they had been the night of Raoul's arrival, before his candid criticism had roused the Sheik's temper and fired his jealousy. The recollection of the miserable week that had preceded the raid had been wiped out in all that had followed it. No shadow could ever come between them again since Raoul had voluntarily stood on one side and sacrificed his own chance of happiness for his friend's.

And with the Sheik's complete recovery his attitude towards Diana had reverted to the cold reserve that had chilled her before— a reserve that was as courteous as it was indifferent. He had avoided her as much as had been possible, and the continual presence of Saint Hubert had been a barrier between them. Unostensibly but effectually he had contrived that Raoul should never leave them alone. Though he included her in the general conversation he rarely spoke to her directly, and often she found him looking at her with his fierce eyes filled with an expression that baffled her, and as each time the quick blood rushed into her face his forehead drew together in the heavy frown that was so characteristic. During meals it was Raoul that kept the conversation from lapsing with ready tact and an eloquent flow of words, ranging over many subjects. In the evening the men became immersed in the projection of Saint Hubert's new book, for details of which he was drawing on the Sheik's knowledge, and long after Diana left them she could hear the two voices, both deep and musical, but Raoul's quicker and more emphatic, continuously rising and falling, till at last Raoul would go to his own tent and Gaston would come—noiseless and soft-toned as his master. Ordinarily the Sheik dispensed with him at night, but since his wound, the valet, as soon as he had himself recovered, had always been in attendance. Some nights he lingered talking, and others the Sheik dismissed him in a few minutes with only a curt word or two, and then there would be silence, and Diana would bury her face in her pillow and writhe in her desperate loneliness, sick with longing for the strong arms she had once dreaded and the kisses she had once loathed. He had slept in the outer room since his illness, and tossing feverishly on the soft cushions of the big empty bed in which she lay alone Diana had suffered the greatest humiliation she had yet experienced. He had never loved her, but now he did not even want her. She was useless to him. She was less than nothing to him. He had no need of her. She would lie awake listening wearily to the tiny chimes of the little clock with the bitter sense of her needlessness crushing her. She was humbled to the very dust by his indifference. The hours of loneliness in the room that was redolent with associations of him were filled with memories that tortured her. In her fitful sleep her dreams were agonies from which she awakened with shaking limbs and shuddering breath, and waking, her hand would stretch out groping to him till remembrance came with cruel vividness.

In the daytime, too, she had been much alone, for as soon as the Sheik was strong enough to sit in the saddle the two men had ridden far afield every day, visiting the outlying camps and drawing into Ahmed Ben Hassan's own hands again the affairs that had had to be relegated to the headmen.

At last Raoul had announced that his visit could be protracted no longer and that he must resume his journey to Morocco. He was going up to Oran and from there to Tangier by coasting steamer, collecting at Tangier a caravan for his expedition through Morocco. His decision once made he had speeded every means of getting away with a despatch that had almost suggested flight.

To Diana his going meant the hastening of a crisis that could not be put off much longer. The situation was becoming impossible. She had said goodbye to him the night before. She had never guessed the love she had inspired in him, and she wondered at the sadness in his eyes and his unaccustomed lack of words. He had wanted to say so much and he had said so little. She must never guess and Ahmed must never guess, so he played the game to the end. Only that night after she had left them the voices sounded in the adjoining room for a very short time. And this morning he and Ahmed Ben Hassan had ridden away at daybreak. She had not been asleep; she had heard them go, and almost she wished Raoul back, for with his presence the vague fear that assailed her seemed further away. The camp had seemed very lonely and the day very long.

She had ridden with Gaston, and hurried over her solitary dinner, and since then she had been waiting for the Sheik to come back. In what mood would he come? Since Raoul's announcement of his departure he had been more than usually taciturn and reserved. The book she held slipped at length on to the floor, and she let it he unheeded. The usual stillness of the desert seemed tonight unusually still-sinister even—and the silence was so intense that the sudden squeal of a stallion a little distance away made her start with madly racing heart Earlier in the evening a tom-tom had been going persistently in the men's lines, and later a native pipe had shrilled thinly in monotonous cadence; but she had grown accustomed to these sounds; they were of nightly occurrence and they soothed rather than irritated her, and when they stopped the quiet had become intensified to such a degree that she would have welcomed any sound. Tonight her nerves were on edge. She was restless and excited, and her thoughts were chaos.

She was alone again at his mercy. What would his attitude be? Her hands clenched on her knees. At times she lay almost without breathing, straining to hear the faintest sound that would mean his return, and then again lest she should hear what she listened for. She longed for him passionately, and at the same time she was afraid, He had changed so much that there were moments when she had the curious feeling that it was a stranger who was coming back to her, and she both dreaded his coming and yearned for it with a singular combination of emotions. She looked round the room where she had at once suffered so much and been so happy with troubled eyes. She had never been nervous before, but tonight her imagination ran riot. There was electricity in the air which acted on her overstrung nerves. The little shaded lamp threw a circle of light round the bed, but left the rest of the room dim, and the dusky corners seemed full of odd new shadows that came and went illusively. Hangings and objects that were commonly familiar to her took on fantastic shapes that she watched nervously, till at last she brushed her hand across her eyes with a laugh of angry impatience. Was the love that had changed her so completely also making her a coward? Had even her common-sense been lost in the one great emotion that held her? She understood perfectly the change that had taken place in her. She had never had any illusions about herself, and had never attempted to curb the obstinate self-will and haughty pride that had characterized her. She thought of it curiously, her mind going back over the last few months that had changed her whole life. The last mad freak for which she had paid so dearly had been the outcome of an arrogant determination to have her own way in the face of all protests and advice. And with a greater arrogance and a determination stronger than her own Ahmed Ben Hassan had tamed her as he tamed the magnificent horses that he rode. He had been brutal and merciless, using no half measures, forcing her to obedience by sheer strength of will and compelling a complete submission. She thought of how she had feared and hated him with passionate intensity, until the hatred had been swamped by love as passionate and as intense. She did not know why she loved

197

him, she had never been able to analyse the passion that held her so strongly, but she knew deep down in her heart that it went now far past his mere physical beauty and superb animal strength. She loved him blindly with a love that had killed her pride and brought her to his feet humbly obedient. All the love that had lain dormant in her heart for years was given to him. Body and soul she belonged to him. And the change within her was patent in her face, the haughty expression in her eyes had turned to a tender wistfulness, with a curious gleam of expectancy that flickered in them perpetually; the little mutinous mouth had lost the scornful curve. And with the complete change in her expression she was far more beautiful now than she had ever been. But with her love was the fear of him that she had learned during the first hours of her captivity, the physical fear that she had never lost, even during the happy weeks that had preceded the coming of Saint Hubert, and the greater fear that was with her always, and that at times drove her, with wide-stricken eyes, wildly to pace the tent as if to escape the shadow that hung over her—the fear of the time when he should tire of her. The thought racked her, and now, as always, she tried to put it from her, but it continued, persistently haunting her like a grim spectre. Always the same thought tortured her—he had not taken her for love. No higher motive than a passing fancy had stirred him. He had seen her, had wished for her and had taken her, and once in his power it had amused him to break her to his hand. She realised all that. And he had been honest, he had never pretended to love her. Often when the humour took him he could be gentle, as in those last few weeks, but gentleness was not love, and she had never seen the light that she longed for kindle in his eyes. His caresses had been passionate or careless with his mood. She did not know that he loved her. She had not been with him during the long hours of his delirium and she had not heard what Raoul de Saint Hubert had heard. And since his recovery his attitude of aloofness had augmented her fear. There seemed only one construction to put on his silence, and his studied and obvious avoidance of her. The passing fancy had passed. It was as if the fleeting passion he had had for her had been drained from him with the blood that flowed from the terrible wound he had received. He was tired of her and seeking for a means to disembarrass himself of her. Vaguely she felt that she had known this for weeks, but tonight was the first time that she had had courage to be frank with herself. It must be so. Everything pointed to it; the curious expression she had seen in his eyes and his constant heavy frown all confirmed it. She flung her arm across her eyes with a little moan. He was tired of her and the bottom had fallen out of her world. The instinct to fight for his love that had been so strong in her the day that Ibraheim Omair had captured her had died with the death of all her hopes. Her spirit was broken. She knew that her will was helpless against his, and with a fatalism that she had learned in the desert she accepted the inevitable with a crushed feeling of hopelessness.

She wondered numbly what would become of her. It did not seem to matter much. Nothing mattered now that he did not want her any more. The old life was far away, in another world. She could never go back to it. She did not care. It was nothing to her. It was only here in the desert, in Ahmed Ben Hassan's arms, that she had become alive, that she had learned what life really meant, that she had waked both to happiness and sorrow.

The future stretched out blank and menacing before her, but she turned from it with a great sob of despair. It was on him that her thoughts were fixed. How would life be endurable without him? Dully she wondered why she did not hate him for having done to her what he had done, for having made her what she was. But nothing that he could do could kill the love now that he had inspired. And she would never regret. She would always have the memory of the fleeting happiness that had been hers—in after years that memory would be all that she would have to live for. Even in her heart she did not reproach him, there was no bitterness in her misery. She had always known that it would come, though she had fenced with it, shutting it out of her mind resolutely. He had never led her to expect anything else. There was no link to bring them closer together, no bond between them. If she could have had the promise of a child. Alone though she was the sensitive colour flamed into her cheeks, and she hid her face in the pillows with a quivering sob. A child that would be his and hers, a child—a boy with the same passionate dark eyes, the same crisp brown hair, the same graceful body, who would grow up as tall and strong, as brave and fearless as his father. Surely he must love her then. Surely the memory of his own mother's tragic history would make him merciful to the mother of his son. But she had no hope of that mercy. She lay shaking with passionate yearning and the storm of bitter tears that swept over her, hungry for the clasp of his arms, faint with longing. The pent-up misery of weeks that she had crushed down surged over. There was nobody to hear the agonising sobs that shook her from head to foot. She could relax the control that she had put upon herself and which had seemed to be slowly turning her to stone. She could give way to the emotion that, suppressed, had welled up choking in her throat and gripped her forehead like red-hot bands eating into her brain. Tears were not easy to her. She had not wept since that first night when, with the fear of worse than death, she had grovelled at his feet, moaning for mercy. She had not wept during the terrible hours she was in the power of Ibraheim Omair, nor during the days that Raoul de Saint Hubert had fought for his friend's life. But tonight the tears that all her life she had despised would not be denied. Tortured with conflicting emotions, unsatisfied love, fear and uncertainty, utterly unnerved, she gave herself up at last to the feelings she could no longer restrain. Prone on the wide bed, her face buried in the pillows, her hands clutching convulsively at the silken coverings, she wept until she had no more tears, until the anguished, sobs died away into silence and she lay quiet, exhausted.

She wrestled with herself. The weakness that she had given way to must be conquered. She knew that, without any possibility of doubt, his coming would seal her fate—whatever it was to be. She must wait until then. A long, shuddering sigh ran through her. "Ahmed! Ahmed Ben Hassan," she murmured slowly, lingering with wistful tenderness on the words. She pressed her face closer into the cushions, clasping her hands over her head, and for a long time lay very still. The heat was intense and every moment the tent seemed to grow more airless. The room was stifling, and, with a little groan, Diana sat up, pushing the heavy hair oft her damp forehead, and covered her flushed face with her hands. A cicada began its shrill note close by, chirping with maddening persistency. Quite suddenly her mind was filled with thoughts of her own people, the old home in England, the family for whose honour her ancestors had been so proudly jealous. Even Aubrey, lazy and self-indulgent as he was, prized the family honour as he prized nothing else on earth; and now she, proud Diana Mayo, who had the history of her race at her fingers' ends, who had gloried in the long line of upright men and chaste women, had no thankfulness in her heart that in her degradation she had been spared a crowning shame. Beside her love everything dwindled into nothingness. He was her life, he filled her horizon. Honour itself was lost in the absorbing passion of her love. He had stripped it from her and she was content that it should lie at his feet. He had made her nothing, she was his toy, his plaything, waiting to be thrown aside. She shuddered again and looked around the tent that she had shared with him with a bitter smile and sad, hunted eyes . . . After her—who? The cruel thought persisted. She was torn with a mad, primitive jealousy, a longing to kill the unknown woman who would inevitably succeed her, a desire that grew until a horror of her own feelings seized her, and she shrank down, clasping her hands over her ears to shut out the insidious voice that seemed actually whispering beside her. The Persian hound in the next room had whined uneasily from time to time, and now he pushed his way past the curtain and stalked across the thick rugs. He nuzzled his shaggy head against her knee, whimpering unhappily, looking up into her face. And when she noticed him he reared up and flung his long body across her lap, thrusting his wet nose into her face. She caught his head in her hands and rubbed her cheek against his rough hair, crooning over him softly. Even the dog was comfort in her loneliness, and they both waited for their master.

She pushed him down at length, and with her hand on his collar went into the other room. A solitary lamp burned dimly. She crossed to the doorway and pulled aside the flap, and a small, white-clad figure rose up before her.

"Is that you, Gaston?" she asked involuntarily, though she knew that the question was unnecessary, for he always slept across the entrance to the tent when the Sheik was away.

"À votre service, Madame."

For a few minutes she did not speak, and Gaston stood silent beside her. She might have remembered that he was there. He never stirred far beyond the sound of her voice whenever she was alone in the camp. He was always waiting, unobtrusive, quick to carry out her requests, even to anticipate them. With him standing beside her she thought of the time when they had fought side by side—all difference in rank eclipsed in their common danger. The servant had been merged into the man, and a man who had the courage to do what he had attempted when he had faced her at what had seemed the last moment with his revolver clenched in a hand that had not shaken, a man at whose side and by whose hand she would have been proud to die. They were men, these desert dwellers, master and servants alike; men who endured, men who did things, inured to hardships, imbued with magnificent courage, splendid healthy animals. There was nothing effete or decadent about the men with whom Ahmed Ben Hassan surrounded himself.

Diana had always liked Gaston; she had been touched by his unvarying respectful attitude that had never by a single word or look conveyed the impression that he was aware of her real position in his master's camp. He treated her as if she were indeed what from the bottom of her heart she wished she was. He was solicitous without being officious, familiar with no trace of impertinence, He was Diana's first experience of a class of servant that still lingers in France, a survival of pre-Revolution days, who identify themselves entirely with the family they serve, and in Gaston's case this interest in his master had been strengthened by experiences shared and dangers faced which had bound them together with a tie that could never be broken and had raised their relations on to a higher plane than that of mere master and man. Those relations had at first been a source of perpetual wonder to Diana, brought up in the rigid atmosphere of her brother's establishment, where Aubrey's egoism gave no opportunity for anything but conventional service, and in their wanderings, where personal servants had to be often changed. Even Stephens was, in Aubrey's eyes, a mere machine.

Very soon after she had been brought to Ahmed Ben Hassan's camp she had realised that Gaston's devotion to the Sheik had been extended to herself, but since the night of the raid he had frankly worshipped her.

It was very airless even out-of-doors. She peered into the darkness, but there was little light from the tiny crescent moon, and she could see nothing. She moved a few steps forward from under the awning to look up at the brilliant stars twinkling overhead. She had watched them so often from Ahmed Ben Hassan's arms; they had become an integral part of the passionate Oriental nights. He loved them, and when the mood was on him, watched them untiringly, teaching her to recognise them, and telling her countless Arab legends connected with them, sitting under the awning far info the night, till gradually his voice faded away from her ears, and long after she was asleep he would sit on motionless, staring up into the heavens, smoking endless cigarettes. Would it be given to her ever to watch them again sparkling against the blue-blackness of the sky, with the curve of his arm round her and the steady beat of his heart under her cheek? A stab of pain went: through her. Would anything ever be the same again? Everything had changed since the coming of Raoul de Saint Hubert. A weary sigh broke from her lips.

"Madam is tired?" a respectful voice murmured at her ear.

Diana started. She had forgotten the valet. "It is so hot. The tent was stifling," she said evasively.

Gaston's devotion was of a kind that sought practical demonstration. *"Madame veut du café?"* he suggested tentatively. It was his universal panacea, but at the moment it sounded almost grotesque.

Diana felt an hysterical desire to laugh which nearly turned into tears, but she checked herself. "No, it is too late."

"In one little moment I will bring it," Gaston urged persuasively, unwilling to give up his own gratification in serving her.

"No, Gaston. It makes me nervous," she said gently.

Gaston heaved quite a tragic sigh. His own nerves were steel and his capacity for imbibing large quantities of black coffee at any hour of the day or night unlimited.

"Une limonade?" he persisted hopefully.

She let him bring the cool drink more for his pleasure than for her own. "Monseigneur is late," she said slowly, straining her eyes again into the darkness.

"He will come," replied Gaston confidently. "Kopec is restless, he is always so when Monseigneur is coming."

She looked down for a moment thoughtfully at the dim shape of the hound lying at the man's feet, and then with a last upward glance at the bright stars turned back into the tent. All her nervous fears had vanished in speaking to Gaston, who was the embodiment of practical common sense; earlier, when unreasoning terror had taken such a hold on her, she had forgotten that he was within call, faithful and devoted. She picked up the fallen book, and lying down again forced herself to read, but though her eyes followed the lines mechanically she did not sense what she was reading, and all the time her ears were strained to catch the earliest sound of his coming.

At last it came. Only a suggestion at first—a wave of thought caught by her waiting brain, an instinctive intuition, and she started up tense with expectancy, her lips parted, her eyes wide, hardly breathing, listening intently. And when he came it was with unexpected suddenness, for, in the darkness, the little band of horsemen were invisible until they were right on the camp, and the horses' hoofs made no sound. The stir caused by his arrival died away quickly. For a moment there was a confusion of voices, a jingle of accoutrements, one of the horses whinnied, and then in the ensuing silence she heard him come into the tent. Her heart raced suffocatingly. There was a murmur of conversation, the Sheik's low voice and Gaston's quick animated tones answering him, and then the servant hurried out. Acutely conscious of every sound, she waited motionless, her hands gripping the soft mattress until her fingers cramped, breathing in long, painful gasps as she tried to stop the laboured beating of her heart. In spite of the heat a sudden coldness crept over her, and she shivered violently from time to time. Her face was quite white, even her lips were colourless and her eyes, fixed on the curtain which divided the two rooms, glittered feverishly. With her intimate knowledge every movement in the adjoining room was as perceptible as if she had seen it. He was pacing up and down as he had paced on the night when Gaston's fate was hanging in the balance, as he always paced when he was deliberating anything, and the scent of his cigarette filled her room. Once he paused near the communicating curtain and her heart gave a wild leap, but after a moment he moved away. He stopped again at the far end of the tent, and she knew from the faint metallic click that he was loading his revolver. She heard him lay it down on the little writing-table, and then the steady tramping began once more. His restlessness made her uneasy. He had been in the saddle since early dawn. Saint Hubert had advised him to be careful for some weeks yet. It was imprudent not to rest when opportunity offered. He was so careless of himself. She gave a quick, impatient sigh, and the tender light in her eyes deepened into an anxiety that was half maternal. In spite of his renewed strength and his laughing protests at Raoul's warnings, coupled with a physical demonstration on his less muscular friend that had been very conclusive, she could never forget that she had seen him lying helpless as a child, too weak even to raise his hand. Nothing could ever take the remembrance from her, and nothing could ever alter the fact that in his weakness he had been dependent on her. She had been necessary to him then. She had a moment's fierce pleasure in the thought, but it faded as suddenly as it had come. It had been an ephemeral happiness.

At last she heard the divan creak under his weight, but not until Gaston came back bringing his supper. As he ate he spoke, and his first words provoked an exclamation of dismay from the Frenchman, which was hastily smothered with a murmured apology, and then Diana became aware that others had come into the room. He spoke to each in turn, and she recognised Yusef's clear, rather high-pitched voice arguing with the taciturn head camelman, whose surly intonations and behaviour matched the bad-tempered animals to whom he was devoted, until a word from Ahmed Ben Hassan silenced them both. There were two more who received their orders with only a grunt of acquiescence.

Presently they went out, but Yusef lingered, talking volubly, half in Arabic, half in French, but lapsing more and more into the vernacular as he grew excited. Even in the midst of her trouble the thought of him sent a little smile to Diana's lips. She could picture him squatting before the Sheik, scented and immaculate, his fine eyes rolling, his slim hands waving continually, his handsome face alight with boyish enthusiasm and worship. At last he, too, went, and only Gaston remained, busy with the *cafetiere* that was his latest toy. The aroma of the boiling coffee filled the tent. She could imagine the servant's deft fingers manipulating the fragile glass and silver appliance. She could hear the tinkle of the spoon as he moved the cup, the splash of the coffee as he poured it out, the faint sound of the cup being placed on the inlaid table. Why was Ahmed drinking French coffee when he always complained it kept him awake? At night he was in the habit of taking the native preparation. Surely tonight he had need of sleep. It was the hardest day he had had since his illness. For a few moments longer Gaston moved about the outer room, and from the sound Diana guessed that he was collecting on to a tray the various things that had to be removed. Then his voice, louder than he had spoken before:

"Monseigneur desir d'autre chose?"

The Sheik must have signed in the negative, for there was no audible answer.

"*Bon soir, Monseigneur.*"

"*Bon soir, Gaston.*"

Diana drew a quick breath. While the man was still in the adjoining room the moment for which she was waiting seemed interminable. And now she wished he had not gone. He stood between her and—what? For the first time since the coming of Saint Hubert she was alone with him, really alone. Only a curtain separated them, a curtain that she could not pass. She longed to go to him, but she did not dare. She was pulled between love and fear, and for the moment fear was in the ascendant. She shivered, and a sob rose in her throat as the memory came to her of another night during those two months of happiness, that were fast becoming like a wonderful dream, when he had ridden in late. After Gaston left she had gone to him, flushed and bright-eyed with sleep, and he had pulled her down on to his knee, and made her share the native coffee she detested, laughing boyishly at her face of disgust. And, holding her in his arms with her head on his shoulder, he had told her all the incidents of the day's visit to one of the other camps, and from his men and his horses drifted almost insensibly into details connected with his own plans for the future, which were really the intimate confidences of a husband to a wife who is also a comrade. The mingled pain and pleasure of the thought had made her shiver, and he had started up, declaring that she was cold, and, lifting her till his cheek was resting on hers, carried her back into the other room.

But what she had done then was impossible now. He seemed so utterly strange, so different from the man whom she thought she had grown to understand. She was all at sea. She was desperately tired, her head aching and confused with the terrible problems of the future. She dared not think any more. She only wanted to lie in his arms and sob her heart out against his. She was starving for the touch of his hands, suffering horribly.

She slid down on to her knees, burying her face in the couch.

"Oh, God! Give me his love!" she kept whispering in agonised entreaty, until the recollection of the night, months before, when in the same posture she had prayed that God's curse might fall on him, sent a shudder through her.

"I didn't mean if," she moaned. "Oh, clear God! I didn't mean it. I didn't know . . . Take it back. I didn't mean it."

She choked down the sobs that rose, pressing her face closer into the silken coverings.

There was silence in the next room except for the striking of a match that came with monotonous regularity. And always the peculiar scent of his tobacco drifting in through the heavy curtains, forcing a hundred recollections with the association of its perfume. Why didn't he come to her? Did he know how he was torturing her? Was he so utterly indifferent that he did not care what she suffered? Did he even think of her, to wonder if she suffered or not? The fear of the future rushed on her again with overwhelming force. The uncertainty was killing her. She raised her head and looked at the travelling clock beside the reading-lamp. It was an hour since Gaston had left him. Another hour of waiting would drive her mad. She must know what he was going to do. She could bear anything but this suspense. She had reached the limit of her endurance. She struggled to her feet, drawing the thin wrap closer around her. But even then she stood irresolute, dreading the fulfilling of her fears; she had not the courage voluntarily to precipitate her fate. She clung to her fool's paradise. Her eyes were fixed on the clock, watching the hands drag slowly round the dial. A quarter of an hour crept past. It seemed the quarter of a lifetime, and Diana brushed her hand across her eyes to clear away the dazzling reflection of the staring white china face with its long black minute hand. No sound of any kind came now from the other room. The silence was driving her frantic. She was desperate; she must know, nothing could be worse than the agony she was enduring.

She set her teeth and, crossing the room, slipped noiselessly between the curtains. Then she shrank back suddenly with her hands over her mouth. He was leaning forward on the divan, his elbows on his knees, his face hidden in his hands. And it was as a stranger that he had come back to her, divested of the flowing robes that had seemed essentially a part of him; an unfamiliar figure in silk shirt, riding breeches and high brown boots, still dust-covered from the long ride. A thin tweed coat lay in a heap on the carpet—he must have flung it off after Gaston went, for the valet, with his innate tidiness, would never have left it lying on the floor.

She looked at him hungrily, her eyes ranging slowly over the long length of him and lingering on his bent head. The light from the hanging lamp shone on his thick brown hair burnishing it like bronze. She was shaking with a sudden new shyness, but love gave her courage and she went to him, her bare feet noiseless on the rugs.

"Ahmed!" she whispered.

He lifted his head slowly and looked at her, and the sight of his face sent her on to her knees beside him, her hands clutching the breast of his soft shirt.

"Ahmed! What is it? . . . You are hurt—your wound—?" she cried, her voice sharp with anxiety.

He caught her groping hands, and rising, pulled her gently to her feet, his fingers clenched round hers, looking down at her strangely. Then he turned from her without a word, and wrenching open the flap of the tent, flung it back and stood in the open doorway staring out into the right. He looked oddly slender and tall silhouetted against the darkness. A gleam of perplexity crept into her frightened eyes, and one hand went up to her throat.

"What is it?" she whispered again breathlessly.

"It is that we start for Oran tomorrow," he replied. His voice sounded dull and curiously unlike, and with a little start Diana realised that he was speaking in English. Her eyes closed and she swayed dizzily.

"You are sending me away?" she gasped slowly.

There was a pause before he answered.

"Yes."

The curt monosyllable lashed her like a whip. She reeled under it, panting and wild-eyed. "Why?"

He did not answer and the colour flamed suddenly into her face. She went closer to him, her breast heaving, trying to speak, but her throat was parched and her lips shaking so that no words would come.

"It is because you are tired of me?" she muttered at last hoarsely, "—as you told me you would tire, as you tired of—those other women?" Her voice died away with an accent of horror in it.

Again he did not answer, but he winced, and his hands that were hanging at his sides clenched slowly.

Diana flung one arm across her face to shut him out from her sight. Her heart was breaking, and she longed with a feeling of sick misery to crawl to his feet, but a remnant of pride kept her back.

He spoke at length in the same level, toneless voice. "I will take you to the first desert station outside of Oran, where you can join the train. For your own sake I must not be seen with you in Oran, as I am known there. If you should by any chance be recognised or your identity should leak out, you can say that for reasons of your own you extended your trip, that your messages miscarried, anything that occurs to you. But it is not at all likely to happen. There are many travellers passing through Oran. Gaston can do all business and make all arrangements for you. He will take you to Marseilles, and if you need him he will go with you to Paris, Cherbourg, or London—whichever you wish. As you know, you can trust him absolutely. When you do not need him any longer, he will come back to me. I—I will not trouble you any more. You need never be afraid that I will come into your life again. You can forget these months in the desert and the uncivilised Arab who crossed your path. To keep out of your way is the only amends I can make."

She flung up her head. Quick, suspicious jealousy and love and pride contending nearly choked her. "Why don't you speak the truth?" she cried wildly. "Why don't you say what you really mean?—that you have no further use for me, that it amused you to take me and torture me to satisfy your whim, but the whim is passed. It does not amuse you any longer. You are tired of me and so you get rid of me with all precautions. Do you think the truth can hurt me? Nothing that you can do can hurt me now. You made me the vile thing I am for your pleasure, and now for your pleasure you throw me on one side . . . How many times a year does Gaston take your discarded mistresses back to France?" Her voice broke into a terrible laugh.

He swung round swiftly and flung his arms about her, crushing her to him savagely, forgetting his strength, his eyes blazing. "God! Do you think it is easy to let you go, that you are taunting me like this? Do you think I haven't suffered, that I'm not suffering now? Don't you know that it is tearing my heart out by the roots to send you away? My life will be hell without you. Do you think I haven't realised what an infinitely damned brute I've been? I didn't love you when I took you, I only wanted you to satisfy the beast in me. And I was glad that you were English that I could make you suffer as an Englishman made my mother suffer, I so loathed the whole race. I have been mad all my life, I think—up till now. I thought I didn't care until the night I heard that Ibraheim Omair had got you, and then I knew that if anything happened to you the light of my life was out, and that I would only wait to kill Ibraheim before I killed myself."

His arms were like a vice hurting her, but they felt like heaven, and she clung to him speechless, her heart throbbing wildly. He looked down long and deeply into her eyes, and the light in his— the light that she had longed for—made her tremble. His brown head bent lower and lower, and his lips had almost touched her when he drew back, and the love in his eyes faded into misery.

"I mustn't kiss you," he said huskily, as he put her from him gently. "I don't think I should have the courage to let you go if I did. I didn't mean to touch you."

He turned from her with a little gesture of weariness.

Fear fled back into her eyes. "I don't want to go," she whispered faintly.

He paused by the writing-table and took up the revolver he had loaded earlier, breaking it absently, spinning the magazine between his finger and thumb, and replaced it before answering.

"You don't understand. There is no other way," he said dully.

"If you really loved me you would not let me go," she cried, with a miserable sob.

"*If* I loved you?" he echoed, with a hard laugh. "*If* I loved you! It is because I love you so much that I am able to do it. If I loved you a little less I would let you stay and take your chance."

She flung out her hands appealingly. "I want to stay, Ahmed! I love you!" she panted, desperate—for she knew his obstinate determination, and she saw her chance of happiness slipping away.

He did not move or look at her, and his brows drew together in the dreaded heavy frown. "You don't know what you are saying. You don't know what it would mean," he replied in a voice from which he had forced all expression. "If you married me you would have to live always here in the desert. I cannot leave my people, and I am—too much of an Arab to let you go alone. It would be no life for you. You think you love me now, though God knows how you can after what I have done to you, but a time would come when you would find that your love for me did not compensate for your life here. And marriage with me is unthinkable. You know what I am and what I have been. You know that I am not fit to live with, not fit to be near any decent woman. You know what sort of a damnable life I have led; the memory of it would always come between us—you would never forget, you would never trust me. And if you could, of your charity, both forgive and forget, you know that I am not easy to live with. You know my devilish temper—it has not spared you in the past, it might not spare you in the future. Do you think that I could bear to see you year after year growing to hate me more? You think that I am cruel now, but I am thinking what is best for you afterwards. Some day you will think of me a little kindly because I had the strength to let you go. You are so young, your life is only just beginning. You are strong enough to put the memory of these last months out of your mind—to forget the past and live only for the future. No one need ever know. There can be no fear for your—reputation. Things are forgotten in the silence of the desert. Mustafa Ali is many hundreds of miles away, but not so far that he would dare to talk. My own men need not be considered, they speak or are silent as I wish. There is only Raoul, and there is no question of him. He has not spared me his opinion. You must go back to your own country, to your own people, to your own life, in which I have no place or part, and soon all this will seem only like an ugly dream."

The sweat was standing out on his forehead and his hands were clenched with the effort he was making, but her head was buried in her hands, and she did not see the torture in his face, she only heard his soft, low voice inexorably decreeing her fate and shutting her out from happiness in quiet almost indifferent tones.

She shuddered convulsively. "Ahmed! I go!" she wailed.

He looked up sharply, his face livid, and tore her hands from her face. "Good God! You don't mean—I haven't—You aren't—" he gasped hoarsely, looking down at her with a great fear in his eyes.

She guessed what he meant and the color rushed into her face. The temptation to lie to him and let the consequences rest with the future was almost more than she could resist. One little word and she would be in his arms . . . but afterwards—? It was the fear of the afterwards that kept her silent. The colour slowly drained from her face and she shook her head mutely.

He let go her wrists with a quick sigh of relief and wiped the perspiration from his face. Then he laid his hand on her shoulder and pushed her gently towards the inner room. For a moment she resisted, her wide, desperate eyes searching his, but he would not meet her look, and his mouth was set in the hard straight line she knew so well, and with a cry she flung herself on his breast, her face hidden against him, her hands clinging round his neck. "Ahmed! Ahmed! You are killing me. I cannot live without you. I love you and I want you—only you. I am not afraid of the loneliness of the desert, it is the loneliness of the world outside the shelter of your arms that I am afraid of. I am not afraid of what you are or what you have been. I am not afraid of what you might do to me. I never lived until you taught me what life was, here in the desert. I can't go back to the old life, Ahmed. Have pity on me. Don't shut me out from my only chance of happiness, don't send me away. I know you love me—I know! I know! And because I know I am not ashamed to beg you to be merciful. I haven't any shame or pride left. Ahmed! Speak to me! I can't bear your silence . . . Oh! You are cruel, cruel!"

A spasm crossed his face, but his mouth set firmer and he disengaged her clinging hands with relentless fingers. "I have never been anything else," he said bitterly, "but I am willing that you should think me a brute now rather than you should live to curse the day you ever saw me. I still think that your greater chance of happiness lies away from me rather than with me, and for your ultimate happiness I am content to sacrifice everything."

He dropped her hands and turned abruptly, going back to the doorway, looking out into the darkness. "It is very late. We must start early. Go and lie down," he said gently, but it was an order in spite of the gentleness of his voice.

She shrank back trembling, with piteous, stricken face and eyes filled with a great despair. She knew him and she knew it was the end. Nothing would break his resolution. She looked at him with quivering lips through a mist of tears, looked at him with a desperate fixedness that sought to memorise indelibly his beloved image in her heart. The dear head so proudly poised on the broad shoulders, the long strong limbs, the slender, graceful body. He was all good to look upon. A man of men. Monseigneur! Monseigneur! *Mon maître et seigneur.* No! It would never be that any more. A rush of tears blinded her and she stepped back uncertainly and stumbled against the little writing-table. She caught at it behind her to steady herself, and her fingers touched the revolver he had laid down. The contact of the cold metal sent a chill that seemed to strike her heart. She stood rigid, with startled eyes fixed on the motionless figure in the doorway—one hand gripping the weapon tightly and the other clutching the silken wrap across her breast. Her mind raced forward feverishly, there were only a few hours left before the morning, before the bitter moment when she must leave behind her for ever the surroundings that had become so dear, that had been her home as the old castle in England had never been. She thought of the long journey northward, the agonised protraction of her misery riding beside him, the nightly camps when she would lie alone in the little travelling tent, and then the final parting at the wayside station, when she would have to watch him wheel at the head of his men and ride out of her life, and she would strain her eyes through the dust and sand to catch the last glimpse of the upright figure on the spirited black horse. It would be The Hawk, she thought suddenly. He had ridden Shaitan today, and he always used one or other of the two for long journeys. It was The Hawk he had ridden the day she had made her bid for freedom and who had carried the double burden on the return journey when she had found her happiness. The contrast between that ride, when she had lain content in the curve of his strong arm, and the ride that she would take the next day was poignant. She closed her teeth on her trembling lip, her fingers tightened on the stock of the revolver, and a wild light came into her sad eyes. She could never go through with it. To what end would be the hideous torture? What was life without him?—Nothing and less than nothing. She could never give herself to another man. She was necessary to no one. Aubrey had no real need of her; his selfishness wrapped him around with a complacency that abundantly satisfied him. One day, for the sake of the family he would marry—perhaps was already married if he had been able to find a woman in America who would accept his egoism along with his old name and possessions. Her life was her own to deal with. Nobody would be injured by its termination.

Aubrey, indeed, would benefit considerably. And he—? His figure was blurred through the tears that filled her eyes.

Slowly she lifted the weapon clear of the table with steady fingers and brought her hand stealthily from behind her. She looked at it for a moment dispassionately. She was not afraid. She was conscious only of an overwhelming weariness, a longing for rest that should still the gnawing pain in her breast and the throbbing in her head . . . A flash and it would be over, and all her sorrow would melt away . . . But would it? A doubting fear of the hereafter rushed over her. What if suffering lived beyond the border-line? But the fear went as suddenly as it had come, for with it came remembrance that in that shadowy world she would find one who would understand—her own father, who had shot himself, mad with heartbroken despair, when her mother died in giving her birth.

She lifted the revolver to her temple resolutely.

There had been no sound to betray what was passing behind him, but the extra sense, the consciousness of imminent danger that was strong in the desert-bred man, sprang into active force within the Sheik. He turned like a flash and leaped across the space that separated them, catching her hand as she pressed the trigger, and the bullet sped harmlessly an inch above her head. With his face gone suddenly ghastly he wrenched the weapon from her and flung it far into the night.

For a moment they stared into each other's eyes in silence, then, with a moan, she slipped from his grasp and fell at his feet in an agony of terrible weeping. With a low exclamation he stooped and swept her up into his arms, holding her slender, shaking figure with tender strength, pressing her head against him, his cheek on her red-gold curls.

"My God! child, don't cry so. I can bear anything but that," he cried brokenly.

But the terrible sobs went on, and fearfully he caught her closer, straining her to him convulsively, raining kisses on her shining hair. *"Diane, Diane,"* he whispered imploringly, falling back into the soft French that seemed so much more natural. *"Mon amour, ma bien-aimee. Ne pleures pas, je t'en prie. Je t'aime, je t'adore. Tu resteras pres de moi, tout a moi."*

She seemed only half-conscious, unable to check the emotion that, unloosed, overwhelmed her. She lay inert against him, racked with the long shuddering sobs that shook her. His firm mouth quivered as he looked down at his work. Gathering her up to his heart he carried her to the divan, and the weight of her soft slim body sent the blood racing madly through his veins. He laid her down, and dropped on his knees beside her, his arm wrapped round her, whispering words of passionate love.

Gradually the terrible shuddering passed and the gasping sobs died away, and she lay still, so still and white that he was afraid. He tried to rise to fetch some restorative, but at the first movement she clung to him, pressing closer to him. "I don't want anything but you," she murmured almost inaudibly.

His arm tightened round her and he turned her face up to his. Her eyes were closed and the wet lashes lay black against her pale cheek. His lips touched them pitifully.

"Diane, will you never look at me again?" His voice was almost humble.

Her eyes quivered a moment and them opened slowly, looking up into his with a still-lingering fear in them. "You won't send me away?" she whispered pleadingly, like a terrified child.

A hard sob broke from him and he kissed her trembling lips fiercely. "Never!" he said sternly. "I will never let you go now. My God! If you knew how I wanted you. If you knew what it cost me to send you away. Pray God I keep you happy. You know the worst of me, poor child—you will have a devil for a husband."

The colour stole back slowly into her face and a little tremulous smile curved her lips. She slid her arm up and round his neck, drawing his head down. "I am not afraid," she murmured slowly. "I am not afraid of anything with your arms round me, my desert lover. Ahmed! Monseigneur!"

THE END

Printed in the United States
132317LV00001B/63/A